The Dummy Run

Mary Baker

Pen Press

Copyright © Mary Baker 2010

All rights reserved

No part of this publication may be reproduced,
stored in a retrieval system, or transmitted
in any form or by any means, without
the prior permission in writing of the publisher,
nor be otherwise circulated in any form of binding or cover
other than that in which it is published and without a similar
condition including this condition being imposed on the subsequent purchaser.

First published in Great Britain by
Pen Press an Imprint of Indepenpress Publishing Ltd
25 Eastern Place
Brighton
BN2 1GJ

ISBN13: 978-1-907172-63-2

Printed and bound in the UK

A catalogue record of this book is available from
the British Library

Cover design by Jacqueline Abromeit

For Jo and Angie who have never been to Ipswich.

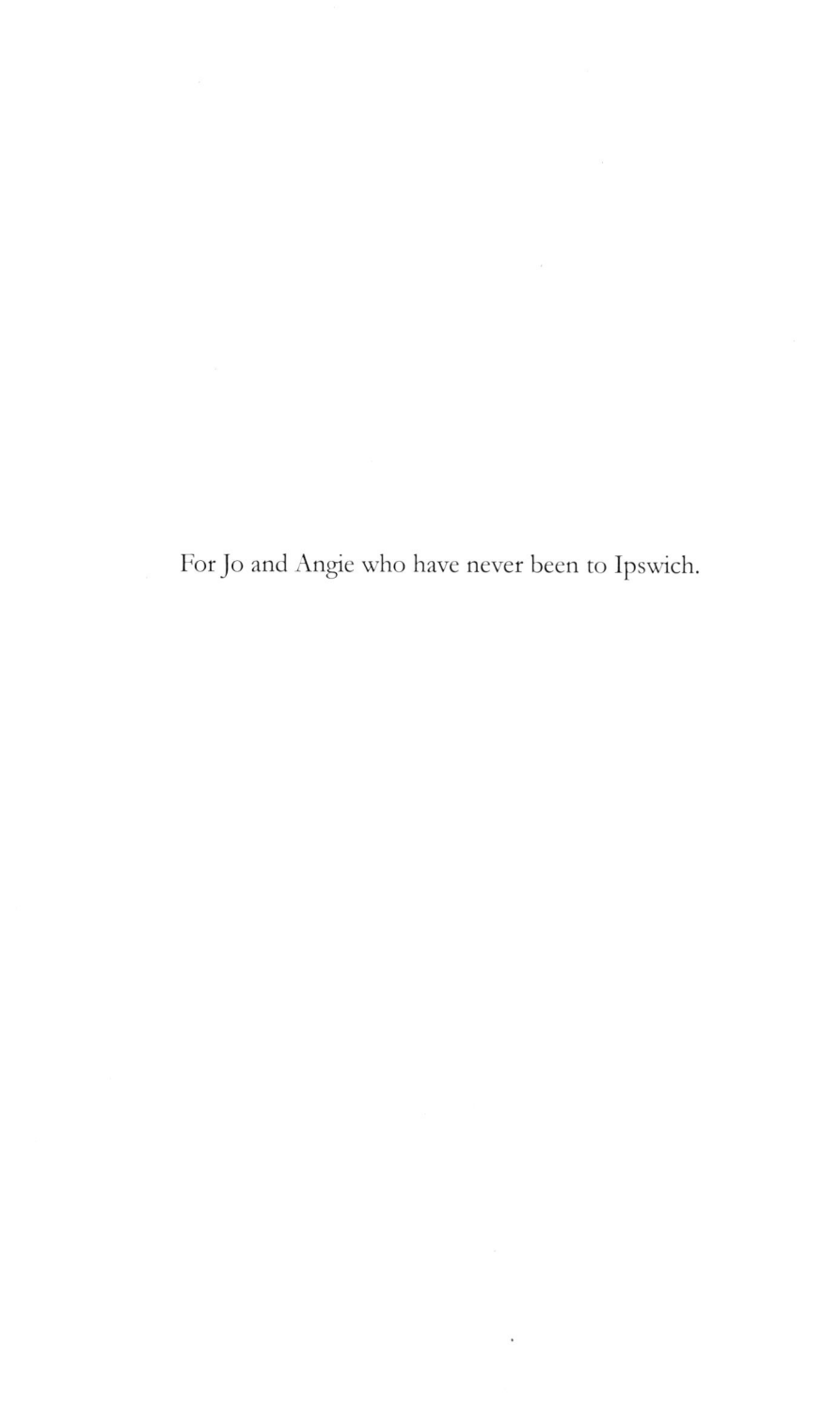

1

Deborah Wainwright had not been looking forward to the day of the disaster exercise. A foreboding, rooted in several months' experience as assistant to Maurice Canning, informed her that something would go wrong. Something always went wrong when Maurice was involved with any type of planning. It was as inevitable as the darkness of winter.

A Sunday morning in early January had been chosen as the ideal time to stage the disaster, presumably because traffic would be light, commuters undisturbed, and holidaymakers nonexistent. It was a considerate decision that made the undertaking somewhat futile, as the whole point was to test the ability of the various emergency services to respond to a full-scale catastrophe that might not treat the daily life of the town with as much courtesy should the worst actually happen. Nevertheless, lured in by the promise of overtime rates of pay, staff members lay around the cobbled courtyard and Regency corridors of the museum, clutching cards that detailed their supposed injuries and the symptoms they were expected to display. But long before lunch, the novelty of reclining on uncomfortably cold stone had departed, and the bored casualties began to check and recheck their watches with increasing frequency until at last it was noon, the disaster officially declared to be at an end, and even the dead were permitted to rise again on cramped limbs. Unfortunately, one of their number, sprawled behind the courtyard's fountain, remained dead.

****

"He had no right to be on the premises in the first place, whoever he was. We never have any members of the public in here on a Sunday morning, never." It sounded as though the matter of a dead man was primarily one of trespass in Maurice Canning's mind. He had toiled for weeks on the disaster, and relished every moment of his importance as he liaised with the local emergency planning team. The intrusion of a real crisis detracted from the smoothness of what should have run with clockwork precision, and Maurice resented the fact. He was in his late twenties, a tall and untidy-looking man, who spent his life yearning for a competence that forever eluded him. His uncle financed the museum, and Maurice was very aware of having acquired his job through family influence. The knowledge made him work twice as hard as anybody else, thereby causing twice as much muddle as he would have done had he been able to relax. "We can't even open the museum this afternoon, because the police say that no one must cross the courtyard. And we all have to be questioned before going home. Do you think the staff will expect to be paid for a full day?"

"Your uncle can write the whole thing off as an allowable expense on his next tax form," said Deborah.

"That's rather a cynical outlook," objected Maurice.

"Realistic." Normally, Deborah had weekends in the museum to herself, but nothing could have separated Maurice from his beloved disaster, and she might as well have stayed at home, with regard to work done, because even before the advent of a genuine victim, Maurice was too restless to settle. He had passed the time rushing in and out of her office, vainly querying details decided months previously, and although Deborah liked to think that she was a fairly self-controlled person, the urge to order him to leave had to be fought back.

At 25, she knew that she should have more patience, but what restraint she had was rapidly running out. A fatality just made the situation marginally worse. Yet for Maurice, who could stride around in pointless circles demanding explanations from an unresponsive universe if he mislaid a biro, a corpse in the courtyard represented a rare and glorious opportunity to go to pieces without anyone being able to tell him that it was an overreaction.

"How on earth did a body get inside the museum grounds, today of all days?" demanded Maurice, dark-brown hair beginning to look decidedly windswept as he pushed it back off his forehead yet again.

"Presumably the body wasn't a dead one when it arrived." Deborah aimed at efficiency, but beside Maurice Canning, her life seemed one of supreme and effortless control. Because he was so harassed and dishevelled, Deborah felt compelled to check her own brown, shoulder-length hair with a few hasty swipes of one hand. Whether tidy or not, she was good-looking, but as those looks had been passed on by a reprobate father, she disliked her appearance, although when working with Maurice, composure was a more attractive quality than any other. "I expect the man simply walked into the courtyard, on the assumption that the museum was open for business."

"But you put a notice on the gate about the exercise," objected Maurice. "And the staff should have spotted a stranger wandering around."

"But could have thought he'd just started to work here, or that he was a part-timer they hadn't encountered before. The police will sort it out. Don't worry." But 'don't worry' were useless words to say to Maurice. He had already started pacing, and Deborah's office was not large. "Why don't you go and see if the detectives need any help?" she suggested, hoping for a respite.

"They told me to stay away while they talked to the staff."

Deborah's estimation of the local police's acumen went up. "I suppose it would feel a bit intimidating to be questioned in front of the boss," she said tactfully.

"But I'm not an intimidating boss," Maurice protested in surprise. "I think of myself more as a friend to everyone who works here. This is a family enterprise, and we're all in the same team." Maurice actually believed what he said, the rapid staff turnover because of low wages having apparently escaped his attention. Nobody regarded any member of the Canning family as a pal, and Maurice's uncle would consider camaraderie from a staff member as insolence. Calvin Canning had managed to acquire a great deal of money, and he despised the less acquisitive as failures. Included among those failures was his nephew, Maurice. Deborah might also be classed as a failure, despite her academic qualifications, because women who could not be rich ought to dazzle the world with a film star beauty, in Calvin's opinion.

"The fuss might increase visitor numbers," remarked Deborah. Because the dead man had as yet no identity, she could not take in the reality of someone having died in the museum that day. It seemed no more genuine than the disaster that had been planned for so long. "At least I won't need to alert the local reporters. They usually have a police source."

"I know any publicity is meant to be good publicity," Maurice said hesitantly, "but I don't think a body on the premises would be something to advertise."

"You mean 'See the Canning Museum and die' might not be the ideal slogan. I must make a note of that."

"How can you joke at a time like this?" demanded Maurice. "The whole thing is simply awful: an absolute tragedy. What if the wretched man was killed off by radon gas or drains or something? The newspapers would totally ignore the fact that he had no business being here, and that whatever happened to him was his own stupid fault. You know what journalists are like. There'll be nothing but negative copy printed about us for weeks and weeks. We won't even be able to attract school parties to the museum."

"So it's not all bad news," commented Deborah, and Maurice was forced to smile, despite his previously fraught tone.

"I must admit, almost anything that keeps out those ghastly little swearing vandals would be worthwhile. Even so, my uncle's going to be really annoyed. It's a definite security breach. Perhaps someone should check the perimeter walls."

"Good idea," said Deborah. "Unfortunately, the security staff are talking to the police. Why don't you check the walls yourself? I'd do it, of course, but I'm to be interviewed next. You're the only one free."

"Yes." But Maurice looked unenthusiastic at the prospect of trudging through the grounds in an easterly wind. "On second thoughts, it's probably part of the police's job to investigate things like that. No point in doing their work for them."

The phone on Deborah's desk began to ring, startling Maurice as much as if one of the hypothetical explosions of Exercise Disaster had suddenly taken place. He snatched up the receiver, completely forgetting whose office he was in, listened for a moment, then covered the mouthpiece and said masterfully, "I'll handle this. It's the local radio station."

Deborah had doubts about Maurice's ability to handle anything, but she knew there was little chance of keeping him away from the media that day, even though publicity remained her responsibility. It was usually difficult to get the attention of the local radio or press, as events at a museum could hardly rival the squabbles of town councillors or the continual failure of holidaymakers to comprehend that North Sea tides came in, as well as went out. It made a change for journalists to phone the museum in search of copy, and Deborah could only hope that Maurice was not on the verge of ruining such an extraordinary opportunity, for opportunity it could be, despite the regrettable circumstances. The museum was housed in the graceful simplicity of a Georgian building, and would look most attractive on television or in newspaper pictures. Maurice had been right for once when he said that any publicity was good publicity; but, all the same, he seemed to be doing his best to sabotage a chance to recover something from the wreckage, as he talked on and on with stubborn determination about the absolute success of Exercise Disaster and ignored the little blip of a real disaster for somebody having occurred right in the middle of it. As soon as Maurice was out of the way, Deborah would have to return the radio station's call, and concoct a restrained statement: one that might clear the museum of callousness, yet retain an aura of mystery and intrigue. Perhaps she should also start to look for a new job.

When Calvin Canning paid the salary of a researcher who doubled as a publicist, he expected the sort of copy to be generated, in both local and national media, that would place him on the fast track towards an honour or two. He had money in abundance, but now he craved recognition, and Calvin would not react well to the idea of the police invading his territory. Rumour was inclined to run a bit wild through Seaborne town, but one of the more persistent scraps of gossip maintained that some of his business dealings had, at times, barely kept Calvin more than a few steps ahead of the Fraud Squad, and any bad press, however remote from him personally, would sully the image of dignified philanthropy that he now hoped to present to the world. A stray dead body was unlikely to help gloss over a doubtful past, no matter how many museums he financed to celebrate the lives of people who were no relation to him whatsoever.

****

George Canning 1770-1827, a politician with a tendency to overestimate his talents and quarrel with colleagues, had spent much of his parliamentary career in the wilderness until he startled everybody by being appointed Prime Minister in 1827. Then he startled himself by promptly breathing his last in Downing Street, after a mere handful of occasions to display his eagerness to speak fluently and at length on any topic to anyone. Despite a great deal of effort, Deborah had been unable to find a connection between the fleeting PM and Calvin Canning; but that did not stop Calvin from choosing to be a direct descendant of George, and founding a museum in honour of the life and times of the shanghaied ancestor. Many of the exhibits had only a tenuous link with the would-be forebear, and Deborah was not sure if she should be proud or ashamed of her ingenuity in stretching the facts of George Canning's life to match the objects on display. It was certainly one way to build up a picture of an existence that had ended two centuries earlier, especially with interactive computer programmes that allowed sanitized tours of long-gone streets that Canning might possibly have journeyed through, and gave glimpses inside houses that he could have visited during those same theoretical excursions. It was a sort of biography, fashioned in the style of Calvin Canning's idea of truth, adaptable as required; and if the police were to start an inquiry into the authenticity of the information presented to the museum's visitors, Deborah would have resigned herself to being denounced as a charlatan.

Luckily, the police were more occupied with the unidentified body discovered in the courtyard, than misrepresentation inside a museum. No one was likely to accuse her of dispatching the corpse, but still Deborah felt uncomfortable as she went into what was normally Maurice's office. The clutter that always covered his desk had been stacked on top of the filing cabinets along with his computer, resulting in a tidiness that Deborah had never before seen in the room; even more bewilderingly, the occasion suddenly turned into a social one.

"Lucas!" exclaimed Deborah in surprise. "How's Phoebe?"

"She's fine." Lucas Rudd answered automatically, and Deborah realized that he did not remember her. He had put on weight since the wedding, but his plain face and drab brown hair were the same. It had struck Phoebe Vale's friends as odd that she should have chosen to marry someone entirely without the flamboyance and allure of her previous men.

"I was at school with Phoebe," Deborah continued, although the intelligence was clearly of no interest to Lucas. "I haven't seen her in ages. Do pass on my regards."

"Yes, of course." But again the reply was automatic. Whatever the attraction of Lucas Rudd, it had patently not been the warmth of an outgoing nature, and he felt no need to pretend that the sight of Deborah had stirred even a vague memory. Phoebe would have fudged up something to be agreeable, but Lucas presumably prided himself on speaking the precise truth at all times. Certainly, he dismissed any further attempt at frivolous chat, and asked, "When did you last see the courtyard?"

When did you last see your father? It had been the title of a painting reproduced in one of Deborah's history books at school. A fair-haired Cavalier boy dressed in blue silk stood before a Roundhead tribunal, and the assumption of the picture seemed to be that the boy would haughtily refuse to speak, because he scorned to tell a lie, even if it were to protect his father. As a child, Deborah had had the uneasy feeling that, under such circumstances, she might have been silent through sheer terror, rather than a noble resolve not to defile her lips with an untruth; as a teenager, she would happily have shopped her feckless father. But there was no reason for

Deborah the adult to feel anything at all. Her father had not put in an appearance for months, and Lucas Rudd was only the dull husband of someone she knew. "When did I last see the courtyard? I didn't go outside during the exercise, so it would have been this morning when I arrived here."

"Did you notice any strangers about, anything different?"

"No. I was early, and the security guard let me in. There didn't appear to be anyone else around. Actually, I haven't had a chance to notice much today. I was in my office, and there were a lot of phone calls about the exercise. If you want details of who was where and when, you should talk to Maurice Canning."

"I already have." Lucas did not sound enthused by the recollection, although Maurice would doubtless have provided a plethora of information without prompting. "Did you look out the front windows at any time this morning?"

"My office is in the back of the building." Deborah wondered if Lucas believed she was being deliberately obstructive, and she tried to think of something, anything, useful to say, but there was nothing. A life had ended that day while she worked close by, but no sixth sense had compelled Deborah to go and glance out of a window. It seemed a self-centred omission.

"So the courtyard was exactly as usual when you crossed it?" persisted Lucas, as if the sight of a corpse might somehow have remained locked inside Deborah's memory, but for his question.

"I just hurried inside the museum. It was so cold in the wind that I—"

Lucas cut into the weather report impatiently. "Nothing at all struck you as being out of the ordinary?"

"No. Was he already there in the courtyard?" But Deborah knew that the body must have arrived after she did. However cold the wind, she could not have failed to spot a cadaver, even if it had been half-hidden behind the fountain.

"We don't know the timetable yet." But Lucas was speaking with pointless caution, and must have realized it, because he added, "None of the other staff members spotted anything either."

Deborah almost asked how the man had died, but then stopped herself. If she were able to picture precise details, it gave the death reality, and the courtyard would be forever haunted by a body. The building was centuries old, had once been a family home, and people would have died in many of the rooms, but without particulars, it was merely a fact of history like a name or date in a book. Deborah stood up to end the interview. "Tell Phoebe I said hello."

"Yes." But Lucas was not listening. He had started to scribble notes, and Phoebe might never learn about her husband's meeting with Deborah.

****

"What did he ask?" demanded Maurice, still pacing up and down Deborah's office.

"He asked if I'd noticed anything when I arrived here today."

"And did you?"

"Of course not; I'd have said something before now, if I had. Besides, I would have been the one to summon the police, if I'd found myself tripping over a dead body on the way in."

Maurice took time out from his pacing to declare, "I can't understand any of this."

"No one can. Why don't you go and ask Lucas if he's discovered an explanation?"

"Who's Lucas?"

"Lucas Rudd: one of our resident detectives."

"You know him?"

"He married a school friend of mine," replied Deborah, and then smiled at the amazed expression on Maurice's face. "There's no rule against knowing a policeman's wife if you work in the Canning Museum, is there? Should I have mentioned it at my job interview?"

"An omission that I'm sure can be overlooked," said Maurice, with his usual heavy-handed attempt at humour. "But it's probably an advantage to employ someone with a police contact. You'll be able to get us all the latest information."

"I doubt it. My wedding present couldn't have been up to much. Lucas made it very clear that meeting me had wholly escaped his memory."

"I bet he only pretended that, to knock your confidence," decided Maurice. "You know what the police are like."

"Actually, I don't. Your experience of their wily methods is obviously greater than mine."

"You've guessed my dark secret." Maurice laughed, liking the implication that his life was not one of total conformity. It seemed odd that what should be an insult was apparently regarded as some sort of compliment, but Deborah had known he would be pleased with words that insinuated a debonair recklessness lurked beneath his fussy disposition. "When do you suppose they'll let us go home?"

"I haven't a clue. Would you like me to find out?"

"I do so value your obliging and good-natured attitude to the job—" began Maurice.

"Oh dear, this sounds ominous," said Deborah. "Are you going to suggest that I now oblige by taking my good-natured attitude to another employer?"

"On the contrary. I was about to offer you lunch at my expense; though perhaps I should say dinner, as it must be closer to that now."

"OK. I'll phone for a takeaway. Sandwiches or pizza?"

"In point of fact, I mean a restaurant." Maurice shuffled his feet and looked as embarrassed as an adolescent. "You deserve some compensation after so unpleasant a day."

"More unpleasant for other people: particularly the dead man and his family, if any." Deborah wished that she had not spoken, because her words might appear reproving, and it would not be a good move to hint that the boss lacked sensitivity, especially as that was her opinion.

"Yes, yes. A terrible business. Of course," Maurice agreed hastily. "Where would you like to have dinner? Which is your favourite restaurant?"

"I've never been paid well enough to find out," replied Deborah, not eager to spend more time with Maurice than she had to. "By the way, don't forget to phone your uncle. He's bound to want a first-hand report of the day's events."

"I did phone, but couldn't get an answer. I'd like to talk to you before I speak to him though; get my ideas clear."

"Clarity is decidedly absent right now."

"I'd still appreciate your input," Maurice declared in best managerial style, doubtless gleaned from a *Guide to Inspirational Leadership* or some other similarly titled paperback.

"You want me to tell your uncle what's happened." Deborah said shrewdly.

"Well, you have such a fluent way of explaining things, it'll seem better coming from you. He'll only blame me otherwise."

"Blame you for what? Bumping off the victim?"

"Hardly," objected Maurice, with another ponderous attempt at levity. "That would require initiative, something my uncle considers I lack."

"The whole purpose of family life is to keep you humble. Years ago, when I told my father that I hoped to go to university one day, he said that only clever people went to college."

"Perhaps he meant to spur you on to greater effort," Maurice suggested charitably.

"I wouldn't know. He waltzed off the next day, and neglected to supply a forwarding address until he ran short of money." Deborah sounded wryly amused, as though referring to a minor foible. It had taken her a long time to achieve a convincing casualness of tone when speaking of her father. "But to return to the subject of the present drama, I better call your uncle now, before he switches on a television or radio."

"He might already have picked up my message."

"The phone would be ringing itself into a frenzy if he had. I'll explain how busy you are, co-ordinating the investigation."

"I am very busy," agreed Maurice, pleased with the consequence of the role allotted to him. "I ought to see if your detective friends want any—any—anything."

"Definitely," said Deborah, hoping to rid her office of Maurice's fidgety presence. "They might need permission to carry out tests, or whatever else has to be done. Someone could be searching for you."

"Give my uncle an in-depth report," ordered Maurice, straightening to his full height. "If you can't contact Calvin, leave a message assuring him there'll be a stringent review of security."

Better late than never, thought Deborah. She dialled Calvin Canning's number, and after several fruitless rings, was put through to his message service. "This is Deborah Wainwright. As Maurice told you earlier, there's been an incident at the museum, but we're carrying out an immediate security review. I'll update you as soon as there's any further information."

Maurice, hovering in the doorway, looked happier. "That's that done. Do you think I should call a news conference?

The media ought to have the facts, instead of relying on wild speculation."

"But we don't know the facts ourselves yet," Deborah pointed out, alarmed at the prospect of Maurice let loose in the middle of a crowd of journalists. "Dignified reticence is the best approach. I'll prepare a statement for the website to say how sorry everyone here is. Anything more would be superfluous. Control the media; never let them control you."

"Yes, that's very true," conceded Maurice, but he was reluctant to allow his moment in the spotlight to get away. "The police must know the ins and outs by now; they've been here hours. I could relay what they tell me to the reporters."

"The police will make their own statement. Besides, it's the lack of detail that the media like. 'Allegedly' is a journalist's favourite word, and the real explanation is bound to be dull."

"You're so level-headed," said Maurice. "I really appreciate your sound advice."

"Are we back to the subject of my sound advice soundly advising me to seek gainful employment elsewhere?" It was clear to Deborah that Maurice was trying to tell her something, and she wished he would get on with it.

"The day you leave is the day I leave too," declared Maurice.

"And are you currently studying the sits vac column?"

"On the contrary. Actually, I'm planning to extend the range of the museum. We could add a section devoted to George Canning's contemporaries, another about the rebuilding of Europe post-Napoleon. And I figured we might do something cultural as well: perhaps host concerts of whatever music Canning would have heard."

"Or not have heard. By all accounts, he deemed music rather a waste of time."

"He would!" said Maurice in exasperation. "George Canning is the most uncooperative man I've ever encountered. I suppose he hated poetry too."

"Only other people's. He thought very highly of his own. We could have readings of the collected works, if you like; although I doubt a politician's poetic reflections will bring the masses to your gate, clamouring for admittance."

It could have been an ordinary day at one of the meetings that Maurice so cherished, during which he would call for ideas, then spend the next hour revealing his own latest brainwave, and he always had a brainwave. "It's a distinct lack that we don't have an arts festival in Seaborne. We ought to celebrate our heritage; remember the famous people who've lived here; perhaps stage re-enactments of the great moments from our past."

It was unfortunate for Maurice's plan that no great moments had chanced to occur in the town, as unfortunate as the fact that famous people seemed to have gone out of their way to avoid the place. Seaborne had a dull and plodding history, consisting of virtuous hard work, rather than battles or coups d'état, and Deborah foresaw that yet again some creative sleight-of-hand would be required, should Maurice stick tenaciously to his intellectual dreams. "There isn't much local interest in the arts."

"Then it's up to us to create the demand, to expand horizons, to educate," declared Maurice. "It's our duty to enrich the existence of those deprived of culture. Giving them music and poetry will be like offering a banquet in the middle of a famine. The town council ought to help with funding, especially as an arts festival is sure to bring in visitors. We could hold it out of season, in November perhaps, or February, when it'd be a real boost to the local economy."

"But would people be keen to visit the seaside when it's perishingly cold?"

"Our festival will make them keen," said Maurice. "What's the best way to get this off the ground? Go to the council, or run a campaign in the local paper?"

"Local paper." Deborah knew the town councillors better than Maurice did. Their response would be to form a committee, and that committee was going to divide itself into several sub-committees, all of which could then squander lavish amounts of public money on trips to study other festivals, where the councillors would be far too busy wining and dining to have time to attend any of the events. At the end of the glorious spending spree, the finance committee would announce that budgetary factors and the need for Spartan economy rendered any financial backing infeasible.

"You don't think much of the idea," said Maurice, suddenly uncertain.

"The idea's interesting. The town might not be the ideal location. But nobody ever achieved anything by listening to someone else's pessimism."

"I value your opinion, as I said," declared Maurice, with team-bonding encouragement. "We'll discuss the matter further over dinner. Well, I better go and take an interest in whatever progress your detective friends have made."

"Yes," said Deborah, noting that the offer of a free meal was now considered by Maurice to be a definite arrangement. "I'll sort out that statement, and get it onto the museum website."

"I can always rely on you."

Deborah did not think that it was much to her credit to treat the morning's incident as a public relations drill, but a response had to be manufactured, if only to deny Maurice a second chance to parade his version of events before another reporter. Deborah scribbled down a few phrases of condolence for the dead man's family, assuming he had one, before she expanded the statement to include a reference to the deep shock experienced by the museum staff. The sentiments were trite, but they would please Maurice, and more importantly, the local media. The sadness belonged to someone else, and it would be ghoulish to linger over a grief that was not hers, yet the uncomfortable feeling persisted that she should be ashamed to have done the job she was paid to do.

"Detective Sergeant Rudd wants to see you again," said Maurice, bustling back into the office.

"Why?" asked Deborah in surprise.

"Some detail or other that he has to check. I'll take over in here, so there's no need to be anxious."

But the idea of Maurice left unsupervised with a telephone was the one thought making Deborah anxious at that moment. "If there are any calls, it's best to read out the website statement, and then say we've no further comment to make."

"Of course; I totally agree. Dignified reticence is our strategy, exactly as planned."

"Yes," said Deborah, certain that Maurice would be in full flow the instant a telephone rang. "Calvin hasn't called back, by the way."

"I expect he's busy." Maurice spoke without the tension that normally entered his voice at any reminder of his uncle, but the importance of liaising with the police, as Maurice would term it, had managed to relegate even Calvin to one of life's minor drawbacks.

"There nothing more to do," continued Deborah. "The website's updated, and some of the local journalists are stringers for the national papers. Everything's covered."

"Then I'll simply hold the fort here."

"Thanks," Deborah said uneasily, but Maurice was in charge, and she could only suggest, not command. Nevertheless, she had to force herself out of the office and down a corridor that was unusually quiet, wholly free of the activity she had imagined automatically accompanied a police investigation. The courtyard would be the centre of

17

their attention, of course, but still it felt odd that such drama should not include the entire premises.

"You wanted to see me, Lucas?"

"No. I wanted to get rid of your boss. That's why I sent him to deliver a message. Can you keep him out of our way?"

"Not if he's determined to stay in your way."

"That appears to be his sole ambition in life," Lucas said impatiently. "I told him to go home, but he took no notice."

"Can I leave as well?" asked Deborah.

"Yes; and take your boss with you."

No, thanks. A little of his company goes a long way. Give him a job. You could tell him to locate his uncle."

"Can't you find him either? I tried to contact the elusive Calvin Canning myself earlier. What do you know about him?"

"Not much. He owns this place and his cheques don't bounce."

"I thought he was a friend of yours." Lucas sounded as smug as if he had cleverly spotted a damaging discrepancy in a suspect's account.

"A friend? Calvin Canning? Good grief, no. Whatever gave you that idea?" asked Deborah in amusement.

"Your boss claims that Calvin saw the name Deborah Wainwright on a list of job candidates, and told him to hire you."

"Then Maurice is clearly hallucinating under the strain of today's crisis," said Deborah, entertained by the carefully blank expression on Lucas's face as he studied her reaction to his unspoken charge of having told him a lie. "I'd never met Calvin before I started this job, and I've only seen him a couple of times since."

"So Maurice Canning has made a mistake?"

"Definitely: unless Calvin's mother and I share a name, and he's emotionally attached to it. Maurice must be thinking of another staff member." And Deborah thought she could pinpoint the one: Chelsea Pritchard, a decorative young blonde, whose idea of a receptionist's duties consisted of varnishing her fingernails and leafing through fashion magazines. Something kept Chelsea gainfully employed, and it was neither enthusiasm for the job nor outstanding proficiency.

"Does Calvin Canning have the final word about who works here?"

"I imagine so, but I'm merely a hireling and it's not my department. Don't forget to say hello to Phoebe for me."

"Yes." But Lucas spoke absently, as if he had already deleted Deborah from his mind.

Although knowing that she should hurry back to her office and supervise Maurice's telephonic activity, Deborah sidetracked down the basement stairs into the staff room, a place deserted now that freedom had been granted to the museum's employees. It was a dismal cavern of leftover furniture and drab green walls, never repainted, as the cellars were not visited by the public. Deborah generally avoided the area, but the attraction that afternoon was a pay phone next to a startlingly modern, bright-red vending machine. She scrabbled in her pocket for some change, and then dialled her mother's number. "Do me a favour; ring my office in five minutes' time. Say it's urgent, and you have to see me."

"You've heard!" Rhoda exclaimed, but Rhoda was usually in a flurry over something or other.

"I haven't had a chance to hear a word. It's been total pandemonium the whole day."

"Yes, I saw the police all over the courtyard, when I went out earlier to get some champagne to celebrate."

Deborah sighed wearily, knowing only too well the single event that her mother would consider worthy of champagne.

"I nearly dropped in to see you," continued Rhoda, "but there was such a kerfuffle going on—"

"Don't tell me. Just call back, and I'll be on my way."

"I'll babble on for hours, if you don't stop me right now." Rhoda was struggling not to blurt out the news, and she laughed at herself. "You better put the phone down this second."

Not wanting to have her suspicions confirmed, Deborah took Rhoda's advice, and then raced back to her office, where she found Maurice engaged in a telephone conversation of his own. The statement she had constructed was lying neglected on the desk, while Maurice elaborated his theme. "Of course the museum's in no way to blame. That's perfectly clear. And we're fully insured anyhow. But I'm a hundred per cent confident that, no matter what happened, none of our procedures were at fault."

Maurice didn't need an assistant, thought Deborah, he needed a minder. She edged out of his line of sight and pulled the telephone wire from its wall socket, wishing that she had had the sense to cut his link with the outside before leaving him unguarded.

"The phone's gone dead," said Maurice in bewilderment. It had taken him over a minute to become aware of the fact, and Deborah congratulated herself on having kept from the world Maurice's views on the clumsiness of visitors crossing the courtyard's cobblestones.

"The wind's getting up. It's probably affected the line. I wouldn't bother about it."

But Maurice proceeded to shake the receiver like a pepper pot and, under cover of his distraction, Deborah pushed the wire back into its socket. "I've got a dial tone," Maurice declared as triumphantly as if his skilled engineering technique had restored communication with the moon. "I'll ring that reporter back. He was doing an interview with me: an in-depth one, to judge by the number of questions."

"Never call back," Deborah said hastily. "Always leave them wanting more. It's an old PR trick to keep the story alive. Don't give the impression that you're frantic to get their attention."

"No, certainly not." But when the telephone rang, Maurice snatched up the receiver enthusiastically, only to look like a child who had opened a gaudily wrapped birthday present to discover a pair of sensible shoes inside. "It's your mother. She says it's urgent."

"Urgent?" repeated Deborah for effect, as she regained control of her phone. "Mum, what's wrong?"

"I'm sure I was convincing enough," said Rhoda, laughing, "because I really can't wait to see you. I've got the most astounding news."

"I'll leave at once." Rhoda could marvel at a bus ticket, and almost anything that occurred in her life would be described as amazing; but Deborah had realized what the news was, and dreaded hearing the words spoken aloud.

"You'll never guess what I'm going to tell you," claimed Rhoda.

"I think I already have, but I'll be with you in ten minutes all the same." Deborah put the receiver down, and turned to Maurice. "It's OK if I skive off, isn't it? There's nothing more to do here."

"Yes, fine. I hope the news isn't too bad?"

"My mother wouldn't tell me over the phone, but she sounded a bit stressed, and she's on her own."

"Of course you must go. In fact, I'll give you a lift, and then you can be there in next to no time. We'll just postpone our dinner."

Mission accomplished without offending the boss, thought Deborah in relief.

****

"What kept you?" demanded Rhoda, opening her front door before Deborah had had a chance to ring the bell of the pink terrace house with the rosebud curtains. "You said you'd leave at once."

"I did, and I couldn't have got here any quicker without chartering a helicopter. What's the big news? And I hope it's not what I think it is."

"Then you better sit down," said Rhoda, giggling nervously like a schoolgirl. She generally appeared younger than her age with a trim figure, fair hair and pretty face, but at that instant, Rhoda seemed so immature that she made Deborah feel old and jaded.

"I have a horrible premonition that I'm not going to like your wonderful news." Deborah closed the door on the darkening afternoon and bitter wind, yet the coldness stayed inside her despite the warmth of the house. "But I hate the post-Christmas gloom at the best of times, so I might as well have a reason to be a misery this January."

Rhoda giggled again, as they went into a living room that looked as flustered as she did. Newspaper pages were distributed over the sofa, a can of polish stood on the edge of the table, while an unplugged hoover cable coiled its way across the carpet. "Guess who rang this morning?"

"Someone who took your mind right off housework," said Deborah, apprehension turning to certainty. She had lived through that moment before.

Rhoda glanced around the disorder of the room without interest. "Oh well, everything's in place for a clean up, when I'm calm enough to tackle it. Your father has never worried about appearances."

"Do I have to listen to any more? I've had a rotten day."

"Oh, I'm sorry." But a dull museum could hardly compete with the prodigal's return, and Rhoda dismissed Deborah's words without further comment. "I bet you can't guess where Gregory's staying."

"I don't feel like guessing," said Deborah. "It's the same monotonous story all over again, isn't it?"

"He's at the Grand Hotel," Rhoda continued impressively, ignoring Deborah's contribution, but Rhoda was expert at hearing only what she wanted to hear. "Gregory said he was on his way over, but I'm not holding my breath. He had to meet a friend first, and you know how very sociable Greg is."

Especially with women, reflected Deborah.

"He sounded marvellous: on top of the world."

"That's because he doesn't worry, especially about us."

"If you don't take care, you're going to turn into a sour, cold-hearted, hatchet-faced type of woman."

"Too late; I've already turned. Please tell me that you're becoming equally warped, because I couldn't bear it if you forgave him yet again."

"There's nothing to forgive," declared Rhoda. "I married your father knowing he isn't a nine to five worker, who mows the lawn in his spare time. Gregory was never the conventional sort."

"No; most people have progressed beyond adolescence by the time they reach their forties."

"I chose to be with him part-time, rather than never be with him at all. When you meet the right man, you'll understand."

"I sincerely hope not."

Rhoda smiled at the fervour in Deborah's voice. "It's better to be happy every so often, than drive away the man you want by trying to make him into somebody he isn't. If I was a navy wife, it would be exactly the same situation, and you'd have accepted your father's absences without a murmur."

"The navy doesn't usually vanish for three years at a stretch."

"There's no need to exaggerate."

"Is it only two and a half? How time flies."

"Someone else doesn't seem to have progressed beyond adolescence either."

Rhoda's refusal to admit that she was being used was the most annoying thing of the whole mess. She made Deborah feel in the wrong, and, in Deborah's opinion, the only person who should have felt that way was her unregenerate father, as he drifted in and out of their lives with the nonchalance of a holidaymaker. "He only ever comes back when he needs money. If he hit the big time, we'd never see him again."

"He can't be skint. I told you; Greg's staying at the Grand Hotel."

"Staying at the Grand doesn't automatically mean that he can pay the bill. I'll ask you to guess something for a change. Guess who he's expecting to pick up the tab? He hasn't even got the courage to come straight here, in case you've regained your senses and sling him out as he richly deserves."

"It must have been a very bad day at work indeed," remarked Rhoda.

Deborah smiled, but with reluctance. "I could have done without the pariah's impending arrival. But I knew all along what you were going to tell me."

"Incidentally, why did I have to summon you here in such cloak-and-dagger fashion?"

"Maurice Canning announced he was treating me to a meal, and I couldn't think of words tactful enough to inform the boss that he wasn't my idea of a fun companion when out on the town."

"Poor man." But Rhoda was uninterested in Maurice's lonely fate, and reverted to her own concerns. "Gregory should be here very soon."

"But not before visiting a few pubs on the way, where he'll invite himself to sing to the great delight of no one but himself. Then he'll bore everybody with an account of the television audition he failed, because the show's compère was jealous of such astonishing talent."

"It's quite true," Rhoda said defensively. "That Joey Slade can never bear anyone who takes the limelight off him. Even when he still worked the clubs, Slade was jealous of the impact Gregory has on an audience."

"Yet Joey Slade went onto fame and fortune, while the impacting Greg Wayne, aka Gregory Wainwright, languishes in obscurity."

"He's very popular in the northern clubs," protested Rhoda. "But there's no point in trying to make you understand when you've simply closed your mind about Gregory. Tell me what happened at the museum instead. Did the disaster exercise go smoothly?"

"Sadly it turned into a real disaster for someone. A visitor died in the courtyard." Not being allowed to continue her rant against Gregory frustrated Deborah, although she knew that nothing she said would convince Rhoda that the absent husband was a freeloader who deserved the life he had. And when Rhoda's fantasy world began to sound like a reasonable way of dealing with a flawed universe containing flawed people, it was definitely time to change the subject. "Do you remember Phoebe Vale?"

"Of course; flighty Phoebe who astounded everybody by actually marrying one of the men she had dancing to her tune."

"I met the husband again today. He's a policeman, a detective, and very officious with it. I thought he seemed a bit distant at the wedding, so he was even more aloof this afternoon. Not Phoebe's type, I would have said."

"It was the warmth of your father's personality that first

attracted me to him." All topics led straight to Gregory for Rhoda.

"Perhaps I better go before he gets here. You don't need the joyous reunion marred by the presence of a sulky daughter."

"But Greg will want to see you," said Rhoda, hurt on his behalf that Deborah should choose to avoid him.

"He could see me any time he liked, if he bothered to visit us a little more frequently."

"He asks about you every time he phones."

"And how often is that?"

"You just won't try to meet him halfway." Rhoda spoke with genuine regret. According to her, Deborah was the one who should adapt to Gregory's wandering habits without expecting any reciprocal effort from him. To her daughter, Rhoda's kind of unconditional selfless love could seem very close to stupidity at times.

****

The telephone was ringing as Deborah opened the front door of the small and dark terraced house that would one day belong to her, should she be able to continue paying the mortgage for a further 25 years. With its narrow rooms and low ceilings, the house was not the home she would have chosen had finances permitted a wider choice, but it represented stability, and Deborah craved security. She reached out to pick up the phone, but it immediately stopped ringing in accordance with a law as strictly enforced by the cosmos as gravity. Deborah waited a few minutes, and then dialled the message service, troubled at the prospect of perhaps hearing her father, but the recorded voice was a more familiar one.

"Deborah, it's Maurice. I still haven't been able to contact Calvin. Let me know if he calls you. Perhaps we can meet up later for a drink somewhere? Anyway, I hope your mother's news wasn't too bad."

Too bad? Maurice could have no idea exactly how bad Deborah considered the news to be. She deleted his message, but before she had time to go into the kitchen and think about her first meal since breakfast, the phone was ringing again.

"Hi, Deb. Bet you can't guess who this is."

Deborah had not heard from Phoebe Vale in over a year, but the confident cheerfulness was unmistakeable, and Phoebe had every reason to be both confident and cheerful, because she was not only clever, but extremely good-looking as well, with a delicate fairness that belied her tough nature. Remembering the sociable and lively Phoebe, Deborah was yet again bewildered that someone with so much going for her, and so many men to choose from, should have decided to marry the drab and unresponsive Lucas Rudd.

"Whatever made you take a job in a museum of all places?" demanded Phoebe, sounding as appalled as if she spoke of a particularly Dickensian factory.

"I was freelancing, and rather liked the idea of a regular wage. As an accountant, you should approve of that."

"The very thought warms my heart. Even so, I couldn't believe it when Lucas dropped by and told me you were currently wasting your PR skills on some long-gone politician nobody's ever heard of."

"I can't be that skilful if I haven't raised George Canning's profile in the town," Deborah pointed out, before adding cautiously, "Phoebe, when you say Lucas dropped by—"

"Didn't he tell you we're getting a divorce? I'm afraid the novelty of marriage rapidly wore off. Lucas is in denial though, and believes a sudden yearning for domesticity will overtake me, as I realize fulfilment can only be mine by yielding to no one with the finesse of my ironing and vacuuming. I'm afraid the emancipation of women has rather passed Lucas by."

"I'm sorry the marriage didn't work out." But Deborah's reply was a mechanical response. She had said the same words too many times, when talking with other friends, to sound overly concerned.

"Don't waste any sympathy on me. I'm incredibly busy having a good time, and that's a vast improvement on the marital state, I can tell you. What about your own life? And how on earth did you get mixed up with a body?"

"I'm not. I merely chanced to be in the vicinity."

"Then, if you didn't actually wield the notorious blunt instrument, you should be fairly safe from Lucas and his cronies."

"You always did build without bricks," declared Deborah, "so I won't bother to demand precise details of whatever your ex told you, even though I found it impossible to guess what Lucas was thinking."

"That's because automatons can't think. They're simply programmed, and I was deluded enough to fall for the romantic programme that came to an abrupt end the instant a wedding ring slid onto my finger. Lucas then moved onto the husband programme, and I was expected to provide a 24-hour laundry and cleaning service, despite going out to work full-time. But never mind the bitterness of my now twisted personality. Who's top of your list of suspects?"

Phoebe's conversation had often been inclined to jump around with grasshopper agility, and Deborah laughed. "What are you talking about? I lost track after the reference to your twisted personality. Who exactly am I meant to suspect?"

"The guilty party, of course. Oh, come on, Deb, you must know everyone who works in that dreary museum of yours. Any psychopaths lurking behind the exhibits? Or did a stray madman wander in off the street, and eliminate the only other stranger in sight?"

"There's no need to dramatize the situation," protested Deborah. "I'm supposed to make the museum an alluring place to visit, remember, and that's difficult enough without people deciding to have heart attacks all over the courtyard."

"No heart attack, if Lucas is a reliable source. Definite foul play, according to him." But Phoebe's tone was untroubled. Like Deborah, she could not take in the reality of a death when the corpse was still both nameless and faceless.

"Lucas is wrong," Deborah said firmly. A Georgian building might very well have housed melodrama during the course of history, but its present role was to be an elegant reminder of a more cultured time. Murder belonged to deprived inner-city areas and ill-educated gang members, whose true deprivation was caused less by poverty than lack of imagination.

"It isn't Lucas who decided what had happened. The medical evidence so far points to—" Phoebe stopped in exasperation. "Oh dear, I sound just like a policeman's wife. The sooner the divorce is finalized, the better."

"What medical evidence?" Deborah asked, and then added hastily, "But no gruesome details. I'm planning to eat very soon."

"Medical evidence is always gruesome."

"Then please don't say another word about it."

"Never marry a policeman if you can't take grisly details along with your food. And while we're on the subject of food, what about meeting for lunch tomorrow? You haven't told me a thing about your life yet."

"That's because there's nothing much to tell."

"I suppose a museum isn't the ideal place to meet interesting men," conceded Phoebe, who judged the success of a woman's life by how many suitors she had trailing in her wake. "What happened to that handsome journalist you brought to my wedding?"

Only Phoebe Vale could have found time to weigh up an unknown man on an occasion when most females were fully occupied being the bride, thought Deborah in amusement. "Nothing happened to Jason. He's still working for the local paper, so I see him now and then." Or, more accurately, Deborah had, until Jason Clenham made the mistake of asking her to marry him.

"You don't sound ecstatic at the mention of his name," commented Phoebe.

"He's OK," said Deborah. "But it's definitely over. Feel free to use all your seductive wiles on Jason, if you find him so very attractive."

Because Phoebe had allowed the conversation to drift back to trivia, Deborah dismissed the wild talk of medical evidence and blunt instruments as Phoebe's usual exaggeration. Dealing with Gregory's return was enough to occupy Deborah's mind, without a stray body complicating her efforts to achieve good publicity for the museum. Gregory made Deborah's relationship with her mother difficult, and the memory of his casual rejection came between Deborah and every man who tried to get close to her. Gregory was the problem, the perennial problem, and she did not need any additional worries.

2

In an endeavour to avoid any contact with Gregory, Deborah had unplugged her telephone after speaking to Phoebe, and did not check for messages before going to work the next day. It was a craven method of coping, but preferable to a confrontation that would upset Deborah but leave her father blithely unconcerned.

To approach the graceful symmetry of a Georgian building, and then cross its cobbled courtyard, had been an agreeable start to Deborah's working day; but that morning, she re-routed her walk to the museum and went inside via the back door. Shunning the courtyard did not alter the fact that a man had been found dead there the previous afternoon, but meant Deborah was able to postpone whatever she would feel at being so close to the end of someone's life. Again, it was evading a situation, but Deborah had enough to contend with: Maurice Canning, for example.

The door to Deborah's office was open, and she could see Maurice inside, already pacing up and down. She reminded herself that he was a well-intentioned man, deserving of friendship and esteem, but still her heart sank as she went into the room.

"Is everything all right?" demanded Maurice.

"I've no idea what the latest news is," replied Deborah, accustomed to the Canning abrupt plunge into conversation. "You're the first person I've spoken to this morning."

"Actually, I meant your mother. I rang you a few times yesterday evening to ask how she was, but there's something wrong with your phone. I kept getting the message service. Is your mother OK?"

"Yes, she's fine. It was just a bit of family turbulence. Nothing that won't resolve itself before too long, but my mother got rather flustered, and I didn't think to check for phone messages. You'll have to update me. Is the museum opening today?"

"Tomorrow at the earliest," Maurice replied gloomily. "And then we're sure to get all sorts of ghoulish weirdoes hanging around, determined to spot a ghost. It's bad enough now, with them wanting to stay here overnight and hold séances."

"As long as they shell out for the entrance fee, you shouldn't complain," said Deborah. "Your uncle will be pleased, how ever visitors are attracted here."

"Talking of Calvin, has he contacted you?" Maurice stood still and tidied the papers on Deborah's desk. She had known him long enough to recognize that he was trying to appear casual while he chose his words carefully. "I haven't been able to do anything but leave Calvin another message."

"Perhaps your phone is the one not working properly."

"It can't be that. I used different phones: land line and mobile; but I couldn't get further than his message service."

"Then Calvin clearly doesn't want to be disturbed. I could send an email, but if he isn't bothering with his phone messages, he's unlikely to be interested in his correspondence either."

"Don't you think that's odd?" Maurice picked up a notepad, and began flicking through its pages too quickly to read any of the writing inside. "Calvin always checks his messages. You know how efficient he is."

"Even the most efficient of mortals is entitled to some time off." Deborah sat down at her desk and switched on the computer. "I'll get in touch with the staff, and tell them there's no need to come here today. I must put a notice on the website too."

"Excellent plan." But the normal team-bonding over-praise was only in Maurice's words, not his voice, as he continued to flip through the pages of the notebook. "They haven't identified the courtyard man yet."

"Haven't they?" Deborah checked the staff rota, and hoped that Maurice would realize she had work to do.

"Dan Rother says it definitely wasn't a staff member," continued Maurice. "The police asked him to take a look at the body."

"I suppose a retired policeman was the obvious choice. Dan's the sole person here who'll have had any experience of that type of situation. Poor Dan; he must have thought getting a security job in a museum would be a career change."

"He hasn't been here more than a few weeks," said Maurice, balancing the notepad on one finger.

"It wasn't Dan's fault that a body wandered in off the street," Deborah stated, before Maurice could attempt to pass the buck. "Dan doesn't usually work Sundays, and he was only here yesterday to be an Exercise Disaster casualty."

"I'm not blaming him in the least," declared Maurice, as he picked the notebook up from the floor. "I just wondered if Dan had ever met my uncle."

"I haven't a clue. Ask Dan, if you really want to know. Does it matter?"

"No, no, of course not," replied Maurice, then added, "but you must admit it's odd."

"Odd? Odd if Dan knows Calvin or odd if he doesn't?"

"Odd that Calvin's disappeared," Maurice said hesitantly.

"But he hasn't disappeared," Deborah pointed out. "He simply isn't answering his phone. That's not odd; that's strategy."

"I rang your detective friend earlier," continued Maurice, still trying to sound nonchalant. "But he said he was too busy to talk."

33

"That doesn't surprise me," Deborah commented, amused.

"I spoke to a detective constable instead." Maurice leaned awkwardly against the wall before immediately straightening up again. "I asked what the courtyard man looked like."

"Why?"

"Well—because no one had said. And I thought—well, never mind what I thought. Tell me, how would you describe Calvin?"

"You don't seriously think it was Calvin in the courtyard?" demanded Deborah.

Maurice shrugged. "He's tall, with dark-brown hair, average build—"

"That describes millions of men, yourself included."

"But why would someone here want to hit a complete stranger over the head?"

"Are you implying that someone here would prefer to hit your uncle over the head?" asked Deborah. Then she registered Maurice's exact words, and added in surprise, "It's true that the man had a head injury? I did hear a rumour about blunt instruments, but I thought it was one of those tales that gets bigger and better as it speeds through the town."

"There's no need for anything to be embellished," declared Maurice despondently. "The man was killed by some weapon or other that the police haven't found yet. It's lucky there were so many people milling around yesterday. If it had only been museum staff, visitors might think twice about coming here."

"No one's going to imagine that we have a maniac skulking among the staff," said Deborah. "I can't picture the emergency services running amok with blunt instruments either. The man who isn't Calvin doubtless tripped and banged his head against something. A dull explanation, but a rational one."

"You're probably right." The solid commonsense of Deborah's words forced Maurice to agree, although with reluctance. "Yes, whatever happened must have been an accident. Anything else is too sensational for a Monday morning. All the same, it's odd that Calvin's vanished for so long."

But the timescale of Calvin Canning's incommunicado status would depend on the charms of the female who had done the vanishing with him, and the staff rota offered Deborah a clue to a possible identification of the siren. Chelsea Pritchard, the museum's fetching receptionist, had her day off on a Monday, and so there was no necessity for Chelsea to hurry to the breakfast table that morning, which could mean Calvin might remain unavailable for some hours. "Don't worry about your uncle. I'm sure he has an excellent reason for neglecting to check his messages."

"Yes, I expect so." But Maurice did not look convinced. In his fraught world of calamity and affliction, the vast majority of which had no existence outside his brain, the only explanation for an unanswered message was the recipient's death. A second corpse might be too much of a coincidence even for Maurice's lurid imagination, and therefore Calvin had to be the battered body in the courtyard. It would be as logical to Maurice as following a map to an inevitable destination. In his mind, Calvin was dead and as good as buried, with the will read and the rest of the world already having moved on. The deduction meant that he could not concentrate on anything else, and drifted in and out of Deborah's office as she made telephone calls, answered emails and opened letters, but his restlessness was a usual occurrence that she had learnt to ignore.

"There's still no news about Calvin." Maurice's words tripped over themselves in his rush to speak, as Deborah put the final letter to one side. "It's almost 24 hours since the first message was left. Something's wrong. I know something's wrong."

"Like everyone else, Calvin's entitled to a day off."

"He's never taken one before."

Maurice was right, yet the idea of Calvin Canning's life abruptly reaching its end in a museum courtyard during a dummy run disaster was absurd; he was too well-known in Seaborne, too rich, for such a slight as remaining anonymous throughout so many hours. "Somebody would have recognized him by now," said Deborah. "I don't like to suggest that your uncle's name is a byword in police circles, but most of them will know Calvin. He's the sort of person who's rather conspicuous in a provincial town."

"But no one's going to check if it's him or not. No one's even going to think of it." Maurice sounded frantic, but that was a normal tone of voice for him, and Deborah only shrugged.

"The police will identify Calvin soon enough if it is him; if it isn't, he'll turn up. You just have to wait. Rather cold advice to give to a family member, I know, but sensible."

"I wish I was half as sensible as you," declared Maurice, but he spoke automatically, having barely listened to what Deborah said, and his disquiet began to put doubts in her own mind. Calvin was a compulsive message checker, and even if he failed to hear the local news bulletins, Chelsea Pritchard would surely not have been able to resist passing on such an extraordinary piece of information, no matter how impassioned their encounter. Deborah had another look at the staff rota, and saw that Chelsea had indeed signed in the previous day to grace the proceedings as a casualty.

"If you're really bothered, why not go around to Calvin's house?" suggested Deborah.

"He can't be there. If he was, he'd have listened to his messages by now. Anyway, he could have checked them, wherever he was. So why hasn't he?"

Assuming Chelsea was the gossipmonger Deborah supposed her to be, the tale of police swarming through his museum should have had an electrifying effect on Calvin. Any chance of a scandal near the Canning surname might tarnish the image, and Calvin's opinion of his nephew's ability to deal with it was unlikely to be high. For a few seconds, Deborah considered phoning Chelsea, but if Calvin were too preoccupied to answer messages, presumably Chelsea was sharing that preoccupation.

"Do you have any idea where Calvin could possibly hide himself so thoroughly?" asked Maurice.

"Your guess is bound to be better than mine," replied Deborah, unwilling to admit that she was making assumptions on very little evidence.

"I can't guess. I never knew that much about Calvin's life. He didn't talk to me, only at me." Maurice hesitated, and Deborah realized that he was trying to think of a casual way to ask a question.

"Yes?"

"Yes?" repeated Maurice, perplexed.

"What do you want to ask me?"

Maurice attempted to smile, but looked self-conscious. "I just wondered if Calvin was a family friend."

"Of my family? Of course not. We don't exactly move in the same circles," said Deborah, amused at the idea of how insulted the pursuer of local MPs and other minor celebrities would be at having his name linked with nonentities like the Wainwrights. "Though Lucas did inform me that I was hired on Calvin's orders. He also claimed you started the rumour."

"It's true," protested Maurice, half apologetic, half defensive, "but I'd have given you the job anyway. You were the best candidate, and have been invaluable from your very first day. You don't owe Calvin a thing."

"As I'd never met him before coming to work here, I definitely owe him nothing. You must have muddled me with whoever Calvin actually recommended."

"He'd soon have pointed it out if I had," declared Maurice.

"Then Calvin muddled me up with someone else."

"He never said so."

"Perhaps he didn't want to tell you he'd made a mistake."

"No, he certainly never admitted to mistakes."

Calvin was already in the past tense for Maurice, Deborah noted, and indeed the continued silence was uncharacteristic; but Chelsea's attractions were doubtless many, and Calvin had a dashingly lascivious reputation to maintain. Deborah gave up, handed the puzzle over to time to sort out, and shut down her computer.

"Are you going to lunch now? We can have our postponed meal," said Maurice, with an eagerness that Deborah would have found flattering in another man.

"Actually, I've promised to meet a friend," she replied, blessing Phoebe for having bothered to renew contact.

"Then we'll just have to postpone our meal a second time." Maurice was let down, but made an effort to appear jovial. "Is Jason Clenham back in the picture?"

"I do know other people, I'm glad to say. And the museum should make the front page of the local paper this week, without the ghost of boyfriend past returning to haunt me."

But at that moment Maurice was the one who seemed haunted, his face frozen in an expression of absolute amazement, as he stared in disbelief at the open door of the office. Deborah turned around to discover what had so disconcerted him, and found herself looking at Maurice's personal spectre.

"What on earth's been happening?" demanded Calvin Canning. "I take a weekend off, and pandemonium breaks out. This is supposed to be a museum, not some kind of circus."

"I didn't know that circuses had bodies lying around as a matter of course," retorted Deborah. "I've obviously led a sheltered life."

Calvin laughed. The best way to deflect his anger was by standing one's ground to challenge him, a strategy that Maurice entirely failed to master. He continued to stare at his uncle as though Calvin really had come back from the dead, and could be expected to dematerialize without warning for a return to the spirit world. The superficial likeness between them, dark-brown hair and height, only emphasized their differences, which were extensive. Calvin knew the value of appearance, and dressed well. He stood bolt upright and confident, totally in command. Although he was nearly 20 years older than Maurice, everything about Calvin seemed closer to youthfulness than his nephew's finicky attempts at self-assurance. "When I checked my messages, Maurice is rambling on about a successful disaster, Deborah talks of an incident, and the police order me to contact them. What's going on?" demanded Calvin.

"A visitor was found dead in the courtyard yesterday," Deborah explained, "but as you weren't here, I don't know how you could help the police."

"Then why are they being so officious?" Calvin spoke impatiently. He did not expect to be pestered by those he considered minions, and would blame either Deborah or Maurice for the affront. "How did the visitor die? Presumably not from straightforward natural causes, if the police are scurrying around."

"There's some talk of a head injury," said Deborah, "but precise details are a bit scarce. No one knows who the man was, or why he should have been here."

"But it wasn't our fault." Maurice abruptly plunged into the conversation, speaking too quickly and too appeasingly. "The museum was closed to the public because of the disaster exercise. And that went off without a single hitch."

"Apart from the slight hiccup of a body left behind in the courtyard," Calvin pointed out.

39

"Well, yes," conceded Maurice. "But it was definitely an accident. Almost certainly."

"That's the most likely explanation," said Deborah, before Calvin could wither Maurice with further scorn. "I'm sure the police will tell you the same thing."

"I'm not talking to them until I have all the available facts, as well as my lunch," declared Calvin. "I overheard you say something about meeting a friend, Deborah. Male or female?"

"Female."

"Is she attractive?"

"Stunningly so."

"In that case, I'll treat you to lunch," announced Calvin, shanghaiing the meal on the assumption that his company was a valued bonus to any party. "Maurice, if the police phone, you haven't seen me and don't know where I am."

"I better warn you that my good-looking friend is the ex-wife of one of the detectives who was here yesterday," said Deborah. "Does this piece of information mean that Phoebe and I have just lost our chance of a free feed?"

"Not necessarily. How ex is the husband?"

"Very ex. Phoebe never changes her mind."

"And what are the ex's failings? Women? Drink?"

"You want the gossip?"

"I want the dirt on the detective. You never know when a few facts might come in handy." Calvin's tone was jocular, but Deborah suspected that he was not joking. Knowledge of people's weaknesses would add to the sense of power that he so enjoyed.

"I don't think Lucas has any dramatic vices. They simply married in haste and repented at leisure. Phoebe acts on impulse, and it takes her commonsense a little time to catch up."

"She's sounding more attractive with each second," remarked Calvin.

****

The café was only a few minutes' walk from the museum, but Calvin insisted on taking his car to get there. "I did enough foot-slogging when I was young and broke, so I've no intention of going on a hike at my time of life."

It was not the idea of some exercise that Calvin disliked, but the thought of being seen in the town without the ostentatiously expensive car that he seemed to regard as much a part of his identity as his name. In that car, he was Calvin Canning, the self-made man who went to the right places and knew influential people; he was Calvin Canning, the generous supporter of local charities. But he was also Calvin Canning who had a reason for all that he did, including the offer of lunch at his expense, and he wanted a return on any investment. "What's the name and rank of your detective pal?"

"Lucas Rudd, DS; but he's not really a friend of mine," protested Deborah, as if denying a slur on her good name. "I've only met him twice: at his wedding, and yesterday. He appears to be efficient, but I don't know more about him than that. You'll have to interrogate Phoebe."

"And if that's Phoebe, I relish the prospect."

Phoebe stood in front of the café, looking like a film star unconvincingly cast as a small-town girl. With shining fair hair, slender figure, perfect make-up, and stylish clothes, she was a dash of Technicolor in a drab and misty street. "Here's a chance to impress with your PR abilities, Deborah. Sell me to Phoebe."

"I'll have a shot at it, but that's generally one PR job you have to do by yourself." The car would help, however. Phoebe had always appreciated luxury, and even before she realized that Deborah was inside, Phoebe's eyes were fixed on the vehicle as it approached her. She was not especially avaricious, but she liked wealth, as others were fond of music or landscapes without needing to possess original scores or the contents of the National Gallery. It was Deborah's emergence from the car that made Phoebe really stare at it.

"This is my good-natured and generous employer, Calvin Canning," said Deborah, "famed for his philanthropic tendencies and wide-ranging intellect. How's that for a PR job, Calvin?"

"Adequate, but you left out my statuesque handsomeness."

"Surely that goes without saying," commented Phoebe, but it was something of an effort to remove her gaze from the car to its owner.

Although two decades older than Phoebe, Calvin looked a more likely companion for her than Lucas could ever have done. Both Calvin and Phoebe had been born in the town, but projected an air of holidaymakers who would return to a more sophisticated background when their week at the seaside ended. It was an impression that came naturally to Phoebe, but was the result of determined effort by Calvin. He wanted to distance himself from his roots, to prove how very far he had travelled. That journey, however, was not as arduous as he habitually implied; the slum, so often claimed as his childhood home, had in fact been a comfortable, three-bedroom terraced house in an area where poverty consisted of only having one television and one car. But Calvin's imagination would doubtless have him trudging barefoot to school in rags before much more time passed. Most of the locals knew what his real background had been, but nobody contradicted his recollections because Calvin's money, unlike his early deprivation, was no illusion.

"I can't have lunch here," decreed Calvin, dismissing the café with a haughty glance. "We'll go to the Sea View." The Sea View sounded as if it should be the name of a dingy bed-and-breakfast with a formidable landlady, but it was in reality one of the more expensive restaurants in the town, and Calvin presumably chose it to impress Phoebe as, before seeing her, he had considered a café quite adequate for a meal with Deborah.

"I'm not paying the Sea View's pretentious prices," declared Phoebe.

"My guests never pay," said Calvin. "No arguments, Phoebe."

"I never argue with benefactors. The Sea View can be as pretentious as it chooses if someone else is picking up the bill." The day was rapidly turning into Phoebe's favourite sort, with a newly met man at her side, who was not only attentive but rich as well. Despite marriage and imminent divorce, she seemed not to have altered significantly from the teenager Deborah had known at school. Having a good time was still Phoebe's priority, and it took very little to make her cheerful, so an unexpected host with money enough to waste on overpriced food was reason for jubilation. "My luck's becoming exceptionally good. I had dinner at the Grand on Saturday, and now lunch at the Sea View."

Mention of the Grand Hotel made Deborah recall her father's presence in the town, and she tried to push the thought away. "I've never dared enter the Sea View before. According to rumour, they charge for the very air you breathe."

"I can afford all the air I want," Calvin said smugly. The Sea View was his type of restaurant, with formally dressed waiters who recognized him, and an obsequious manager prepared to grovel before the sums that resided in Calvin Canning's bank account. Nonetheless, price excluded, there was nothing remarkable about the food they were served, but quality of cooking would never be Calvin's main concern when selecting somewhere to eat.

"I'll be far too high and mighty after this servility to be bothered with receipts and allowable expenses when I go back to work," said Phoebe.

"What receipts?" asked Calvin.

"Phoebe's an accountant," explained Deborah.

"But I prefer to hear my job described as financial consultant. It sounds less dreary."

"I thought you'd be a model or an actress." Calvin looked surprised, and also disappointed. In his opinion, Phoebe's career should have matched the glamour of her appearance. He could not boast about having had lunch with an accountant.

"Wherever could I act or model in Seaborne?" said Phoebe, laughing. "Besides, fate doomed me to accountancy. It's in my blood."

"Phoebe's grandfather founded Vale and Son." Deborah's contribution went unacknowledged, but Calvin had heard. There were branch offices of Vale and Son across the county, and Calvin was always on alert in his quest to know people with influence. Deborah had ceased to be present, as far as he was concerned, and no further attempt on her part to be sociable was required. Untroubled, Deborah accepted the invisibility, and lapsed into silence. After a morning with Maurice, it was a pleasure not to speak.

"No family business cushioned my start in life," Calvin informed Phoebe with pride.

"You don't realize how lucky you were," said Phoebe. "I had a calculator instead of a rattle when I was a baby."

"Then you must know everything about tax loopholes and the other dodges."

"You bet. The Inland Revenue mob hates me. I stop them getting their clutches on thousands of pounds a year."

"Then where do I sign on? You've just acquired a new client. Have you got a business card? And write your home phone number on the back."

"It's not usually this easy." Phoebe did not believe a word Calvin was saying, Deborah could tell. Vale and Son, not to mention Granddaughter, had no need to chase work, and their clients rarely had Calvin's reputation, whether justified or not, for shady dealing. That reputation might be modified if a firm as respectable as Vale and Son accepted him, but Calvin was not thinking of image; he was thinking about Phoebe and how to impress her. Normally, he could assume that a woman would be impressed by stories of his wealth, but the Vale family knew the rich and their money with a thoroughness denied to the majority. His surname meant little to Phoebe, and Calvin grasped that he would have to make an effort to intrigue her.

"I'm going to London next week to discuss a business project, and it'd be helpful to have a financial expert with me. We'll have dinner together this evening and decide on our strategy."

"Sorry. My evening's already spoken for, and I've got appointments here in Seaborne all next week." Phoebe could not have made a reply more apt to beguile Calvin further. He did not value anyone or anything readily available.

"Then I'll reschedule the London meeting until the week after," Calvin announced grandly. "You can't abandon your latest client in his time of need. What about dinner tomorrow evening?"

"Well, perhaps—"

Deborah pushed back her chair and stood up. "I'll have to leave you to your negotiations. My lunch hour's practically over. Thanks for the meal, Calvin."

"You're welcome." But the response was automatic, and Phoebe's goodbye was a trifle abstracted as well. Deborah's company would not be missed.

****

Maurice was behind Deborah's desk, leaning back in the chair, and apparently fully occupied with staring at the wall. Such unusual stillness from the fidgety Maurice compelled Deborah to ask, "What's wrong?"

"Nothing. How was the lunch?"

"OK."

"Did Calvin invite you to dinner this evening?" There was distinct resentment in Maurice's voice.

"Your uncle was far too taken with Phoebe to remember that I was there too," replied Deborah, uncomfortably aware of how she had avoided Maurice's invitation to a meal, but permitted Calvin to gatecrash an arranged lunch. "Phoebe's an accountant, and it appears that the Canning finances might be entrusted to Vale and Son in future."

But a piece of information that would normally absorb Maurice's whole attention was ignored. "Did Calvin say where he'd been all weekend?"

"No. You'll have to ask him."

"He never tells me a thing." Maurice sounded almost sulky. Instead of dutifully rejoicing at his uncle's return from the dead, he seemed more depressed than relieved. It occurred to Deborah that if Calvin had been the corpse behind the fountain in the courtyard, Maurice's life would have improved immensely, especially should he inherit his uncle's money. Calvin was not fond of Maurice, but there were no other family members, and the nephew might have hopes of a substantial legacy. If Maurice had allowed his imagination to picture a wealthy future free of disparagement and contempt, sheer guilt would explain the atypical peevishness.

"Why don't you go and have lunch?" suggested Deborah.

"I phoned for a takeaway," Maurice replied austerely. "I'm far too busy to waste time going out."

But still Maurice sat at Deborah's computer, doing absolutely nothing. She could not ask him to leave, so picked up a few loose papers from her desk and shuffled through them as a hint that she was ready to start the afternoon's work. "Are there any calls I should return?"

"I dealt with them. The local paper wanted an update." Maurice paused, and then added, "It was Jason Clenham who phoned. You'd think he'd have more tact than to try and use you as a source."

"There's no need for him to be tactful. We never shrieked insults at each other, even when splitting up. In fact, we were tremendously civilized."

"He still shouldn't think that he can just phone you and get an exclusive," Maurice said stubbornly.

"Did he ask for an exclusive?"

"No," conceded Maurice, "but that's what he expected. Why else would he ring? He can get all the info he needs from the police statement."

"Is there some news? Have they identified the man yet?"

"Presumably not, or Jason Clenham wouldn't have tried to extort details from you."

"It is part of my job to speak to the press," Deborah reminded Maurice. "Whether or not I want to talk to a specific journalist doesn't actually matter. The idea is to get publicity."

"We've got more than enough publicity this week," declared Maurice, his petulance overtaken by gloom. The museum represented his main interest in life, and Deborah tried to sympathize, although she regarded her job as temporary, because when Calvin considered that his cultural credentials had been established in Seaborne, the museum project might be abandoned. He was unlikely to continue throwing money at an enterprise that brought him so little financial return.

"The courtyard's own particular disaster is a 15-minute wonder that'll be forgotten next week," said Deborah, but she knew that memories were long in the town.

"I put a hundred per cent into everything I do, and yet life always sticks barriers in front of me," complained Maurice.

"Do you think I was simply born unlucky?"

"Of course not; no one is." Because she suspected Maurice of hoping for a more intimate relationship with her than that of manager and assistant, Deborah did not want to listen to any confidences from him, and she changed the subject. "Will the museum be opening tomorrow?"

"I don't know." Then Maurice frowned, and demanded irritably, "What's happening?"

Deborah glanced at him in surprise, on the assumption that she was being addressed, before realizing that Maurice's attention had shifted to Detective Sergeant Rudd who stood by the door. Lucas ignored Maurice, and looked at Deborah. "Inspector Atherton needs to talk to you."

"Has there been a development?" asked Maurice, leaping to his feet.

"It's Deborah we have to see," said Lucas, and Phoebe's automaton managed to sound both awkward and apologetic, almost as if he had learnt a new programme: one of Maurice's.

"Deborah's already told you that she doesn't know anything," Maurice declared indignantly. "I won't have my staff harassed like this. What possible questions are there left to ask her?"

"It's OK, Maurice," said Deborah, "though you're quite right about me not knowing a thing. I can't add a word to what I told you yesterday, Lucas."

"It's not—well, Inspector Atherton will explain."

"The Inspector can do his explaining to me," announced Maurice.

"Perhaps you should be there too," agreed Lucas, astonishingly meek in the face of Maurice's antagonism. "Actually, it might be better if you go and have a word with Inspector Atherton first. I'll wait here with Deborah."

"I'm not planning to do a runner, Lucas," remarked Deborah. "My conscience is clear."

"I've no intention of leaving Deborah alone with you," Maurice stated. "You can forget that idea right now."

"You ought to have more confidence in the fact that I'm innocent," said Deborah, smiling.

"Of course you're innocent." But Maurice spoke so emphatically, he seemed to be denying an accusation already made against Deborah. "This is obviously a misunderstanding. I'll sort everything out for you."

"I can't say I'm relieved to hear it, because I wasn't worried in the first place."

"Why should you be worried? But if Inspector Atherton insists on perpetrating this charade, he can come in here to do it," decreed Maurice.

"I'll tell him." Lucas turned away, and walked down the corridor as obediently as a servant.

"That showed him, the arrogant bully," said Maurice, but possibly a little staggered that he could be forceful enough to send policemen scurrying around like underlings. "Don't worry, Deborah. I won't leave you alone with them."

"As I keep telling you, I'm not worried." But worry was so permanent a state of mind for Maurice, he could imagine no other, and reverted to the security of managerial guise, determined to tackle what he would term a challenge rather than a problem. His despondency had been banished by a situation he apparently considered to be a crisis, after which Deborah might find herself in a police cell on trumped-up charges. She abandoned the attempt to persuade him that she had no apprehension about talking to sergeants, inspectors or even chief constables, and sat in the chair newly vacated by Maurice, who had resumed his habitual pacing.

"This interference with the museum's routine is ridiculous. They must have done all that's necessary by now, and I'm determined to open the place to the public tomorrow, whatever happens." Maurice paused to draw attention to his decisiveness, before adding hastily, "Not that anything's going to happen. It's a ludicrous mistake."

"What's a ludicrous mistake?" asked Deborah, but she had started to check emails, and was only half-listening to Maurice.

"The whole thing's a stupid mistake. Inspector Atherton is just being officious. I bet it's only a few weeks since he was promoted, and the job title has gone to his head. He's so eager to prove what a hot-shot detective he is, anyone within sight gets arrested. Not that you'll be arrested, of course. I won't let it happen."

"Thanks awfully," said Deborah, aware that Maurice was picturing himself as the hero who stood between her and the calamitous results of police incompetence. "However, I don't think my chances of being sent to Devil's Island are all that great."

"Yes, I know I'm overreacting, as usual," admitted Maurice, trying to laugh, "though you do hear about completely innocent people getting into difficulties with the law through no fault of their own."

"Yes, you do. But I'm still not worrying." There was an email from Jason Clenham asking Deborah to telephone him, and she knew that Maurice had been right in his assessment of Jason, who was an ambitious man with no intention of spending the rest of his career reporting charity fêtes and Rotary Club speeches. An ex-girlfriend, close to the scene of a local sensation that had made the national papers, would be regarded as an excellent source.

"There's really no need to bother Deborah with further questions, Inspector," Maurice was saying defiantly. "She can't tell you anything more than what she's already said."

"I'm not here to ask questions."

At the sound of an unfamiliar voice, Deborah glanced up and saw Lucas walk into her office with a man who was presumably the officious Inspector Atherton. He was in his forties, tall and thin, with light-brown hair and so unremarkable a face, he did not look different enough to have such an authoritative title. Maurice's bluster seemed to pass him by, as if Atherton hardly registered it, but Maurice was not prepared to give up that easily.

"If you've no more questions for Deborah, why are you demanding to see her?" Maurice sounded triumphant, believing he had somehow tricked Atherton into an admission of Deborah's probable innocence.

"We know the identity of the man who died here," said Lucas, but he spoke to Deborah, not Maurice.

"Who was he?" demanded Maurice, sidetracked from his mission to protect Deborah.

Both Atherton and Lucas were silent for a moment, and their discomfort was evident. "Deborah, this is Inspector Atherton," Lucas said at last.

Deborah nodded an acknowledgement, but Maurice was impatient with the formalities. "Who was the man?"

"It took a while to identify him, although he turned out to be a local. He was staying in a hotel, and no one realized he was missing." Atherton looked at Deborah as if he expected her to join in the conversation, and she understood that the information was directed at her. In Atherton's opinion, Maurice was simply a bystander.

"He was at the Grand Hotel," added Lucas, but Deborah did not respond. If they were trying to tell her that Gregory could not be located, and was therefore considered a possible candidate for the role of body in courtyard, the police had made a mistake. Gregory occasionally vanished, but he always turned up again sooner or later.

"He signed into the hotel under an alias for some reason," said Atherton, and he made the use of a stage name seem very suspicious behaviour indeed.

"Gregory Wainwright sounds like someone who works in a district council office for 50 years because of a secure pension at the end that he'll be too feeble to enjoy. Now, Greg Wayne takes chances, lives life on impulse. Anything could happen to Greg Wayne." It must have been on a Sunday when Gregory had explained to a puzzled child why her father's name was pliable. During the week, he was away, either working or chasing work; and work, of course, meant singing in provincial clubs, or touring in second-rate musicals and second-rate pantomimes. However, Gregory saw himself as a star in waiting, and stars did not lower themselves by stacking shelves in superstores or washing glasses in pubs, even on a temporary basis. Obviously, there would be no more financial difficulties in the future, a future so gloriously golden, it entirely eclipsed the present for Gregory. As soon as his talent was acclaimed, he could forget about cadging handouts from Rhoda, forget failed auditions, supercilious agents, and half-drunk audiences in back-street clubs. Greg Wayne was to conquer the West End, have his own television series, receive film offers from Hollywood. It was his destiny and without belief in that astounding destiny, existence would be futile, because he did not value life without success and fame. Gregory had to be the person he pictured in his imagination. There was no other option, and even languishing in the wilderness of provincial clubs and theatres could never tarnish his perception of himself.

"He called himself Greg Wayne at the hotel," continued Atherton, waiting for Deborah's reaction.

"That's his stage name."

"You knew him?" Maurice stared at Deborah in astonishment. "You knew the man in the courtyard?"

"They think it's my father, but he isn't missing. He's at my mother's place. He phoned yesterday to tell her that he was on his way there."

"You talked to him?" asked Atherton.

"No, he talked to my mother." Gregory knew which side his bread was buttered when he ran short of money, and more importantly, Rhoda saw him as he liked to be seen.

"You've made a mistake," Maurice informed Atherton. "I gave Deborah a lift to her mother's yesterday evening, hours after all the fuss here."

Atherton was clearly unaccustomed to being told that he had made any sort of mistake, and his features hardened as he asked Deborah, "Did you actually see your father last night?"

"No, but he was definitely on his way."

"And did he arrive?"

"I don't know. I've been at work all morning, and we're not allowed to have personal calls."

"Except in emergencies," Maurice added hastily, to distance himself from Simon Legree. "And they don't have to be dire emergencies; even quite minor situations would count. It's very flexible. Deborah's perfectly free to phone anyone she—"

Atherton cut into Maurice's rambling self-justification with an impatient sigh. "Your parents are divorced?" he asked Deborah.

"No."

"Then why was your father staying at the Grand?"

"You'll have to ask him. He usually goes straight home when he's in town." But Deborah could guess the probable reason for the change in Gregory's habits, and that reason would be female. He had wanted to secure the favours of the latest in a long line of attractive yet gullible women by convincing her that Greg Wayne was successful, wealthy and with influence enough to ease her route into show business. To avoid tiresome commitments should the lady prove clinging, Gregory would then spin a tale of being unable to divorce Rhoda because the heartless wife threatened to deny him access to his treasured little daughter if he did so. A few of the deluded females had actually contacted Rhoda to protest at such callousness, and Rhoda would triumphantly point out that the age of the treasured little daughter rather put her beyond maternal control.

"Why do you let him get away with treating you like this?" Deborah had demanded more than once, and Rhoda would seem surprised at having to explain yet again her free as air marriage.

"Women are forever chasing after Gregory, and he shakes them off in his own way. He isn't a possession I bought in a shop, and so when he comes home, it's by choice, not compulsion. I'll never understand how Greg and I managed to produce such a suburban-minded daughter."

Atherton had said something, and Deborah hurriedly tried to free her head of both Rhoda and Gregory. "I'm sorry?"

"I asked if you need a lift." Atherton had difficulty masking his irritation, as if he thought Deborah were being deliberately obstructive.

"You've already been told that the man in the courtyard can't possibly be Mr Wainwright." Maurice could not have sounded more irate had he just witnessed a flagrant example of police brutality. "You've no right to worry Deborah. And don't say you're merely doing your job. That's no excuse."

With a visible effort, Atherton refrained from ordering Maurice to keep his mouth shut, and Deborah tactfully intervened. "What made you think it was my father?"

"Deborah, we know it's your father." After Atherton's prickliness, Lucas appeared almost sympathetic. "Warren Forbes identified him."

"Then Warren Forbes, whoever he might be, is plainly wrong," stated Maurice.

But Deborah knew Warren Forbes. He was a young police constable, the son of Rhoda's neighbour, and he ought to be able to recognize Gregory. The first uneasy doubts crept into Deborah's mind, and a sickly warmth began to spread through her body. "I'll phone my mother," she decided, after a few seconds of dithering.

54

"Good idea," said Maurice. "That'll put a stop to all this nonsense."

"Perhaps it would be better if we took you straight to your mother, Deborah," suggested Atherton, arrogance dented by an unexpected trace of compassion in his voice.

"I'll take Deborah anywhere she wants to go," announced Maurice. His over-protectiveness would probably make Atherton assume that Deborah and her boss were an item, as Maurice's participation in the interview went beyond dutiful support of an employee. He apparently felt himself to be under attack, because Deborah's fight was his fight. Except that there was no fight, Deborah reminded herself.

"I don't need to go anywhere," said Deborah, trying to regain control of her life. "I'll phone my mother. The whole thing's ended if my father's with her." *If. If. If.* As she dialled the number, Deborah realized that she had said *if*. But Gregory was immortal, a perennial problem, a perpetual problem to worry her all through life. He could not really disappear forever, because he never did. It was as simple as that.

"Hello?" Rhoda's voice was jumpy, and Deborah's heart sank. Her mother was still waiting for Gregory, hoping that he would be at the other end of the line.

"It's Deborah." There was nothing more for her to say. She knew what she had called to find out.

"Gregory hasn't put in an appearance yet, but I should have known better than to expect promptness. Time has never meant much to him."

"Have you had any word since yesterday morning?"

"He didn't make an appointment," protested Rhoda. "He's knows it's my day off. Greg will turn up when he's ready."

"There might be a problem." Even as she spoke, Deborah could not accept what she was saying. A mistake had to have been made.

"A problem? Are you still talking about Greg or do you mean at work?"

"I'll explain when I see you. Ten minutes or so."

"Fine." But Rhoda was hardly paying attention. Her mind had stayed with Gregory.

****

Damn Gregory. Deborah had despised him for years, but the memories that filled her head were of childhood, when she believed his stories, believed herself to be at the centre of his world, just as he was the centre of hers. The Sundays Gregory had been at home were Christmases out of season, parties with music and fun and laughter, the highest of high holidays. He had a gift of making the dullest hour bright for the child who loved him more than anyone else, even Rhoda, because when he was not there, everything seemed second-best, predictable, monochrome, time to be endured until his return. If Gregory had died then, her whole existence, whether long or short, would have been blighted.

But Gregory had not died. Instead, his visits became less frequent, promises were forgotten, and arrangements ignored. He could take Rhoda's adoration for granted, but Deborah knew that she had been abandoned, and the pain was one of betrayal. His absence meant Gregory did not need or value his daughter's company, and also meant that he had once duped her in the way he continued to dupe Rhoda. Deborah wanted to erase her father, to relegate him to a past so distant, it could no longer hurt. But Gregory refused to be banished, refused to be obliterated.

Gregory had stood in handsome profile by the kitchen window, and warmed his fingers around a coffee cup. "No one at the audition had half the talent I've got. In fact, there's more talent in my shoes than most of them will be able to acquire in a lifetime. Somebody got to the casting director." But somebody always turned directors, producers and agents against him, according to Gregory. Treachery was the only explanation for his inability to conquer the world of show business.

"Of course you'll make enemies, Greg. People hate anyone better looking or more talented than they are," said Rhoda, whole-heartedly in agreement with Gregory's assessment of himself and his gifts. It never occurred to Rhoda that she might be married to a second-rater who tried to work in a profession full to overflowing with other second-raters. In looks, talent and personality, Gregory was an average hopeful who had nothing original to offer, nothing unique. He sang other people's songs and repeated other people's jokes: just another handsome face, with the sort of voice that could be heard in any nightclub or touring show. Gregory was adequate, but entirely without the indefinable something that separated top-of-the-bill bold letters from the smaller-print names. Only two individuals believed in his imminent stardom, and they were Gregory and Rhoda.

Rhoda. Rhoda had to be told that her husband was dead. Deborah pictured her mother sobbing hysterically, collapsing with grief, unable to go on. Life for Rhoda would stop at that moment, because Gregory was the principal thought behind everything she did. Yet Rhoda had to learn that he was gone for good. Leaving her behind seemed the most thoughtless act that Gregory had ever done.

"Your father must have gone to the museum to see you," said Maurice, as if offering consolation. Because Deborah was in his car, he apparently imagined that, akin to a latter-day Scarlet Pimpernel, he had rescued her from the grasp of malign authority. Lucas and Atherton were only a few vehicles away, but Maurice regarded himself as already having outwitted them. "Of course, it might not be your father at all. Coincidences happen, so you mustn't give up hope. It could be someone who looked exactly like him."

"And by a couple of further coincidences, the someone chanced to be called Greg Wayne and was staying at the Grand Hotel." Deborah struggled not to sound curt, but the tension made Maurice's blundering attempt at kindness more exasperating than usual.

"I didn't know your father was on the stage," continued Maurice, for whom silence deeper than words would never be an option.

"His career wasn't worth mentioning."

"It's still more interesting than most people's jobs: mine, for example. Have you met lots of actors?"

"My father didn't bring any home, but it was a rare enough event when he brought himself home."

Maurice looked uncomfortable at the criticism of one so recently departed, but he ploughed on. "This is all too much for you. Stay off work as long as you want. You don't have to worry about a thing. I can cope."

Coping was what Maurice did least well, but Deborah thanked him, certain that she could never go back to the place where Gregory's life had ended. Everything at the museum would be a reminder of him, and she did not wish to be forced to remember someone she had tried so hard to forget.

Maurice stopped his car at a pedestrian crossing, and Deborah watched shoppers with loaded carrier bags exchange one side of the High Street for the other. She longed to join them, to hurry away and hide in the anonymity of a crowd while somebody else lifted from her shoulders the burden of telling Rhoda. But cowardice was an inheritance from Gregory, who had ducked responsibility all his life, and Deborah was ashamed to realize how like him she could be. She was not thinking of Rhoda, but of herself.

"I'll go inside with you," said Maurice, as they approached the house. "You and your mother shouldn't have to deal with Atherton at such a time. The man's a downright bully."

"There's no reason for him to bully my mother, but if he tries it, I'll kick him out."

"I'll do any kicking required. You don't need the aggravation today."

But Maurice himself had been the aggravating factor for Atherton. However, that was the Inspector's problem; Deborah had more than police sensibilities to think about. Maurice parked his car at the kerb of a street so placidly small-town, it felt impossible that Rhoda's world was soon to be shattered. The terrace was Edwardian, too old not to have opened front doors to bad news before, but the incongruous pink of Rhoda's house looked absurdly frivolous: a colour scheme that belonged in a fairy tale with a happy ending; although, for someone who chose to live with rosebud curtains and bluebell wallpaper, Rhoda had an odd streak of realism in her that could accept Gregory as he was, not as she might have preferred him to be. The illusion had been a belief that he came home because he wanted to see her, rather than to replenish his finances. It was a fantasy that Deborah had scorned for years, but now wished Rhoda could have kept forever.

If Maurice had not been there, Deborah would have shirked going straight to the house, but it did not occur to him that she might need a little time before facing Rhoda. Maurice thought of Deborah as capable and self-possessed, requiring only minimal backup. Like most people lacking confidence, Maurice was convinced that everybody else in the world had been born with supreme ability to tackle any contingency without flinching, and he was unable to imagine that Deborah could feel as hurled around by events as he regularly did. He also gave her more credit for sensitivity than she deserved, because Deborah would have abandoned Rhoda to Atherton given any excuse, no matter how feeble, to avoid being the one to break the news to her mother; but that was precisely what Gregory would have done, and so Deborah forced herself to walk towards the house.

Rhoda must have been watching from behind the living-room curtains because the front door opened before Deborah reached it. "Well? What's going on?" demanded Rhoda. She looked tired, perhaps after having stayed awake all night as she waited in vain for Gregory.

Deborah did not reply, could not reply, and walked past Rhoda into the house, closely trailed by Maurice. Most people would have felt awkward to gatecrash such a traumatic moment, but awkwardness was so usual a feeling for Maurice that he regarded it as the normal human state. "I'm Maurice Canning, Mrs Wainwright: a friend of Deborah's," he said, offering Rhoda a hand to shake, his solemn tone of voice the only concession made to a sombre occasion.

"It's about Gregory, isn't it?" declared Rhoda, ignoring Maurice's hand, scarcely aware of his presence. "Something's happened to Greg."

Deborah tried to speak, but could only nod.

"He's dead, isn't he?"

"How did you know?" asked Maurice in surprise, under the impression that he was the one who had been addressed.

Deborah went to put an arm around her mother, but Rhoda turned away. A daughter was no substitute for the lost Gregory, especially a daughter whose life would not be devastated by removal of the paragon. Deborah felt as inadequate as a Maurice, because she suspected that Rhoda was already promoting Gregory to sainthood. He would become the peerless husband, the devoted parent, in Rhoda's memory, and therefore any differences between father and daughter must have been entirely Deborah's fault. It was why Rhoda had spurned the attempt to comfort her; she blamed Deborah for cold-heartedly rejecting Gregory. As all disputes seemed petty in the face of death, Deborah began to think that her mother might be correct. Gregory could not have changed; it had been up to Deborah to accept him the way he was, as Rhoda did. Better an intermittent father than none at all.

"I'll go and tell Atherton that he can't ask his questions today. He won't get by me, whatever he tries to do," announced Maurice, although the Inspector was hardly likely to force an entrance.

Deborah nodded again, and then made herself follow Rhoda into the living room.

"Who was that man?" asked Rhoda as the front door closed behind Maurice, but she was talking to herself, as if in an effort to make sense of a confusing dream that she knew to be unreal, even as she slept. "This is all a mistake. It must be a mistake."

"I don't think so," said Deborah, but her throat was so tightly constricted that she had difficulty making the words audible.

Her back to Deborah, Rhoda stood by the mantelpiece, and began to rearrange the treasured collection of pink glass animals. "What happened?"

"I'm not sure. Do you want to talk to the police?"

"I don't want to talk to anybody."

And that included Rhoda's daughter, but Deborah floundered on. "Someone said something about a head injury. I think he must have tripped over in the courtyard."

"Gregory's the man in the museum courtyard?" said Rhoda in bewilderment. She was silent for a few seconds, and then abruptly turned around to glare at Deborah. "He went there on purpose to see you."

It sounded like an accusation: an accusation that Deborah was responsible for Gregory's death. If he had not gone to the museum, he would still be alive. It was so logical a conclusion that Deborah felt miserable with guilt. "He never came to see me at work before."

"But yesterday he did."

"I'd no idea he was going to."

"Of course not. When was the last time that you condescended to speak to him?"

Rhoda's voice was hostile, and Deborah did not reply. She wanted to cry, not because her father had died, but because her mother spoke with such anger. Rhoda was not falling apart; she was fighting, and the enemy appeared to be her daughter.

"Who's that?" demanded Rhoda, as somebody rang the front door bell.

"I expect it's Maurice, my boss. I'll tell him to go."

"Go with him."

It was an order that Deborah would have liked to obey immediately, unable to recognize her mother in the contemptuous figure whose eyes were filled with hatred. But bereavement was supposed to be a time when family members came together in best Hollywood fashion to heal old wounds, not inflict brand new ones, and so Deborah said tentatively, "Will you be all right?"

"No, I won't be all right. I'll never be all right again. Stop asking stupid questions and get out."

Deborah had always known that she came second in her mother's affections, but to have lost even that lowly place was hard to bear. Uncertain how Rhoda would react to any further words, Deborah went into the hall without saying goodbye, and opened the front door. Maurice, prepared to re-enter the house, was taken aback to have to retreat a few steps when Deborah joined him in the street, closing the door behind her.

"Atherton's gone. I made it very plain he was being too intrusive," Maurice reported, under the impression that he had single-handedly vanquished a modern version of Attila the Hun. "You won't be troubled by that loud-mouthed bully again today."

"Thanks." Deborah started to walk down the road, and Maurice hurried after her.

"Can I give you a lift? Or should I stay with your mother? She ought not to be alone at a time like this."

"But she wants to be left alone. For a little while. She said so." Deborah hoped that she had made her mother's wishes seem a reasonable method of dealing with grief. The prospect of blame from Maurice, in addition to Rhoda, was too daunting to face. Deborah, who normally had most of her life under control, felt adrift on a rough sea.

"Where are you going?" asked Maurice. "I'll drive you there."

It was easier for Deborah to get into the car, and let Maurice take her home, than invent a tactful excuse to be free of him. The dismissal by Rhoda was too raw a pain to pass on, even in a minor way.

"It does get bearable after a while," ventured Maurice. "My parents died in a car crash when I was nine, and I thought I'd die too, but—Oh well, time's a great healer, as they say."

But the usual rules were irrelevant in Rhoda's world. Gregory would never be dislodged, and time seemed more likely to inflame wounds than heal them. Deborah knew that she was on her own.

3

For a day or so, Deborah wilted, alternately worrying about Rhoda and feeling sorry for herself. Sympathy cards began to drop through the letterbox, but the English horror at actually having to face the newly bereaved in person meant that nobody knocked on the door or telephoned, with the single exception of Maurice. His persistence roused Deborah into beginning an internet search for another job, although it was difficult to imagine a new life in new surroundings with new people, because a void seemed to separate her from the rest of the world, almost as if she had been the one who died. But were she dead, Maurice would not have appeared on the doorstep with such regularity.

"I've brought some lunch with me. Just sandwiches, but better than nothing. I know you won't be able to face the bother of cooking. We could go around to your mother's house and eat there, if you like."

"I saw her earlier. She needs some time to herself right now," said Deborah, too ashamed to admit that she had been banished.

"You won't feel very lucky at the moment, but you are, to have your mother. When my parents died, there was nobody but Calvin, so he packed me off to boarding school. He didn't know what else to do with the kid who'd been dumped on him, and I don't blame Calvin in the least. Well, that's what I tell myself anyway."

"You're right; I am lucky to have got through childhood so easily." But Maurice's story just made Deborah feel more guilty to have let Rhoda down at such a time. A daughter should be a support, not an impediment. "What's happening at the museum? Have you been allowed to open the place again?"

"Not yet; perhaps tomorrow. But it's always 'perhaps tomorrow' whenever I ask." Maurice moved gratefully onto a less emotional subject, and sat down at the kitchen table. Then he recalled the reason why his museum was closed, and added quickly, "Don't even think about work."

"But why are the police still there? Surely they've done all the necessary tests by now."

"Presumably not." But Maurice shied away from the awkwardness of the topic, and looked around the kitchen for inspiration. "You know, this is a nice little house."

The house was certainly little but not particularly nice, being dark and cramped and relentlessly filled with dust. Over two centuries old, its history was of low wages and manual labour; and even Deborah's spin would be hard pressed to find romance in the mundane past of gruelling work and limited lives. Something inside her, instilled from earliest days by Gregory, regarded ordinariness as defeat. She too wanted success and achievement, and understood why Calvin Canning had chosen to identify with a long-gone Prime Minister, rather than his own undistinguished ancestors. "Working in a beautiful building has raised my standards considerably," said Deborah. "It's a comedown, having to return here each night."

Maurice resolutely ignored the reference to the museum. "Little houses feel homelike to me. Anything manorial reminds me of school. I know everyone says they hated school, but I really loathed the place."

"I didn't mind it that much," claimed Deborah, unwilling to let Maurice assume they were in sympathy on any issue. "I suppose that means I was the school swot."

"I was the dunce."

Deborah smiled as if she thought Maurice must be joking, despite his matter-of-fact tone of voice. She did not want to trade memories with him, even though minor annoyances were meant to fade away, mirage-like, before the actuality of death. But mirages could seem very real while they lasted, and it was a relief to hear a knock on the front door.

"I'll go," said Maurice, crashing the back of his chair against the wall. "It might be that tiresome Inspector. Atherton has no idea of what constitutes an appropriate time. This is simple persecution, badgering you day after day."

"Actually, I haven't heard from him or Lucas Rudd."

But Maurice was not to be talked out of his knight champion role. "Don't worry. I'll get rid of them."

"I'm not worried," Deborah protested yet again, as Maurice strode from the kitchen. She heard the front door open, and then went into the hall herself because the man, being repelled so vehemently by Maurice, was not Detective Inspector Atherton, but Jason Clenham, journalist.

"Deborah isn't speaking to the press." Maurice sounded angry, but Deborah did not blame Jason, who had a living to earn, and Gregory's fate would sensationally fill the local front page, more usually the terrain of planning application disputes and centenarian birthday celebrations.

"Come in, Jason," said Deborah, glad of a third person to deflect Maurice's attention.

"I just dropped by to tell you how sorry I am," declared Jason, thrusting a bunch of snowdrops at Deborah. "I swear I haven't arrived to doorstep you in the expectation of an exclusive interview."

But Deborah was fairly certain that Jason did hope to glean details withheld from the news media, as he had never before given her flowers, even in the heyday of their relationship. Ignoring Maurice, Jason walked confidently into the house, and took one of Deborah's hands in both of his to prove how sympathetic he was; then, point established, Jason led the way to the kitchen with the ease of someone thoroughly at home. Deborah had grown accustomed to his handsomeness during her involvement with him, but after not seeing Jason for a few months, she was struck anew by his appearance: the looks that Phoebe had taken time out from her wedding day to notice. "Oddly enough, Jason, I was talking about you only the other day with Phoebe Vale. Do you remember Phoebe?"

But of course Jason would remember. He had everybody filed in his mind as a possible future source; exactly as Phoebe appeared to keep a mental inventory of good-looking males, and Jason was very good looking. He had the fair hair of so many of the local families, and even in the most casual of casual clothes, gave the impression of being well groomed. Maurice, in comparison, seemed more dowdy and dishevelled than before. "I was trying to prise some info out of Phoebe's ex-husband earlier on," said Jason, attempting rueful amusement. "But Lucas Rudd entirely fails to comprehend that a question is meant to be followed by a reply."

Maurice frowned in disapproval as Jason helped himself to a sandwich. "Deborah doesn't need reminders of what happened."

"It's OK, Maurice. You can't be reminded of something you haven't forgotten," said Deborah. "What are you doing these days, Jason?"

"Pretty much the same as I've done the past five years."

"Still headed for London?"

"You bet!"

"When?" demanded Maurice, brightening with sudden hope.

"As soon as the opportunity comes along," replied Jason. "I'm a stringer for one of the less salubrious tabloids, but it's all experience, if not a very dignified newspaper to add to your CV. Anyway, they like what I've given them up to now, not that it's been much. Seaborne isn't the liveliest town in the universe."

"So now you've decided to prise details out of Deborah, and invent some turgid rigmarole to further your career prospects," snapped Maurice.

"If I invent my copy, I won't need to ask Deborah a thing," Jason pointed out, unconcerned.

"Just as well, because I've no intention of letting you bother her," Maurice stated belligerently.

"Jason will already have more facts than I do," said Deborah. "I know nothing."

"Haven't you seen a family liaison officer?" asked Jason.

"That's none of your business," declared Maurice.

"Probably a mistake to offend the press, Maurice." It was a respite for Deborah to be able to relegate Rhoda to the back of her mind, even though making conversation felt as heavy-going as trudging through a muddy field. "If you want nice things printed about the museum, flattery works better than truth."

"Deborah's absolutely right, Maurice. Affront my sensibilities, and I could be tempted to demolish your most cherished endeavour with one stinging paragraph." Jason went to take another sandwich as he spoke, but Maurice promptly moved the cellophane box out of reach.

"I got these sandwiches for Deborah."

"Sorry to have snaffled a free feed, but every true journalist is born with a reflex action to grab at whatever he can. You should know that by now, Maurice."

"What I know is that you ought to leave Deborah alone at a time like this." Maurice's voice was so hostile, he seemed to have become a different person. The dithering was gone, along with the nervous agitation. He, who normally worried about the impression he made, did not care what Jason thought of him. "Nobody should be harassed and hounded."

"Maurice is the person you should hound for a story, Jason. He's got some big plans for a local arts festival." Deborah had imagined that she would easily sidetrack Maurice's attention, but he was not to be diverted from his animosity.

"Nobody in this benighted town gives a hoot for the arts. And you can print that."

"My editor doesn't like sweeping generalizations," said Jason. "And insulting the intellectual capacity of our fine townspeople wouldn't do much for sales figures."

"But I'm sure you can interest your editor in the idea of a festival." Deborah was not in the least sure, and Jason's unenthusiastic expression confirmed her doubts, but she made herself add, "You must ask Maurice about his plans, Jason."

On any other day, Maurice would have seized the opportunity to speak to a journalist about anything whatsoever, but when Jason Clenham happened to be that journalist, the whole situation altered, and even realism had a chance to creep in. "The festival's a non-starter. You said this town wasn't the place, Deborah, and you were right."

It was obvious that Maurice intended to outstay his adversary to monitor all conversation with Deborah, and so Jason stood up. "I better get going. There's a council planning committee that unfortunately I'm expected to celebrate in vibrant prose."

"Thanks for calling round," said Deborah, as she followed Jason out into the hall. "And thanks for the flowers."

"Oh, that's OK." Jason closed the kitchen door and muttered, "I really didn't come here to cross-examine you."

"I know," said Deborah, although unconvinced by Jason's newfound altruism.

"I got thinking about the past, about us."

"Why? Has another girlfriend just run off?"

"Certainly not. She walked away at quite a slow pace. Anyhow, I've since met a woman who doesn't seem totally resistant to my charm, so I'm able to hope again. Phone me, Deb, if you want to talk or you need any errands done."

"I'm all right. Maurice has practically restocked my kitchen." Gregory had died, and she was chatting: his daughter was actually chatting.

"Poor Maurice," said Jason.

"Why poor?"

"Because he's in love with you, and you don't even like him."

"I wouldn't say I disliked him."

"I repeat, poor Maurice." Jason put his arms around Deborah, and if he had chosen that moment to ask her again to marry him, she might have weakened. She felt so alone that affection, anyone's affection, seemed more valuable than it had ever done before. But Jason released her, opened the front door, and was gone. For a few seconds, Deborah had to struggle against tears, aware that any emotion would have to wait until after Maurice's departure.

"I'll tell Jason Clenham's editor that you're being persecuted. There's no other word for it," declared Maurice.

"I think friendship might be an alternative word. I've known Jason for years. And, if I were you, I wouldn't ever make a complaint to any newspaper about anything. You need the goodwill of the press."

"Not to the extent of allowing Jason Clenham to browbeat you. He came here with the sole aim of demanding an exclusive." Maurice was unable to disguise his sulky resentment, and also unable to stop himself demonizing Jason.

Commonsense had never been Maurice's chief characteristic but, even for him, the silliness was extreme. "Jason Clenham wouldn't care if he destroyed you, as long as he got a byline. He only thinks about what he can get from a situation. Nobody else's feelings stand a chance. If Clenham had any talent worth mentioning, he'd have been working on a London daily by now, instead of reporting golden wedding anniversaries and school sports. He's trying to use you as his passport onto what he trusts will be a higher rung of the ladder. Clenham isn't a friend; he's a leech."

"What did Jason ever do to give that impression?" asked Deborah. She could not tell her boss that he was being ridiculous, especially as she hoped to get a fulsome reference from him in the near future, but Maurice sounded perilously close to sullen adolescence. "I've never noticed any bloodsucking tendencies in Jason. He's actually rather kind, and very good at getting items about the museum into the paper."

"Only because he wants to impress you." Maurice's tone defied the world to contradict him.

****

Later that day, Maurice returned bearing daffodils, a huge bunch of them, top-heavy and yellower than rancid butter. Against the delicate beauty and simplicity of Jason's snowdrops, the daffodils looked garish, and as ungainly as Maurice himself. "Don't leave me," he declaimed, trying to sound light-hearted. "Don't ever leave me, Deborah. I won't be able to go on, if you desert me."

Deborah, with an armful of daffodils and no suitable vase in the house, attempted to show interest in Maurice's dramatics. "You'll have to explain. I haven't a clue what you're talking about."

"I had an email from some advertising agency. They want a reference for you. Tell me it's a mistake."

"You didn't really think I could go on working at the museum, did you?" Deborah was unable to keep apology from her voice, although it would be more surprising if she chose to return, instead of finding another job.

"You can work from home," announced Maurice. "You know I wouldn't last a minute without you; in fact, I'd be booted out by Calvin in less than 59 seconds. You mustn't leave me, and that's that. I'll bring all the paperwork and your computer here."

"No," said Deborah.

"Yes," said Maurice, suddenly cheerful and determined. "I'll pay for extra shelves and whatever else you need. The whole thing's solved. We can run the museum from here."

Deborah noted his use of the word 'we' and wondered if Maurice intended to take up residence in her front room, along with the office paperwork, but he scurried out of the house, eager to start the move, before she could demand particulars. He might ignore all requests to provide a reference, a thought that made Deborah feel more trapped than valued, because a new job was a priority. She had to escape, not only from the museum, but perhaps also from the town. Deborah wanted a fresh start, needed a fresh start. It was the sole answer to her difficulties.

But then the telephone rang, and as though to accentuate the power of the past, Jason Clenham was on the other end of the line. "Deb, I've got a favour to ask. What do you know about Calvin Canning?"

"Probably less than you do," replied Deborah, unsurprised that Jason should regard his condolence obligations as effectively covered by a handful of snowdrops and a five-minute visit. He had a reporter's mentality; after one aspect of a story had been followed up, it was time to find the next twist.

"I've heard you were lunching at the Sea View with the enigmatic Calvin. You must have gathered something about the origin of his money."

"Not an earthly. But if he's prepared to reveal anything, it might be to Phoebe Vale. She was at the lunch too, as I'm sure you were informed, and Calvin is greatly taken by her." Deborah realized that she still did not know the sequel to the meal. Phoebe had not bothered to telephone.

"Were you involved with Calvin Canning?" asked Jason.

"Good heavens, no."

"Pity. I hoped you'd give me the dirt on him, especially if he chucked you over for Phoebe. How did Calvin get planning permission to build an industrial estate on the old Trope Manor site?"

"I don't know, but I have a feeling you're about to tell me the suspicions of Jason Clenham, hot-shot reporter."

"Bribery, of course: bribery and corruption. It's the only way he could have got those plans through. Can you get something out of Maurice?"

"Calvin would never confide in him."

"Then see if you can get some info from Phoebe."

"Calvin was talking of her becoming his accountant. If he's accepted as a client, I think you can guarantee the money's legit. Vale and Son are above reproach."

"No one's above reproach when it comes to dosh," declared Jason, in best cynical journalist manner. "At 18, Canning left Seaborne, flat broke; at 40, he's back, rolling in it. How did that miracle occur?"

"If I knew how people get rich, I'd have made some money myself. Why do you think there's a story in Calvin's finances? He's bound to have covered any incriminating tracks."

"Only too well. Surely Maurice has to know where his uncle vanished to for 20-odd years. The man can't have dematerialized."

73

Clearly Jason expected Deborah to rally round his flag, drop a casual interrogation into her next chat with Maurice, and then con Phoebe into letting slip details about the hopefully ill-gotten gains of Calvin Canning. Jason knew that Deborah had not been close to Gregory, and therefore he believed it was perfectly justifiable to ask her to give a young journalist a helping hand on his way to London fame, if not fortune. "Jason, why are you so sure Calvin's harbouring a guilty secret?"

"Because instinct tells me that he's a crook."

"Calvin's reputation might owe more to idle gossip than fact," warned Deborah. "Not many people in Seaborne make much of their lives, so sheer jealousy compels them to knock someone who's got a bit of drive."

"Yes, but humour me. Anything I can do for you in return?"

"You could push the arts festival idea. Maurice would love to see his name in the paper. He'd talk more freely."

"I can't quite visualize the stolid burghers of this prosaic town taking to chamber music and poetry recitals, but I'll sell the idea to my editor if necessary. Anything else you'd like?"

"Yes," said Deborah, recalling her daffodil-filled kitchen sink. "Find me a vase the size of a bucket."

****

When the telephone rang again, Deborah picked it up, hoping not to hear Maurice wittering on about paperwork and shelves, but the sound of Rhoda's voice was worse.

"Deborah, I'm sorry. I'm really sorry. I wasn't thinking straight."

"That's OK," mumbled Deborah, ashamed not to have made the first move to heal the breach, and then equally ashamed to experience such a trivial emotion when her mother's world had come to an end.

"I didn't know what I was saying," claimed Rhoda.

But both had known exactly what the words meant, and Deborah would be unable to forget them. It had not occurred to her that she should contact Rhoda, because the rejection seemed absolute. Rhoda wanted Gregory, not a superfluous daughter, and that situation would never change. "I was going to visit you," lied Deborah, "but I thought the sight of me might upset you more."

"I can't be more upset than I am, and you didn't know that Greg was trying to see you. I suppose he thought neutral ground would be easier."

But the museum was not neutral ground; it had been part of Deborah's territory, and an estranged father turning up out of the blue would not have eased anything. "I didn't think he knew where I was working."

"You make it sound like Greg didn't take the slightest interest in you." Rhoda's voice was suddenly cold, and Deborah hastily recanted.

"I mean that I've changed jobs so often, even I can't keep track at times."

"You always did underestimate Gregory," snapped Rhoda, then she too backed down. "But it doesn't matter now."

It did matter, and was going to matter for the rest of their lives. Deborah would have to speak carefully, walk carefully, whenever Rhoda was there, because the old casual relationship had died with Gregory. When big events drove people apart, it was futile to expect unity to come out of mediocre days. "Do you need any shopping done?" asked Deborah, to steer the exchange towards safer ground.

"Only you could think of food at a time like this," snarled Rhoda before, with a lightning switch of mood, she was apologizing again. "I know I'm taking it out on you. Ignore what I say."

"I'll send Maurice Canning round with some sandwiches. He won't mind." It was the coward's way, Gregory's way, to act via an intermediary, but more sensible than risking another rejection that might never be undone.

"Thanks." But Rhoda had to force herself to say the word, before she slammed down the telephone.

****

Maurice, arriving in a car filled with boxes of paperwork and Deborah's computer, was only too pleased to have been volunteered for the role of food deliverer. He probably thought that it meant a giant step had been taken in the relationship he hoped to have with Deborah, and did not realize he was chosen because he might fail to discern any hostility on Rhoda's part. Maurice was convinced that everybody but him belonged to an uncomplicatedly warm and close family: a world as imaginary as Rhoda's, and as saccharine.

"How's Calvin dealing with the hassle?" asked Deborah, recalling Jason's expectation of a detailed account from her in relation to the activities of Calvin Canning, past and present.

"Calvin deals well with every situation," replied Maurice. "Atherton couldn't get a thing out of him."

"That doesn't altogether surprise me, with Calvin not actually in our midst on Sunday morning."

Maurice hesitated, but then said, "I glanced out of a window at one point, and thought I saw him in the courtyard. But when he didn't show up later on, I decided I must have made a mistake."

"It was definitely a mistake. Calvin wouldn't stand around the courtyard, and then meekly leave without checking up on what was happening inside the museum."

"He might have wanted to see how Exercise Disaster was going."

"If Calvin had been anywhere in the vicinity, he'd have taken over and run the disaster single-handedly. Why would he skulk in the shadows?"

"Calvin likes to pretend that he's a man of mystery."

"He is quite mysterious though," said Deborah, hoping that she sounded guileless. "No one seems to know exactly how he managed to transfer himself from dole queue to riches."

"He used his initiative," reported Maurice with a rueful sigh. "He grabbed opportunities. He took chances and created his own good luck. I've heard the lecture a million times at least, and I'm sure you don't want a précis."

"But I do. I haven't a clue how to make real money."

"Nor have I, and it doesn't matter how many pep talks are directed at me."

"What were the opportunities that Calvin grabbed so gainfully?"

"He's never gone into specifics. It's all as uselessly vague as those school-spirit and playing-the-game speeches that headmasters spout."

"Then where did Calvin find his opportunities?"

"No idea. I didn't often see him when I was at school. At the end of each term, I got packed off to so-called adventure holidays, which were less adventure than being trapped in a permanent gym lesson, complete with shouting teacher."

"Where was Calvin living?" asked Deborah, to guide the subject back on track.

"I'm not sure; he moved about. It was a good excuse to send me straight from school to whichever nightmare holiday had been selected. I fell off horses, discovered I suffer from vertigo when ordered to abseil down what looked like the north face of the Eiger, and entirely forgot how to swim after going headfirst into a Cumberland river. The only useful thing I learnt was to avoid any activity that's described as an adventure."

"What was Calvin doing while you were trapped in a hell of character-building activities?"

"I haven't an inkling what he does now, never mind all that time ago. He doesn't exactly take me into his confidence."

"Why did he come back here to live, after making his money?"

"Probably to show everyone what a success he is." Maurice paused, suddenly aware that Deborah had displayed no interest whatsoever in reminiscences from his childhood, because she wanted to know about Calvin: only Calvin.

"Shall I put something on the website to begin the arts festival discussion?" Deborah asked, to deflect any suspicion that she had tried to conduct a cross-examination on behalf of Jason. "Once the notion of a festival is started, it'll take on a life of its own, and getting money out of the town council might not be as difficult."

"There isn't going to be a festival," Maurice declared moodily.

"Why not? You've got a perfect venue in the museum for small concerts, and the town hall can accommodate anything larger. Rope in the school for an exhibition of children's painting, and the rest will take shape as more people get involved. You just need to decide on the festival's theme."

"You really think the idea's got a chance?" Maurice looked doubtful, but he wanted to be persuaded. "What if the town council won't cough up?"

"It doesn't need to be a huge event in the first year. You simply have to demonstrate the possibilities." Deborah did not know if she were being kind or cruel to encourage Maurice, but the frustration of dealing with the council would keep him fully occupied for months and, by that time, she might have found another job far away.

"I'll get your computer out of the car, and you can start the preparatory work," said Maurice, with an enthusiasm that was likely to grow and grow, until he saw himself as director of an international gathering that would be a date in the diary of the world. Then he recalled the reason why he was transporting a computer about town, and added hastily, "But if you can't face work yet, there's no hurry. Why not visit your mother with me?"

"I have to stay here," claimed Deborah, unwilling to tackle Rhoda, even with a peacekeeper present. "I'm waiting for a phone call."

"From Jason Clenham?" Maurice had asked before he could stop himself.

"No, not from Jason."

"Has Calvin contacted you?" Maurice sounded too casual, and apprehension was not far behind the façade. His whole life had been overshadowed by Calvin, and were there to be any sort of competition between uncle and nephew, uncle would win.

"Calvin? Why should Calvin contact me? If he's contacted anyone of late, it's almost certainly Phoebe Vale."

****

Phoebe: somebody who might be more forthcoming with information about Calvin. Questions should seem gossipy rather than sly while chatting to Phoebe, but Deborah put off the telephone call. Maurice had emptied the contents of his car into her front room, and left boxes of paperwork on chairs and windowsill, resulting in a clutter that bore a strong resemblance to the usual state of his office. Depressed by the sight of such untidiness, Deborah did her best to restore some order in the room, but it was too small an area to cope with the influx, and she had to admit defeat. Deborah closed the door on the confusion, angry with Maurice for spoiling her house; but she knew that his habitual carelessness just reminded her of Gregory's self-centred, happy-go-lucky attitude, and he was the one who had actually made her angry. A distraction, any distraction, was necessary to evade slipping into a futile and childish tantrum over times long gone. Deborah picked up the telephone, and dialled Phoebe's number.

"Calvin, I hope you're not ringing to cancel, because I bought myself a new dress today," declared Phoebe, without preamble.

"I wondered if Calvin Canning would still be in the scene."

"Deborah!" Phoebe's cheerful tone abruptly changed, as if she had been cornered, and would have to use her wits to bluff a way out. "I'm awfully sorry about your father. I meant to call you. I really did. But what could I say or do to help the situation?"

"That's OK. It'd be a kindness to let me talk about something else." But Deborah felt equally uncomfortable to have committed the social error of telephoning Phoebe at so embarrassing a time. "Where's the new dress going to be worn?"

"At a charity fundraising dinner. The sort of occasion when you're surrounded by pictures of starving children while you tuck into five courses, and then pacify your conscience by shelling out for a couple of raffle tickets." Relief, at having got the condolences over and done with, made Phoebe more buoyant than usual, but it was a forced liveliness.

"So you and Calvin can now officially be classed as an item?"

"That's a bit of an exaggeration, although I have gone out with him a few times, and met him for lunch as well."

"I think I'd describe that as being an item." Poor Chelsea, thought Deborah; but Chelsea Pritchard with her glitter make-up, shrill voice, short skirts and fake jewellery could never be Calvin's satellite at the classy dinners he graced with his presence. Chelsea belonged to the world of noisy bars and cheap nightclubs: the sort of places where Gregory might have featured on the bill. Socially poised and elegantly dressed Phoebe would be considered a much more suitable candidate for the role of Calvin's companion when he was in public.

"I'm just having fun with whoever fate chances to send along," said Phoebe. "Calvin's merely the current pastime, an entertaining one though."

"It's odd, but I don't know much about Calvin, even if he does pay my wages." Deborah felt more awkward, certain that Phoebe would realize she was being pumped for a journalist's copy. At least when Jason asked questions, people knew he was a reporter and that whatever they said might find its way into a newspaper. To assuage her conscience, Deborah added, "Jason Clenham wanted to know how Calvin made his money, but I couldn't tell him a thing."

"Is Jason back in your life?" Phoebe demanded, immediately sidetracked. "I can't understand why you let him get away in the first place."

"But you've no idea what Jason's like. He could have a vilely bitter personality for all you know. You only spoke to him for about three seconds at your wedding."

"OK, so I'm totally superficial and judge entirely by appearance, but his appearance is rather alluring. I took one glance at Jason, and couldn't think why I'd been fool enough to limit my options by getting married. Perhaps I should cite Jason Clenham as the cause of my divorce. If I'd known you weren't really interested in him, I'd have dumped Lucas at the wedding reception. But now that I've finally liberated myself, I suppose you've come to your senses, and won't let Jason wander off a second time."

It might have been ten years earlier, and a schoolgirl Phoebe babbling on eagerly about the latest crush on the latest boyfriend. For a woman with a responsible job and an intelligent brain, Phoebe could be remarkably juvenile at times. "Feel free to vamp Jason. He only contacted me to ask what I knew of Calvin, and I wasn't the slightest help, so if you phone Jason with some info, he'll be thrilled."

"Alas, I'm not supposed to discuss a client, no matter how enticing the interrogator. Does Jason think there's something shady in Calvin's background?" Phoebe made an effort to seem nonchalant, but she wanted a precise answer to her question. The accountant had resurfaced.

"I don't expect it's more than Calvin choosing not to tell all and sundry his business, and Jason having a sceptical mind. If there was anything shifty about Calvin's finances, you would have spotted it."

"Perhaps, and perhaps not."

"Calvin must have given you an explanation of his money. I presume he didn't just tip sacks of £50 notes on your desk, and tell you to square it with the Inland Revenue."

"I never meet men that dashing. What type of nefarious activity does Jason suspect Calvin of?"

"Ask Jason, not me. But I think his suspicions might owe more to a journalist's hope of uncovering a scandal, than one actually having taken place. What's your opinion of Calvin?"

"He's good company," said Phoebe, "and he doesn't ramble on with dreary details of some boring hobby. My father warned me not to get involved with a client, so naturally that makes Calvin appear more attractive than he probably is. Apart from those idle reflections, I haven't given Calvin much thought. In fact, I don't even know if he was ever married, although Lucas has been thoroughly discussed."

It was the Calvin Canning speciality, to gather information on other people, but to give none in return. Such caution had to indicate extreme reserve or a guilty secret, and Deborah could understand Jason's curiosity. "You'll have to ask Calvin a few direct questions, especially if you want to curry favour with Jason."

"As indeed I do. Jason will benefit from all the dirt I can dig up, but he might be disappointed to learn that Calvin can't have a criminal record. When Lucas heard I'd been wined and dined by Calvin Canning, the indignant ex-husband entirely forgot we're in the process of getting a divorce, and came charging round to protest. If Calvin had so much as a parking fine in his past, Lucas would certainly have informed me."

A pristine record hardly tallied with local gossip, but the assumption would be that Calvin Canning had simply outwitted the police. A town of low wages and lower aspiration was bound to believe that anyone with money had to be a crook. "I'm beginning to think that there's a dull explanation of Calvin's dosh," Deborah said. "He's merely an astute businessman."

"But you're the one who's just persuaded me that Calvin's a devious spiv about to bring disgrace on the proud name of Vale and Son," complained Phoebe. "It's not fair to turn sensible when I'm all geared up to uncover a sensational story for Jason. Besides, what business did Calvin so astutely make his original dough in? He'd talk, if it was respectable. People love to drone on about how clever they are."

Phoebe was right. Calvin liked to flaunt his wealth, but not the source of it, and even his nephew had no idea of the particulars. There might be a secret, after all.

****

When she heard somebody knock on the front door, Deborah assumed it was Maurice, returning from his mission of mercy to Rhoda. The prospect of another bout of his company was disheartening, but the sight of Lucas Rudd did not seem much of an alternative.

"Inspector Atherton wants to talk to you," said Lucas. He appeared so impassive that it was difficult to imagine him charging around indignantly to demand details of his ex-wife's relationship with Calvin Canning. "Is now OK?"

"No worse than any other time," replied Deborah, but her permission was evidently unimportant, as she could see Atherton already getting out of a parked car. Lucas had been sent on ahead, presumably because Detective Inspector Atherton considered himself far too dignified to knock on a door. That was a job for lesser ranks.

The disorder still spread across her front room bothered Deborah, but the other option was a kitchen, and that would be altogether too informal a location when policemen were on an official call. She tried to assure herself that the state of the house was none of their business, but felt compelled to apologize. "I'm going to do some work from home, but I haven't had a chance to sort things out yet. Maurice Canning only brought the stuff a little while ago."

"Your boss isn't here now, is he?" Lucas did not look enthusiastic at the possibility of another clash with Maurice.

Atherton was clearly impatient with the banal nature of the question, not even attempting to hide his testiness. "Why did your father go to see you last Sunday? Did you ask him to visit you at the museum?"

Perhaps Atherton thought it would be easier for Deborah if the interview were conducted quickly, but he sounded abrupt enough to have made an accusation, and her reply was defensive. "We had a disaster exercise going on. I wouldn't have asked anyone to the museum on Sunday. The place wasn't open to the public."

"Your father was able to get inside."

"You'll have to take that up with the security guard." But Deborah's mind wandered back to the untidiness of the room, as she glanced around despondently. "I expect half of these files could go back to the museum. I haven't the space to store them."

Atherton ignored Deborah's words, making her feel humiliated to be preoccupied with something so petty. "Did you know that your father wanted to see you?"

"I didn't even know he was in Seaborne. I only found that out when I spoke to my mother after work on Sunday." After work on Sunday: a time that belonged to a far-distant past, with Rhoda still happy and Gregory still assumed to be alive.

"So you didn't meet your father at the Grand on Saturday."

"Of course not. I'd no idea then that he was staying there."

"Your father was seen at the Grand Hotel on Saturday evening with a fair-haired woman, described as young enough to be his daughter."

"My hair's brown," Deborah pointed out.

"Hair colour is hardly a constant in a woman's appearance these days," remarked Lucas, and he tried to continue the casualness as he added, "You had lunch with Calvin Canning the next day."

Despite Lucas's pose of indifference, his statement had seemed more of a rebuke than anything else, and Deborah was bemused that the truth should sound so lame. "I'd arranged to meet Phoebe for lunch. Calvin arrived at the museum as I was leaving, and he decided to gatecrash the meal."

"Why?" Lucas demanded.

"Because he was hungry, I suppose."

"Did he know you were meeting Phoebe?"

"Yes." It was the answer that Lucas had not wanted to hear, and Deborah guessed that he was imagining a lecherous Calvin wangling an introduction to a woman he had seen from afar and determined to seduce. "I mean, Calvin just knew I was meeting a friend," Deborah added, to soften the blow.

"You didn't give the impression of being surprised that your father should be seen with a young woman at the hotel," commented Atherton, not to be sidetracked by Lucas's marital problems.

"No, I'm not very surprised," admitted Deborah.

"Do you know who that particular young woman might have been?"

Deborah shook her head, but a memory stirred at the back of her mind. The lunch with Calvin: a café haughtily disdained in favour of the Sea View restaurant, and Phoebe saying that her luck had turned when lunch at the Sea View followed dinner at the Grand on Saturday evening. Then another memory raced after the first: Gregory declaring with appreciation that the teenage Phoebe was attractive enough to be a film star. There were no grounds for imagining that Phoebe and Gregory had kept in contact over the years, but they might have re-met on Saturday and arranged to have dinner. Flighty Phoebe would not regard it as an important decision, merely a way of passing time agreeably, and that would be Gregory's opinion too. Even if they went on to spend the night together, it would mean little to either of them, and certainly not have been cause enough to deter Phoebe from telephoning Deborah for a chat on Sunday evening. In fact, any encounter might actually have served to jog Phoebe's memory concerning the existence of Gregory's daughter. Two good reasons stopped Deborah from mentioning a possible identity for her father's mysterious companion: Phoebe had no connection with the death, and Lucas Rudd did not need to know further details of his ex-wife's social life.

"Have you any idea what your father might have wanted to discuss with you?" asked Atherton.

Deborah shook her head again. If Gregory had hoped to cadge some money, he knew that Rhoda would readily provide it. He also knew that his unforgiving daughter no longer believed a word he said, and Gregory needed to be admired. He would not willingly have approached someone who scorned him.

"Perhaps your father chanced to walk past the museum, and decided to pay you a visit there and then," suggested Atherton.

"Perhaps." But Deborah found that explanation no more credible than Atherton's face suggested he did. She could sense that he thought she might have hidden something from him, and Deborah felt indignant to be suspected of withholding information, before recalling that Atherton was right. But it would be futile to drop Phoebe into a pointless hassle with the police, and futile to mention suspicions that were mostly conjecture.

****

Years previously, in another world, Gregory had been at home, an increasingly rare occurrence: so rare that a 15-year-old Phoebe, dashing down the hallway, had stopped at the unexpected sight of Gregory at the kitchen table. "Hello, Mr Wainwright. I didn't know you were in town."

"Surely this can't be little Phoebe all grown up? I think it's about time you started to call me Greg. When did you turn into a beauty? You look like a film star." Gregory had smiled in the way that he always did when he saw a woman who attracted him, and Phoebe had smiled back.

In Deborah's memory, it seemed that Phoebe assessed Gregory's looks at a glance because she, like him, judged by appearance. Both were also flirts. "It depends on which film star you think I look like. If you say Frankenstein's monster or the Hunchback of Notre Dame, I'll probably burst into tears."

"No need to reach for the pocket handkerchief. You're a Hollywood princess: Grace Kelly, perhaps, the one who actually married a prince."

"There's a sad shortage of princes in Seaborne." Even as a teenager, Phoebe had never been tongue-tied or disconcerted, and she knew how to accept a compliment without awkwardness.

"Don't underestimate your luck," said Gregory. "This could be the day when you meet the genuine article."

****

It was unreal that somebody so in love with life as Gregory could die, because he still seemed more alive than the daughter left behind, with her limited and controlled world. As a child, Deborah had never imagined office work to be her future, nor had she pictured herself in the cramped confines of a backstreet terrace house. She was the daughter of a star, and the mundane existence that other people were forced to endure would never trap her, just as it had never persuaded Gregory to be sensible.

The song that Gregory liked best had been his favourite from childhood. *When You Wish Upon A Star* told him everything he wanted to know, and reinforced those beliefs throughout his life. He had often closed his nightclub act with it, when audiences were at a maudlin stage of drinking and in the mood for syrupy sentimentality, before the more aggressive phase of drunkenness took over. The song had also been Deborah's favourite, because Gregory sang her to sleep with it when she was a small child, offering his view of the universe as a magical place in which you only had to believe, and wishes were fulfilled as dreams came true. Phoebe's father had taken his daughter to London on instructive visits to the Science and Natural History museums. Deborah's father took his daughter nowhere, but taught her how to dance and sing. They had no need to travel, because Gregory brought the world to Deborah, and the air around them was filled with more life than Phoebe would ever see from the windows of her father's car. Yet Deborah had grown up to be the one sleepwalking through her days in jobs that were chosen solely for the amount of money she would earn. It was so far from the land of wishing on stars that Deborah felt she had let her former self down by turning out to be unexceptional. The child had confidently expected to be happy ever after; the adult forgot that she was meant to grab hold of existence and cling on tenaciously until it gave her whatever she desired. Gregory never forgot, and even in the most tawdry of nightclubs, had managed to find a little of the enchantment that his daughter no longer chased. For him, the dream came first, and everything else had to look after itself.

But the everything else that Gregory disregarded had become Deborah's life, and she was depressed by the mediocrity of her CV and by the equal mediocrity of the jobs on offer, as she did yet another internet search. It might have been easier if she had a definite idea of a goal she wanted to achieve, but she was as devoid of unique talent as a Gregory, and in the meantime, a less than perfect job awaited her attention.

The museum website would need updating, unless Maurice had already dealt with it, in which case some urgent editing might be called for; but Deborah put off the task, unwilling to face the bland statement she had concocted, imagining it to be her only connection with a stranger's demise. Maurice's arts festival was a good way to fill empty time, and yet persuade her conscience that some work was being done. Deborah jotted down a few possible sponsors, possible themes, and possible events. Probable expenses would have been a more practical approach, but she did not want to dampen Maurice's enthusiasm for the scheme. With any luck, he could be kept fully occupied running around town in pursuit of his festival until Deborah had moved on to another job.

Then, as though her thought had summoned him, Maurice arrived at Deborah's front door bearing two takeaway meals, and obviously expecting to eat his share of the food in her kitchen, because he walked inside the house without waiting for an invitation to do so. "Your mother's coping really well. I made her some tea, and she talked about your father the whole time. It's meant to be a good sign when people can talk, isn't it? She showed me some photo albums too."

Deborah immediately felt guilty not to have been the one looking at old photographs with her mother, and hastily sought a less sticky conversational topic. "I've worked out a few plans for your festival. It won't be difficult to get a piece in the local paper about your ideas."

"Has Jason Clenham phoned you?" Maurice appeared to think that he had every right to ask the question, and also to receive an answer. In his mind, the relationship with Deborah was apparent advancing with every hour.

"Jason's promised to talk to his editor about the festival," replied Deborah, not caring to inform the boss, from whom she still hoped to prise a reference, that it was none of his business who telephoned her at home. "There's the local radio station too. I'll contact their newsroom, and suggest that somebody interviews you."

"You really think we can get this idea off the ground?" Maurice demanded, temporarily sidetracked from thought of Jason by the prospect of media attention.

"Well, you might have to do a lot of talking to journalists."

"Oh, I can manage that," Maurice assured Deborah.

"I think you should chair a public meeting as well, and form a committee of volunteers. When I've arranged a time and place, I'll print some posters for shop windows etc."

"A public meeting!" repeated Maurice, impressed with such unaccustomed importance, and doubtless imagining himself fluently addressing a rapt and deferential audience.

"The town hall would be the best place," said Deborah, knowing that the Victorian municipal excesses of oak panelling and carved arches would make Maurice feel he was presiding in the House of Commons.

"Yes, you're right. This isn't an individual undertaking; it's for the whole town," declared Maurice. "You must have some help delivering the posters. Shall I send the receptionist over? She isn't doing anything much with the museum closed."

The receptionist never did anything much, be the museum open or shut, but Chelsea Pritchard would have even less than usual to fill the vacant hours, with Calvin Canning's desertion of her for Phoebe Vale. There was, of course, the possibility that Calvin's favours were not exclusively Phoebe's, but Chelsea was unlikely to be content with part-time attentiveness. Parading her charms about town would comfort Chelsea, and she was certain to persuade male shopkeepers to exhibit as many museum posters as her heart desired. "Yes, send Chelsea round. It'll cheer her up."

"Why should she need cheering up?" asked Maurice, but he was not interested enough to wait for a reply. Maurice had more vital matters to occupy him. "I'll start work at once on a speech for the public meeting. Book the first available town hall date. Perhaps you should send personal invitations to the councillors?"

"Good idea," said Deborah, glad of an opportunity to squander more blank time, during which she might escape having to think.

****

Chelsea Pritchard had always seemed impervious to cold and, even during the bitterest weather, she wore flimsy blouses, short skirts, and open-toed high heels. The only concession made to that day's east wind was a jacket, but it had been left unbuttoned in a gesture of defiance to January, and as much of her eye-catching figure as could decently be displayed remained on show because Chelsea, although down, was not out.

"They said at the museum that the man in the courtyard was your father," began Chelsea, with a directness that took Deborah by surprise after everybody else's caution. Either Chelsea had determined to grasp the nettle, or she lacked imagination enough to realize that her words might be inopportune. The latter appeared the more probable explanation, when she added, as though Deborah were somehow at fault, "You never told me your father was in show business."

"It didn't occur to me that you'd want to know."

Chelsea ignored Deborah's reply, glanced without comment around the front room, moved towards a wall mirror, and proceeded to rearrange long strands of dyed-blonde hair. "I'm going to be a model."

"I'm sure you'll be a successful one." But any career in which Chelsea's shrilly high-pitched voice went unheard was undoubtedly a wise choice.

"There's a course in London starting in a few months, but I need to pay for it now." Chelsea looked aggrieved, and then blurted out, "They say you're the person who introduced Calvin Canning to that Phoebe Vale."

"Guilty." Deborah wondered if Chelsea had intended Calvin to pick up the bill for the modelling course, because the advent of a rival appeared to annoy Chelsea rather than upset her. Something of the self-centred ruthlessness of early childhood had lingered on, and nobody was ever going to break Chelsea's heart, for people were there to be used, not loved. If Calvin had escaped her grasp, she would simply hunt for another career sponsor.

"You're lucky I'm still speaking to you," said Chelsea, forcing a smile as she reluctantly tore herself away from the mirror.

"I'm sorry, but I can't be held responsible for Calvin's wandering ways."

"You didn't have to introduce him to that Phoebe Vale though," retorted Chelsea. "She's not only got looks, she's got a rich father as well. It's not fair."

"Life rarely is," said Deborah. "Do you plan to move to London?"

"Yes, of course," replied Chelsea, clearly surprised at the question. "I'll have my own flat when I'm modelling. There's real money in it. And I'll get some television work too: acting, I mean."

Deborah was reminded of Gregory, and the seven years between her and Chelsea suddenly seemed many more. "Whatever you do, you'll find it an improvement on the museum."

"There are worse jobs, and I've done some of them."

"So have I. Today's task isn't much better, I'm afraid. Maurice Canning wants you to promenade through the town, persuading shopkeepers to put posters in their windows. The only consolation on offer is the fact that you were specially chosen for the mission, because it's assumed no man will have the strength to resist granting your wishes."

Chelsea laughed, pleased with the compliment. "Is that what Maurice Canning said?"

"Word for word," lied Deborah, and watched a speculative expression cross Chelsea's face. Maurice was not the owner of the Canning money, but he was close to it, and could presumably get his hands on the amount necessary for Chelsea's course. If Maurice were distracted by the attentions of a would-be supermodel, Deborah would benefit too by finding herself freed from his gallantry, and the thought was heartening. "Maurice is a bit shy, but he's certainly aware of Chelsea Pritchard. Yours happened to be the only name he suggested when a persuasively attractive staff member was called for."

Chelsea laughed again. Admiration brought her to life, even when the appreciation came from a man not previously considered a possibility. Because a youthful appearance would be essential for a career as a fashion model, Chelsea had little time to waste while achieving her aims, and Maurice was likely to find himself a targeted prey before many hours passed. It was to Chelsea's credit that any purpose at all had emerged from a background of shiftless parents and social security handouts, but the aspiration that had sprung from such unpromising soil seemed as great as Gregory's ambition.

"Do you know where Maurice is now?" Chelsea asked, too nonchalantly. Her strategy was back on track

4

Deborah preferred the seafront in winter, when she had the shore to herself, and could walk by the waterline without having to struggle through an invasion of holidaymakers. Being alone by the ocean usually gave a sense of freedom, but that day Deborah felt hemmed in, more than she ever had been by the hoards of day-trippers, because memories of Gregory filled the promenade, filled the beach.

Gregory had liked the picture of himself strolling by the sea. He wore the sort of crisply new clothes that only summer visitors sported, and could not be parted from his sunglasses even on the dullest of days. He was Greg Wayne, star, unspoilt by fame, graciously returning to his roots, and the family game had been to pretend that the camera of a documentary film director followed them along the sand to record the event. Rhoda and Gregory would reminisce about early hardship before the inevitable success of Greg Wayne, while Deborah was supposed to demand extra details in a breathlessly excited yet natural way, something she found difficult to master, even though the camera filming them was imaginary.

"We have to make it look spontaneous," Gregory had decreed. "Hold onto my hand, Debbie, and skip to keep up with me. I can't have an elderly daughter hobbling in my wake. I'm the perennially youthful Greg Wayne, and therefore no child of mine is allowed to age beyond her fifth birthday."

That non-existent camera still seemed to be following Deborah 20 years later, and she stood self-consciously at the water's edge, watching waves retreat from the wet sand while, on the horizon, dark clouds drifted by. The microphone would pick up the sound of the surf and a distant gull's cry; but the real scene was taking place behind her as, on a sunny afternoon, Greg Wayne's elderly six-year-old daughter clung to her father's hand and skipped along the beach.

"Hello, Deborah." The sense of being observed had not been total paranoia after all. Lucas Rudd, looking ridiculously formal in suit and tie, crossed the sand towards her.

"You can't conduct an interrogation on the sea shore," objected Deborah, glad to have the ghosts routed. "This simply isn't an appropriate place."

"I wasn't planning an inquisition. In fact, I came down here to get away for a little while, just as you did, I suppose." But Lucas appeared to be making excuses, and Deborah waited for the questions to begin. "Atherton's in a mood, so I decided to take a breather."

Deborah wondered if Lucas were attempting phoney confidences to catch her off-guard, in the hope of hearing an inadvertent remark that would confirm whatever suspicions he had, and she was forced to remind herself that she was actually innocent. "What's wrong with the Inspector?"

"Problems with a son who dropped out of university, and is now ungainfully employed stacking shelves in the local superstore." Lucas sounded almost chatty, and Deborah became more convinced of an agenda, not quite as well hidden as Lucas believed.

"Surely it's the son's decision what he does with his own life."

"Don't try telling that to Atherton." Lucas hesitated, but then asked, "Has Phoebe rung you lately?"

All was explained. Lucas hoped to find out the exact nature of his ex-wife's relationship with Calvin Canning, but Deborah thought he could hardly expect her to reveal scintillating details, even if she knew any. Phoebe had been a school friend; Lucas was an outsider. "I talked to Phoebe the other day, but not for long."

"What did she have to say about Canning?"

"That she was off to a charity fundraiser with him. If you want to ask Calvin's intentions, I suggest you haul him into the nearest police station to assist with your inquiries."

"Unfortunately, it's not that simple." But Lucas smiled, and Deborah reckoned she could detect some life in him at last. It was obvious that more than a frozen-faced official had to be concealed inside Lucas, or Phoebe would not have been attracted to him in the first place, but his camouflage was singularly effective.

"I don't know a lot about Phoebe's life these days. I haven't seen much of her since school," Deborah said, to avoid a cross-examination concerning Phoebe's activities. But mention of Phoebe brought Gregory back into Deborah's mind, and his rendezvous at the Grand Hotel with the fair-haired woman young enough to be his daughter. As though she could leave the thought behind in the place where it had been remembered, Deborah began to walk along the tide line again, but the recollection kept pace with her, and so did Lucas.

"It turns out that Calvin Canning is a family friend after all."

"Of my family?" said Deborah. "Definitely not. Maurice made a mistake."

"Calvin Canning knew your father, and that's why you got the museum job. You really didn't know?" Lucas's voice was decidedly sceptical.

"Calvin told you that he knew my father?" demanded Deborah in astonishment. "I don't believe it."

"Why would he lie?"

"But my father never said a word about Calvin. It can't be true."

"They met years ago, according to Canning. That's why he recognized your name on the list of job applicants. Anyway, he's unlikely to have insisted that the daughter of a complete stranger be hired."

"But my father would have said something about Calvin; I know he would." Gregory had always belittled anyone with either success or money, and Calvin Canning was never reluctant to make a splash around town.

"Then why does Canning claim to have been a friend of your father's?" asked Lucas, plainly eager for Deborah to give him a reason that would be to Calvin's discredit.

"He must have known another Gregory Wainwright."

"Who uses Greg Wayne as his stage name and also has a daughter called Deborah? A bit improbable. Did Canning never ask about your father?" Lucas's tone implied a deviousness that went beyond minor deception, whether on Calvin's part or Deborah's. "Not even on the day he invited you to lunch with him?"

"Calvin didn't invite me; he invited himself." Deborah attempted to recall what she and Calvin had discussed before meeting Phoebe. It was like trying to remember a conversation from a previous decade, but Deborah had no real need to tax her memory. She knew that Calvin had not mentioned Gregory.

"You never ask for details," remarked Lucas, as he awaited further information in vain. "It's odd how people react. Your mother wants to hear everything."

"I'm pretending none of it happened." But Deborah spoke awkwardly, knowing that she was a fraud, in distinct contrast to Rhoda.

"It must make it more difficult, believing your father had gone to the museum that day to see you." Lucas seemed sympathetic, but Deborah was not fooled. He cared nothing for her feelings. He was also on a fishing expedition. "I wonder if

Canning could have been the actual person visited. He denies it, of course, but—"

"You want Calvin to turn out to be a psychopath," said Deborah, and Lucas smiled again.

"Have you any proof that he isn't a raving madman?"

"He doesn't rave, for one thing. Not that I've met him often. He's rarely at the museum, and wasn't there on Sunday. At any rate, I didn't spot him."

Lucas glanced questioningly at Deborah. "That sounds as if you know of somebody who did see him."

"Well, Maurice thought he saw his uncle at one point during the morning, although he wasn't certain." But Deborah's spirits suddenly lifted, and she could have laughed aloud in sheer relief. It was akin to being freed from captivity to think that Calvin, not her, had drawn Gregory to the museum.

"Canning told me he was in London on Saturday night, and only arrived back in the town on Sunday afternoon," said Lucas, pleased at the prospect of confronting Calvin with an accusation of having lied. "Did you contact him at any time on Saturday or Sunday morning?"

"No, but Maurice might have. You should talk to him."

"I fully intend to." As if to carry out his intention immediately, Lucas turned and, without saying goodbye, strode off in the direction of the promenade. Deborah hesitated, and then ran a few paces to catch up with him.

"Maurice only caught a glimpse of someone through a window. It probably wasn't Calvin. We were right in the middle of the disaster exercise, and there must have been hundreds of people milling about."

"It's still something I have to dig into," declared Lucas.

"Maurice wasn't sure."

"All the same, I'd like to know why he failed to say anything about it."

"Presumably because you didn't ask him if he'd seen Calvin on Sunday morning."

"Then it's high time I did ask. Something doesn't add up here, and I want an explanation."

Deborah watched Lucas hurry up the steps of the sea wall and onto the promenade, along which elaborately embellished Victorian houses had what the local estate agent described as panoramic coastal views. Calvin Canning was one of the owners of those views, and Deborah felt certain that he must have observed her talking to Lucas, something Calvin would regard as betrayal. A cold wind, previously unnoticed, trickled under Deborah's collar, making her shiver, although she had undoubtedly done her civic duty, and to have withheld information from Lucas was probably enough to find herself charged with obstructing police inquiries. The real shame was that she wanted Calvin to have been at the museum on Sunday, and she also wanted him to have arranged a meeting there with Gregory. Indeed, it was necessary if Deborah were ever to know peace of mind again.

****

Deborah pressed the bell with a hand that actually trembled, and the moment Rhoda opened her front door, Deborah was saying, "He went to see Calvin Canning at the museum on Sunday. It was nothing to do with me, nothing at all."

Rhoda looked more distracted than grief-stricken, as she stood in the doorway, but there was still hostility in her eyes, and she did not move aside to let Deborah into the house. "What are you claiming? That Gregory went to see your boss? Don't be ridiculous. Why on earth would Greg do that?"

"They knew each other. That's what Calvin told the police. He said I only got the job because he recognized my name."

"Rubbish. Gregory never once mentioned Calvin Canning."

"But why would Calvin lie?"

It had been Lucas's question, and there was no logical answer to it, so an illogical one had to be found, and Rhoda paused before replying. "If Gregory had met Canning, he wouldn't have thought much about it. Greg was never impressed by money."

Gregory the covetous, who resented anybody else's good fortune, had always been Gregory the flawless in Rhoda's mind, and Deborah accepted that version of her father without objection. "Calvin must have arranged to meet him at the museum."

"Why?" snapped Rhoda.

"I don't know. You'll have to ask Lucas Rudd."

"No one said anything about this to me." Rhoda had in all probability not slept for nights, and tiredness made her as fractiously stubborn as a teething baby.

"It's only just come to light. Lucas didn't know anything himself the last time he saw you."

"Has Canning been arrested for murder?" demanded Rhoda.

"No, of course not," Deborah replied, taken aback. "Whatever happened, it must have been an accident."

"You have the nerve to maintain that Canning accidentally hit Gregory over the head with a metal bar? What sort of accident could that be?"

"I'm only telling you what Lucas Rudd is investigating right now."

"Gregory's gone, and that's that." Rhoda was abruptly defeated. She turned, and went into the front room, while Deborah dithered on the threshold, uncertain on which side of the door she was supposed to be when she closed it. But if Deborah walked away then, the rift might never be mended, and so she followed Rhoda.

"How much money have you got?" asked Rhoda.

"With me, you mean?"

"In the bank," Rhoda said impatiently. She began to pace up and down the room, as though Maurice's habit had become contagious. "Gregory's going to have the best send-off this town has ever seen. He had such good taste, and despised cheapness."

Especially when his wife was there to foot the bill; but Deborah felt uncomfortable to think such a thing in Rhoda's presence. If buying her way back into approval was the only method of doing it, Deborah was prepared to spend on whatever grandiose funeral Rhoda wished to give her paragon, even if Gregory himself might have protested at the waste. Money had been for living, according to him; the dead had lost their chance to enjoy worldly things. His own father had vanished shortly after Gregory's birth, but even the more durable mother had not rated a posthumous parade. Rhoda, however, chose to block out Gregory's views. She had been raised, often unhappily, in foster homes, and from earliest days, fantasy had been the essential that got her through life.

"There's so much to decide: what music and flowers to have, which people to invite."

"I'm not sure you send out invitations," said Deborah. "Don't people just turn up?"

"Of course they'll turn up," Rhoda retorted, as if Deborah were suggesting otherwise. "Gregory had hundreds of friends. Everyone liked him."

Everyone except his ungrateful daughter, Rhoda's barbed tone implied, and Deborah hastened to defuse her mother's acerbity. "Shall I ask Jason Clenham to write an obituary for the local paper?"

"That's a good idea," Rhoda said grudgingly. "Get Jason to phone me. I'm the only person who can tell him all about Greg's career. Do you think Jason would write something for the service too?"

"Yes, I'm sure he will," replied Deborah, in the knowledge that she had a good bargaining position as regards Jason. The news about Gregory and Calvin's friendship and their meeting at the museum would presumably be of interest, and Jason might also be pleased to get a chance to interview Rhoda, and perhaps secure a picture for the newspaper of the widow gazing at a photograph of her departed. The rare moment of harmony seemed a good opportunity for Deborah to leave, before relations were again soured, and she stood up. "I'll go and email Jason now."

"How you can continue working at that museum is beyond me," said Rhoda, with an abrupt return of animosity.

"I haven't been back there. Maurice has let me work from home, but I'm looking for another job."

"And, in the meantime, you take that murderer's money."

"I can't afford to live without a wage coming in. Besides, Calvin's no killer." Deborah knew that she sounded too defensive, and tried to think of a convincing character reference for Calvin, but the best she could dredge up was hardly irrefutable proof of his integrity. "He's going out with Phoebe Vale."

"Then why couldn't he have murdered her? She'd be no loss," Rhoda declared crossly

"I'll tell Jason to phone you," said Deborah, glad to make an escape. Perhaps Rhoda would shut her out forever, but there was nothing that Deborah could do to improve the situation. It was Rhoda's call what happened between them in the future.

****

The email to Jason had only been sent a few minutes prior to the ring of Deborah's telephone, but she knew it would be him on the other end of the line. When Jason was chasing copy, he devoted his whole being to the pursuit.

"What's the info?" he demanded.

"It turns out that Calvin Canning was a friend of my father's."

"But you'd have known about it," objected Jason. "Why didn't you?"

"Because neither of them mentioned the other to me. There's more gen, but I want you to promise something before I hand over all my cards."

"If it's connected to money, I have to warn you that my present financial standing is more of a wobbly teeter."

After Rhoda's frostiness, a friendly voice made Deborah feel that she had reached shelter in a storm, and she allowed herself to relax. "My mother wants an obituary written. She'd like you to do a eulogy as well."

"Consider it done. And there's no need to rehash certain occasions in the past when I'd promise faithfully to be somewhere, but you'd find yourself waiting in vain outside cinemas and cafés."

"Oh, I knew I couldn't compete with holidaymakers floundering around in rip currents and town councillors fiddling their expenses."

"Yet which other escort would have given you a glimpse into the corrupt world of local produce judging at the summer fête? And I still maintain that bonny baby competition was rigged in favour of the town clerk's puny grandson. But enough of the highlights of my career as an investigative reporter. What's the rest of your info?"

"Maurice thought he saw his uncle in the museum courtyard on Sunday morning, so it's possible that my father went there to meet Calvin. But it's also possible Maurice made a mistake, because Calvin told the police he was in London, and didn't get back here until Sunday afternoon."

"Another possibility is that Calvin Canning lied about his whereabouts," said Jason, as Deborah had hoped he would. She wanted Gregory to have gone to the museum to see Calvin. She wanted it to be true as much as she had ever wanted anything in her life. "I wonder what Calvin's trying to hide."

"I can't make any sort of guess. Even my mother didn't know there was a connection with Calvin."

"Your father went to the local comp, didn't he?"

"But Calvin's five or six years younger, and that's a tremendous gap at school. They never lived in the same part of town either. My grandmother was permanently broke, while Calvin's family hardly struggled for every penny, despite his claims of having been raised in direst poverty."

"There's no law saying that they must have met here, even if they both grew up in Seaborne." Jason sounded intrigued, and very willing to believe there was a mystery that might be his passport to a London career on a London newspaper.

"The odd thing is not that they knew each other, but that my father never mentioned Calvin, and Calvin never mentioned my father, yet I'm supposed to have been given a job because of their friendship. I thought Maurice had muddled me with someone else when he said his uncle knew my family, but Lucas Rudd confirmed it."

"If Maurice is right once, he could be right twice, and he must recognize his own uncle when he sees him; *ergo* Calvin lied to the police when he claimed to have been in London on Sunday morning."

"Perhaps," said Deborah, realizing that, like Lucas, Jason yearned for Calvin Canning to harbour a disgraceful secret. Everybody seemed to be ganging up against Calvin, and it felt unfair, whatever had or had not happened during the disaster exercise. Even Deborah hoped to use Calvin as a scapegoat so that her relationship with Gregory had not been a factor in his death, and the thought made her cautious. "We're probably jumping to conclusions. Calvin opts to cultivate a reputation for being a ruthless businessman, but it's only a performance. He's very generous to local charities."

"I expect that's what people said about Vlad the Impaler. Deb, I have to know what Calvin was doing in London last weekend. Did you get anything out of Phoebe Vale?"

"No, but I told her you'd be interested in what she could unearth. Contact Phoebe, and you'll find her more than eager to help. Calvin's merely someone who's passing through her life." Just as Gregory had also passed through Phoebe's life. Uncertain if she wanted to discover the schedule of events at the Grand Hotel on Saturday night, Deborah was still compelled to add, "Phoebe knew my father quite well: very well, actually."

Although fairly skilled at reading between the lines, Jason was not skilled enough, and he let Deborah's words go by him, oblivious to the fact that she had hinted at something she did not wish to explain. "Calvin clearly needed to keep in with your father. After all, that's why you were given a job. It's odd this purported friendship never came to light before."

"You think my father was blackmailing Calvin." For the first time since Gregory's death, Deborah laughed, although she immediately felt remorseful to have done so, but the idea of Calvin cold-bloodedly eliminating an adversary in the museum courtyard belonged nowhere but in Jason's headline-fuelled mind.

"I didn't mean to suggest that your father was a blackmailer," Jason said hastily.

"Yes, you did."

"Well, what theory do you have?"

"That you're determined to find a sensational scoop, whether one exists or not."

"All right, so I read *Barney Rex, Boy Reporter* at an impressionable age. But none of this Calvin business adds up, does it?"

"No," admitted Deborah.

"I'm just sorry it involves you."

"Jason, you're thrilled to have a source right at the centre of this mess. Don't forget I know you of old."

"Glad of a source; sorry it has to be you." Jason was defensive; however, he could not deny the ambition that lurked behind all he did. "I might get a byline in a national out of this, but that's no reason to talk to me if you don't want to."

"You mean, we can communicate silently through email," said Deborah, not taken in by Jason's show of finer feelings.

"Of course I didn't mean that. Emails aren't secure." Jason tried to sound light-hearted, but there was enough instruction in his tone to entertain Deborah. "Give me Phoebe's number, and I'll call her. Are there any museum staff members I should chat to?"

"If anybody knows anything, it's Maurice. He's the one who saw Calvin on Sunday morning. If you do an interview with him about his arts festival, you could easily slip in a few extra questions."

"The only snag in your scheme is that Maurice hates me."

"Maurice is far too diffident to hate anybody."

"You're wrong: you're very wrong. Maurice Canning views me as a rival for the favours of one Deborah Wainwright, and he entirely fails to grasp that you're as indifferent to my magnetic allure as you are to his. He'd refuse to speak to me."

"You don't know Maurice. He lives for attention. Tell him you can get a piece about his arts festival idea into the paper, and I'm sure he'll burble on unstoppably."

"And I'm sure he won't. You don't understand Maurice."

"I never aimed to. But if you're not prepared to tackle him, try Calvin himself, instead of going all around the byways."

Jason sighed wryly at the straightforwardness of the plan. "I've dialled Calvin's phone number, and left umpteen polite messages requesting his gracious consent to an interview. I door-stepped his house for hours on end, and when the novelty finally wore off, I shoved an elegantly worded note through his letterbox, saying how much an unworthy local reporter would appreciate the honour of a few minutes spent in his presence. Nothing works. Calvin Canning chooses to remain incommunicado. I've never known him to be so shy. Keeping him out of the paper is normally the problem."

"Calvin won't like being associated with an unpleasant story. He longs for deference and admiration. If we still had a manor house in the vicinity, Calvin would want to be lord of it." Again Deborah was sorry for Calvin, hounded by both Jason and Lucas. A few hefty donations to local good causes would be Calvin's response to the negative publicity, but mud was inclined to stick, and the townspeople made *schadenfreude* their pastime. Deborah wished that she had not contacted Jason, but he was going to delve into Calvin's secrets with or without her help, and nobody on earth had the power to persuade Jason Clenham to abandon an investigation when it might lead to a byline.

Deborah said goodbye, put the telephone down, and was instantly conscious of being alone in a silent house. She thought that even Maurice's company might lessen the sense of isolation, yet when somebody knocked on the front door, Deborah changed her mind, and decided to pretend that she was out should the caller prove to be Maurice. But as she cautiously approached the window, she was astonished to see Calvin Canning outside, with a cellophane-wrapped bouquet held upside down in one hand.

****

"I would have dropped by sooner, but I figured you'd need a little time to yourself first," said Calvin. He handed his flowers to Deborah, and walked into the house as casually as if he were a frequent visitor.

There was no polite way of telling Calvin to get out because her mother believed him to be a murderer, and so Deborah accepted the bouquet. She automatically raised it to her face but the pink roses were scentless.

Calvin opened the door of the front room, glanced at the stacks of paperwork, and said, "It looks like Maurice has moved his office here."

"No, it's my office that's been moved. Maurice told me I could work from home."

"Good, I was going to suggest that myself. I know you won't want to go back to the museum." Calvin spied the kitchen, led the way down the hall to it, and sat at the table. "I owe you an explanation. Maurice shouldn't have said anything but, yes, you did get the job because you're Greg's daughter. I knew you'd be the best applicant."

"How could you possibly know that?"

"Because you're Greg's daughter."

"But he was the most irresponsible person in the world."

"And yet totally trustworthy."

"Trustworthy! Are we talking about the same Gregory Wainwright?"

"The very same." Calvin's voice was sympathetic as he added, "But you wouldn't have been able to recognize that in Greg. You saw him through your mother's eyes. It must be a difficult way to grow up, caught in the middle of an unhappy marriage."

"Their marriage wasn't unhappy," Deborah said, as she forced Calvin's roses into a temporary home amongst Maurice's daffodils. The vase shortage had again become acute.

Calvin looked surprised. "But your parents got a divorce."

"No, although I can understand why you'd think that. My father never needed a bit of paper to give him his freedom. What did he tell you?"

"Nothing," Calvin said hastily. "I misunderstood."

"What did he tell you?" repeated Deborah, smiling. Unexpectedly, Gregory had become a joke she could share. "I suppose he described my mother as an atrocious harridan, who blighted his life with her carping bitterness."

"No; Greg told me she was gentle and easy-going."

"Then why did you think their marriage was unhappy?"

"I made a mistake, especially as Greg talked about you a lot more than Rhoda. He said how pretty you are, and how well you can sing and dance. He assumed you'd follow him into show business."

"I like a regular wage too much," declared Deborah, immune to the attempt at distracting her with flattery. "Actually, I'm not a hundred per cent certain that you're quoting my father with much accuracy. You don't want to say it, but you imagined there'd been a divorce because, the last time you saw him, he was shacked up with some woman or other."

"And I was trying to be so very tactful," admitted Calvin. "Yes, Greg did talk of a girl who'd left her husband for him. I thought he said something about marrying her, and assumed he'd got a divorce. But I bumped into him at Liverpool Street station, and I was hurrying to an appointment, and he was rushing to catch a train, so I obviously misheard."

"When was this?"

"Around ten o'clock."

"Ten o'clock when?"

"Saturday morning. I'd just arrived in London."

"You mean, last Saturday?" Deborah demanded in astonishment. "You met him on his way here? Was that when you arranged to meet at the museum on Sunday?"

"We didn't arrange to meet anywhere," said Calvin. "Anyhow, if Greg needed to see me, he'd have gone to my house, not the museum."

Calvin's words were like a slap across the face. Deborah told herself that Calvin must be lying, because there would be no reason for Gregory to have wanted to see his daughter, particularly when he was preoccupied with Phoebe. And even if Phoebe had never existed, there would still be no reason for Gregory to have wanted to see his daughter. Calvin was lying. He had to be lying. "When did you first get to know my father?" Deborah asked, to escape the feeling that she was somehow to blame for Gregory's death.

"We met years ago in a northern club," replied Calvin. "That reminds me, though I've no idea why it should, there's a nuisance of a reporter hanging around my house when he isn't leaving me messages. Maurice reckons that you have the ability to halt this Jason Clenham in his tracks."

"Nobody has that ability, and avoiding Jason will only make him suspect you've got something to hide. I'd grant him a long, detailed and dull interview, if I were you. Maurice hopes to organize an arts festival in Seaborne, so you could waffle on about that, and fob Jason off with a firm 'I don't know' to anything he asks."

"An arts festival?" queried Calvin. "Do you think one would work in this town?"

"I'll have to do a bit of fobbing off myself, and say that I don't know," replied Deborah. "Calvin, why did you never mention my father? And why did he never mention you?"

"I didn't want you to think you hadn't got the job on your own merits."

"But I hadn't," Deborah pointed out, remembering Jason's theory of her father as a blackmailer with a hold over Calvin.

"The other applicants were illiterate. About Greg's reason for not acknowledging fearlessly and frankly that he knew Calvin Canning, I can only speculate, but I suppose he never deemed being acquainted with me a noteworthy topic of conversation." Calvin was also doing a little fobbing off, and Deborah sensed that he had no intention of further enlightening her. "Tell me more about this arts festival. Is it to be museum-based?"

"Semi: song recitals and chamber music would be fine, but anything on a larger scale might have to be in the town hall. The school could get involved as well: a children's choir perhaps, or a painting exhibition. Anyway, Maurice has a lot of plans."

"It might just take off, especially if we can inveigle a famous name to take part." Calvin was doubtless already picturing himself as an erudite patron of the arts. He would pick up a few facts about Beethoven or the French Impressionists, and then manage to imply that his meagre grains of knowledge were a burgeoning wheat field of culture. "Were any celebrity musicians born in this town?"

"Alas, not a single one; no artists or poets either. Perhaps Maurice could claim that's because there's never been an arts festival here."

"Good selling point. I must ask Phoebe about tax dodges for artistic stuff. She's bound to know. You certainly did me a favour, Deborah, introducing her."

Deborah disagreed; however, Calvin could not know that Phoebe was prepared to collect information about him for Jason's benefit. But everybody seemed willing to betray Calvin, and that included Deborah. Even Maurice had not appeared unduly distressed when he thought there was a possibility that his uncle might have been the one to perish in the museum courtyard. For all his wealth and influence, Calvin was as alone as Deborah felt.

"Phone this Jason Clenham pest, and tell him to come here now," ordered Calvin. "There's nothing like the unexpected to put people at a loss. Let's get this twaddle over and done with."

"I think I've got Jason's mobile number somewhere," said Deborah, knowing that it was stored inside her telephone. She went out to the hall, made a show of looking through a notebook, and then dialled, conscious that Calvin could both see and hear her.

"More info, Deb?" Jason's voice demanded. "What's the latest low-down? I hope you've gleaned a few lurid details about our elusive Calvin."

"Hello, Jason. This is Deborah Wainwright. I believe you left a message requesting an interview with Calvin Canning."

"Terrific! You've persuaded the crook to talk. And I gather he's listening."

"He's at my house now, but has only a few minutes to spare in his schedule, so the interview will have to take place immediately."

"You bet! I'm on my way. Thanks a million, Deb. Incidentally, why is Canning ensconced at your place? Is there something you've neglected to tell me about your relationship with the mysterious Calvin?"

"Definitely not."

"You wouldn't care to volunteer for the Mata Hari role, should Phoebe back out?"

"Again, definitely not. Goodbye, Jason."

"What's so definitely not?" asked Calvin, as Deborah put the telephone down.

"Oh, Jason wanted to interview you this evening. He'll just have to rearrange his timetable. By the way, there's a public meeting in the town hall next week about the arts festival. Maurice is chairing it."

"Maurice!" Calvin made a wry face.

"The idea is to get a committee of volunteers together. You couldn't mention the meeting to Jason, could you? There are posters around town, but the more publicity the

113

better." Deborah sat down opposite Calvin, and all at once the craziness of the situation struck her anew. Gregory could not really be dead, not Gregory, and the enigmatic Mr Canning could not be seated at her kitchen table. But Calvin was, and apparently had no intention of removing himself in the near future.

"Maurice can't be chairman of anything, if this festival is to have a chance," declared Calvin. "My worthy nephew does his best, I admit, but he wouldn't have an earthly against the sort of people who gravitate towards committees."

It was Deborah's opinion too, but an outsider could not possibly join in the denigration of a family member. "Maurice will be fine, I'm sure. He got a very clear concept of what he wants the festival to be, so if people don't like his plans, they needn't sign on."

"But they will," predicted Calvin. "Every faultfinder and wet blanket in Seaborne will clamour to be involved, and then spend the next ten years thinking up reasons why we can't possibly go ahead. I'll chair the public meeting, and make sure all the committee members are the type who get things done."

Calvin spoke so decisively that Deborah knew Maurice's scheme had been hijacked. As regards establishing a festival in Seaborne, it was probably the best thing that could happen, but Maurice was going to be very disappointed. "The town councillors might not be enthusiastic," warned Deborah. "They're hardly the most cultural and aesthetic of mortals."

"No, but they think they're leaders of men. Send each one a personal invitation to the meeting, as if we couldn't make a move without them on board."

"Their invitations have already gone out. I wrote to the school as well."

"Good. I can easily fudge up some claptrap about educational aspects. I wonder if there are any government grants? But

Phoebe will check. She has to be on the committee as financial adviser."

Phoebe's notion of an evening's entertainment did not include meetings in the town hall, but Calvin would discover that for himself soon enough without Deborah bothering to spell it out. Besides, flighty Phoebe might have taken off long before any committee had time to form. "You don't want too many people involved, or nothing will ever get done."

"This festival is going to happen," announced Calvin. "I've made up my mind."

Just as he had also made up his mind not to part with further information about Gregory. The lack of detail concerning the nightclub in which they had originally met indicated that Gregory might have been accompanied by a woman: a circumstance that Calvin was reluctant to reveal to Gregory's daughter. The identity of the northern enchantress could not matter after so many years, but Deborah found herself trying to picture the unknown woman, and the picture insisted on shaping itself into Phoebe. Then a memory surfaced.

It had been the sole fine day in the midst of a wet August. Holidaymakers were out in force, ambling along the High Street with over-hot, red-faced babies and groups of irritable children whining for sweets and toys. Deborah, 16 years old and intolerant of delay, had alternately walked in the gutter and pushed her way through the crowds. She was on a special mission: to buy one of the French-style loaves that were the only bread her father would condescend to eat. White sliced was good enough for Rhoda and Deborah, but when Gregory was at home, catering standards were upgraded.

Then Deborah had seen Gregory: Gregory and Phoebe. They were standing together at the end of the High Street, laughing, chatting, and eating ice cream, oblivious to the day-trippers milling about them. As Deborah approached, Gregory put his left arm around Phoebe, circled her lips with his right forefinger to remove traces of ice cream and, still looking at Phoebe, he slowly licked his finger.

"Hello, Debbie. I've just treated Princess Phoebe to an ice cream. Would you like one?" Gregory did not release Phoebe's waist, but the nonchalance of his tone, and Phoebe's ease of manner, made Deborah feel in the wrong for having misinterpreted an innocuous scene. Nine years later, Deborah believed that her first impression had been the accurate one. Gregory and Phoebe were a couple.

"Jason Clenham must be eager to get at his story," Calvin remarked as somebody knocked on the front door, "unless he chooses to haunt this part of Seaborne for old times' sake."

"Doesn't he live around here any more?"

"He moved last month, and now graces the other side of town. He's got a flat not far from the lifeboat station."

"You have done your homework," said Deborah, amused.

"Know the enemy; not that Clenham seems a particularly formidable one. He's simply a fly, buzzing round and round a room: irritating, but no worse than that. Why did you ditch him? Come on, tell all. I'm an old family friend, remember. You can confide past heartbreaks to me. Is Clenham a notorious womanizer, or does he have a vicious streak in him? What's the dirt behind that masquerade of dull respectability?"

"The respectability is no masquerade," replied Deborah, noting that Calvin expected her to have more loyalty to him than to Jason. "You're doomed to disappointment if you want scandal. Jason works hard, and pays his bills. He doesn't drink to excess, do drugs or gamble."

"Then let the peerless paragon in, before he dazzles passing motorists with the splendour of his radiant integrity. The more I hear about this Clenham, the less I like him. I bet he never forgets his mother's birthday, and always has his Christmas cards posted by the end of November. He's a walking reproach to flawed humanity."

Deborah was tempted to warn Calvin against underestimating Jason, but any words of caution would be an underestimation of Calvin himself. Jason was unlikely to garner much copy from somebody so in control, and so determined to stay in control. However, it was not Jason, primed with questions, on the front step. Deborah opened the door to discover Maurice, holding a pizza box before him like a shield.

"Your mother said she didn't want anything to eat, but I'll check again later on. I'm sure she ought—" Maurice stopped, decidedly taken aback, as he looked down the hall to see Calvin sitting at Deborah's kitchen table. "What are you doing here?"

"Waiting to be interviewed by a righteous predator," replied Calvin.

Deborah stood aside to let Maurice into the house. "Jason's going to interview your uncle."

"Why here?" demanded Maurice.

"Why not here?" retorted Calvin. "Have you any objection?"

"Of course I don't." But Maurice sounded sulky, and also suspicious, perhaps regarding Calvin as another rival for Deborah's attention. He glanced at the pink roses, but said nothing. Then, as though to point out that his relationship with Deborah was on a very domestic footing, Maurice deposited the box he held onto the table, but the action merely resulted in Calvin lifting the lid, and helping himself to a slice of pizza.

"When's the museum opening again?" But Deborah spoke in an attempt to divert her own thoughts, rather than Maurice's. She did not like the assumption that she had become his possession, his exclusive possession.

"I've decided to reopen the place on Monday."

"Don't be ridiculous, Maurice. The museum isn't opening until next month at the earliest, if then," decreed Calvin.

"I meant the first Monday in February," claimed Maurice, too hastily.

"I'll tell you when you can go ahead," said Calvin, ignoring Maurice's words.

Deborah guessed that Calvin was thinking of the funeral, and his consideration made her the complete hypocrite. The only Gregory she could mourn ceased to exist with her childhood, and perhaps that Gregory was an illusion anyway: a fairytale she had told herself. Once upon a time, a child lay awake in the dark, confidently expecting her father to run up the stairs and say goodbye, before he went to catch his train. But then she heard the front door slam, and could not believe that he had forgotten her. Debbie pushed back the duvet, hurried to the window, and pulled the curtains apart to look down at the lamp-lit street. It had been snowing for much of the day, and as Gregory, suitcase in hand, trudged along the pavement, he left a trail of footprints behind him. Even at the corner of the road, he did not sense that Debbie was watching, and so failed to turn and wave. All that remained were his footprints, but the snow had started to drift down again, and soon every trace of Gregory was obliterated with such completeness, he might never have been there. It seemed to Deborah that she must have had a premonition of the emptiness she would feel, years later, at his death, and that was why Debbie had been too desolated to cry.

"I'm sorry, Calvin. Did you say something?"

"Indeed I did, Deborah. I think the demigod of all the virtues has just arrived to favour us with his presence."

Maurice had gone to the front door, and returned looking sullen, accompanied by Jason, who took in the roses and open pizza box with one glance. He had probably not expected to find Calvin sitting unceremoniously at a kitchen table, rather than presiding in the front room, but Jason let no trace of surprise escape him.

"I can't give you more than five minutes," announced Calvin, to start as he meant to go on: the person who dictated the agenda.

"Do you mind if I record the interview?" asked Jason.

"I'd prefer you to. It might mean less chance of being misquoted," replied Calvin.

Deborah had known that her kitchen was small, but she had not realized how small it actually was. With four people squashed around the table, there did not seem to be enough air to breathe, and she got to her feet, understanding claustrophobia for the first time in her life.

"Stay here, Deborah," ordered Calvin. "I like to have a reliable witness around when I talk to the press." He appeared unaware that he had just insulted his nephew, but Maurice would not expect a better opinion of his abilities from Calvin, although to have been dismissed as inadequate in front of both Deborah and Jason would stay in Maurice's mind. Calvin had money and success, but he was not overburdened with imagination.

"I've heard that you were a friend of Deborah's father," began Jason.

"Yes, but I don't think this is either the time or place to discuss the matter." Calvin glanced at Deborah, implying that she might be unable to cope with the tactlessness of the query. It was a clever touch that made Jason look as blundering as Maurice, and also limited the range of further questions, but Jason was not daunted.

"You were at the museum yourself on Sunday morning, I hear."

"Then you hear incorrectly," retorted Calvin.

"It's what my sources tell me," declared Jason.

"Then they're not the most reliable of informants."

"But you were seen in the museum courtyard on Sunday morning."

"Your sources are indisputably defective," remarked Calvin. "Exactly who is supposed to have seen me at the museum?"

Maurice was getting increasingly anxious, and Deborah nudged Jason's arm under the table, but his ruthlessness could equal Calvin's when he was chasing copy. "Your nephew told the police that he saw you in the courtyard on Sunday morning."

"I made a mistake," Maurice said quickly.

"You definitely made a mistake," agreed Calvin. "I wasn't even in Seaborne on Sunday morning."

"So you deny the story?" asked Jason, feigning astonishment.

"Naturally, as it isn't true." Calvin had not lost his composure, and it was clear that even shock tactics would extract nothing from him. Deborah suspected that he might even be enjoying the blank denial that left Jason with nowhere to go, unless he accused Calvin of lying.

"I made a mistake," Maurice said again. "Lucas Rudd asked me to name all the people I saw in the courtyard on Sunday morning. I had to tell him, but I knew I couldn't really have seen you."

"Then why pass on misinformation?" Calvin's tone remained untroubled, but Maurice was no less on edge.

"Where were you on Sunday morning?" asked Jason.

"I'm sure you already know that, despite the inaccuracy of your celebrated sources," replied Calvin. "There's nothing I can add to the investigation. However, my plans for an arts festival are certainly worth your attention. I'm going to chair a public meeting in the town hall next week."

"*You're* chairing it?" demanded Maurice.

"Yes, of course. Who else? It's a Canning project." Calvin dismissed Maurice with the wave of a hand.

"Deborah's kept me fully informed about the festival," said Jason, displaying no interest whatsoever in the topic. "I'd really like to know more details of the years you spent away from the town: where you lived, how—"

"There'll be concerts, arts exhibitions, poetry—" Calvin paused, having run out of cultural pursuits, and then, with a hint of patronizing amusement, asked, "Do you write poetry?"

"Goof grief, no," protested Jason, as vehemently as if accused of an unspeakable perversion.

"I thought you looked the type who'd go in for verse," said Calvin. How such inoffensive words could be classed as a slight, Deborah did not know, but Calvin made his comment sound very near to disparagement.

"I've no idea what the poetic type is, except that it's not me," declared Jason. "I'd like to do an in-depth interview: your early struggles, the first success, people who helped. You know the sort of thing. It would be good publicity for your festival."

"Deborah's handling the publicity." Calvin stood up as he spoke, to inform Jason that the audience was at an end. "Sorry; no more time to spare. Let me know if you want help with anything, Deborah: anything at all."

"Thank you," said Deborah, following Calvin out into the hall.

"I'm not just talking; I mean it."

"Thank you," repeated Deborah. She closed the front door behind Calvin, knowing that she could never turn to him for help. He seemed sincere, but he was also Calvin Canning, who despised dependency and faint-heartedness. Any request for help would be an admission of failure in his eyes.

"It says on the posters that I'm chairing the town hall meeting," Maurice grumbled, as Deborah returned to the kitchen. Even Jason's presence could not postpone Maurice's lament for his shanghaied moment of glory. "People will expect me to chair the meeting."

"It shows what a good idea Calvin thinks the festival is," said Deborah, although aware that Maurice was probably beyond consolation.

"Do you know anything about your uncle's early business ventures, Maurice?" asked Jason, doubtless hankering to profit from an umbrage that might result in secrets being relinquished.

"I've worked hours on my speech," Maurice complained, ignoring Jason. "It's practically finished."

"I better get going," announced Jason, forsaking his chance to quiz Maurice with a willingness that surprised Deborah. Delaying only to help himself to a slice of pizza from the box still on the table, Jason hurried out, to leave Deborah feeling abandoned with hours of a whining Maurice ahead of her. It was a stay of execution to hear the telephone ring.

"Calvin always does this, always," griped Maurice. "The next thing, he'll be maintaining it was his idea in the first place."

Deborah tried to look sympathetic, but went to answer the phone wishing that Maurice would take himself and his woes elsewhere. She had enough problems of her own, without somebody else's being added, and she regretted Jason's departure. Bur he was not that far away. As Deborah picked up the receiver, she heard Jason's voice in full commanding mode.

"Don't say my name, Deb. Maurice mustn't know it's me."

"OK." Deborah could guess why Jason had phoned the very second the front door shut. He wanted her to cross-examine Maurice while the rancour against Calvin was at its most acute.

"Get some info from Maurice."

"I figured you'd say that."

"If he knows anything, you can wheedle it out of him now," declared Jason. "Even unsubstantiated suspicions will be fine. I'll do any substantiating that's necessary. And, Deb, while I'm on the subject of suspicions—"

"Yes?"

"Are you involved with Calvin?"

"Whatever makes you ask that?"

"It looked very cosy: a meal together in the kitchen."

"With a chaperon."

"Oh, Maurice!" Only Calvin could have matched the impatience in Jason's tone. "Are you holding out on me, Deb? Calvin seemed very attentive."

"Then appearances were deceptive."

"Did he explain why he never mentioned knowing your father?"

"Sort of."

"And did he say how they came to meet?"

"Sort of."

Jason paused, and then asked, "Are you still on my side?"

"Sort of."

"Oh well, I can't expect anything more. Have a go at Maurice. If there's anything at all, he'll part with it today. I'll ring again later to hear what Calvin fudged up for you about your father."

"OK."

Deborah felt certain that Maurice would have deduced exactly who had been on the other end of the phone line, but he was too slumped in gloom to be inquisitive, too dejected even to get up and start his customary pacing. He sat with his elbows on the table, chin cupped in both hands, absorbed in misery.

"You're the person who'll really run the festival," said Deborah, sitting down opposite him. "Calvin won't want to bother with all the details of organization."

"Though he'll make sure that he gets the credit for everything." Maurice was right. He had lost control of his festival, and would be regarded as no more than a minion under orders.

"I suppose that's how entrepreneurs make their money: by latching onto other people's good ideas," Deborah suggested, in an attempt to disarm Maurice that was not entirely for Jason's benefit. She too had become curious about Calvin's background and the link with Gregory, because there had to have been more to the history of their friendship than Calvin was willing to disclose. "It's probably just habit for your uncle to take over: something he's done from the start of his career."

"I wouldn't know," Maurice replied sullenly. "And I also didn't know that he paid you visits at home. Why was Calvin here?"

"Jason's been pursuing him, and Calvin imagined I could put a stop to it. I'm afraid he overestimates my influence."

"Calvin was asking about you," said Maurice, unconvinced by Deborah's explanation. "He asked if you were dating anyone. Why would he need to know that?"

"Calvin wants the gen on everybody, but he doesn't divulge much concerning himself. Phoebe Vale is his latest conquest, and yet she told me that she didn't even know if he'd ever been married."

"That's not surprising. I only knew his wife existed after she no longer did. Calvin used her funeral as an excuse to avoid a school Speech Day."

"A rather watertight excuse," commented Deborah, intrigued by the unexpected news. "I never imagined Calvin to be the type with a tragic love story. How did his wife die?"

"No idea; after that one phone call, she wasn't referred to again."

"Calvin would only be 30-ish at the time. She must have been very young. No wonder he can't bring himself to talk about her."

"I wouldn't put it past him to have invented both wife and convenient funeral," declared Maurice with a stubbornness that was probably the single family trait he had in common with his uncle. "Calvin will say anything to get what he wants."

"A wife's funeral is a bit of an over-elaborate invention merely to dodge a school Speech Day, particularly when the pretext of a business trip would do just as well."

"I suppose so," admitted Maurice, but he was reluctant to concede that there could be any straightforwardness in whatever Calvin did. Maurice had not moved far from moody adolescence in dealings with his uncle. "Although he called her Babette, and no woman would really go around with that sort of name."

"With the exception of Calvin's wife, it seems. Where was she from?"

"How should I know?" replied Maurice, cross at the way the absent Calvin had managed to monopolize the conversation.

"Didn't you ask about her?" But even as she spoke, Deborah knew that Maurice would never dare probe into matters Calvin considered private. "Did you ever see any photos of Babette?"

"You can't take photos of someone who's invisible."

"I must admit that a dour name like Calvin doesn't go well with Babette." But a woman who allowed herself to be known to the world as Babette would have to present a frivolous and happy-go-lucky façade to chime in with the nickname, and Calvin favoured women who were not in awe of him. However, he also favoured achievers, and Babette sounded too fluffy to be a shrewd businesswoman or a cultured academic. Of course Chelsea Pritchard was no high flyer, and Calvin had certainly dallied with her, but for his wife, he would never select a Chelsea. Babette must have been closer to Phoebe, and that could be why Calvin had promptly discarded the would-be supermodel after his very first meeting with somebody who reminded him of the lost love. It was more like a précis of one of the romantic films that Rhoda so enjoyed, rather than an episode from the hardheaded Calvin Canning's life, but Babette had already started to take on Phoebe's features in Deborah's imagination. "Where was Calvin living in those days? Your school must have had an address for him, if only to send the bills to."

"Presumably, but no one confided it to me."

"Calvin said something about the north, when I asked where he'd met my father."

"That's more information than I've ever got from him about anything." Maurice paused, but could not resist adding, "Why are you interested in knowing about Calvin?"

"Because he wouldn't tell me exactly how and where he got to know my father. It makes me think there's a story he's holding back. Why is Calvin so secretive?"

"Because he's got something to hide," declared Maurice. "Is he going to take you out to dinner tonight?"

"Of course not. Phoebe Vale is the current companion. He's even entrusted his financial stuff to her."

"Calvin doesn't limit himself to one woman at a time." Flighty Phoebe had never been inclined to restrict her choices either. If Calvin were seeking another Babette, he would probably lose the second version even quicker than the first.

"Phoebe can look after herself. What do you imagine Calvin's hiding?"

"Is it Jason Clenham?" demanded Maurice. "Are you trying to find out things for him?"

"Jason!" exclaimed Deborah, and could only hope that she had not overdone the amazement. "Jason scorns amateurs, and lives in terror of somebody appropriating his byline. He'd go totally paranoid if he thought there was any chance I might uncover an enthralling fact that he'd missed. A rival news gatherer buzzing around Calvin would be Jason's worst nightmare. He yearns for a sensational story that will help him escape this town, along with its gardening club shows and craft bazaars."

Maurice did not appear reassured, and Deborah longed to remind him that her motives were none of his business, whatever questions were asked about Calvin. Maurice was beginning to regard any interest she had in another man as some sort of infidelity, and there was enough of Gregory in Deborah to make her want to flee restriction. But perhaps help was at hand.

****

"Come in, Chelsea," urged Deborah, as warmly as to an old and valued friend.

"I've run out of posters." Chelsea was fed up. Everything about her said fed up: fed up with traipsing around town and fed up with wasting her face and figure on provincial shopkeepers. The bright lights of London and the even brighter lights of a photographer's studio were very far away.

"Go and keep Maurice company, while I get you some more posters." But Deborah spoke to an empty hall. Chelsea had come to life at the first sighting of Maurice, and hurtled towards the kitchen.

On the assumption that Chelsea's enticing wiles would be enough to overwhelm any quarry, and that nothing more than a few minutes alone with the temptress would be required to clear the house of Maurice, Deborah retreated to the chaos of her front room, and pretended to search for posters. The alluring Chelsea offered everybody the perfect solution. She would acquire a patron to finance her modelling career, Maurice could consider himself a sophisticated man of the world, and Deborah gained freedom from his gallantry. That Maurice might be immune to Chelsea's attractions did not occur to Deborah, or indeed to Chelsea. It was a surprise to both of them that he should choose to vacate the kitchen, and seek refuge in the front room.

"I simply can't carry that many posters. They'll be much too heavy for me," Chelsea stated, clutching Maurice's arm like a police officer with a captive. "You'll have to come along and help."

"I'm too busy to go anywhere," Maurice said firmly. "I've a ton of work piled up."

"You should take time off, relax a bit," Chelsea declared with equal firmness. "There can't be much to do now the museum's closed."

Maurice tried to shake off Chelsea's grip, as he sat down in front of Deborah's computer. "I've got an arts festival to organize."

"That's why you should go with me." Chelsea's voice became coaxing, and she rested her free hand on Maurice's shoulder. "Everybody wants to know about the festival, and I can't tell them a thing."

"Ask Calvin for details," retorted Maurice, and all was explained to Deborah. He knew more of Chelsea and her activities than anyone had realized.

"I'm not speaking to Calvin." Chelsea's pout was wasted. Maurice ignored her, picked up a sheaf of letters, and began to read. After a moment or two, Chelsea released him and made a face at his back, but it would not be the end of her campaign. Maurice was the objective, and she had no intention of accepting defeat so easily. Whether described politely as tenacity of purpose or bluntly as pig-headedness, Chelsea possessed that quality in abundance. Nothing would be allowed to thwart her modelling career, and Maurice was still a possible sponsor. His seduction had merely been postponed.

"You shouldn't hurt Chelsea's feelings. She's rather keen on you," remarked Deborah, as the front door slammed behind the wannabe superstar. She had imagined that Maurice would be flattered by the attention of such a showy girl, but he seemed as disapproving as a chapel elder.

"Chelsea Pritchard is involved with Calvin," stated Maurice.

"Phoebe's replaced her."

"Perhaps, and perhaps not. He was at the museum on Sunday morning to meet Chelsea."

"But you didn't see Calvin on Sunday," Deborah reminded Maurice. "You made a mistake."

"Calvin was in the museum courtyard, whatever he says," declared Maurice. "I saw him, and he knows it."

"Calvin was still in London."

"That's his story."

"If he had been at the museum, other people would have spotted him and told Inspector Atherton or Lucas Rudd."

"Calvin pays the wages around here."

"Even so, I don't think the staff will have formed a conspiracy to lie to the police on his behalf."

"I saw Calvin," declared Maurice, surprisingly certain for somebody who, as a general rule, became doubtful when anything he said was queried. "I recognized that awful blue-striped jacket of his: the one he wears because he's under the impression it makes him look young."

"I'm not sure that Inspector Atherton would be inclined to hold an identity parade for a jacket, no matter how striped."

But Maurice was not to be jollied out of his belief. "Calvin hasn't worn that jacket since, and it's not in the hall cupboard where he keeps his coats. I checked when I was at his house."

"Perhaps he's altered the habits of a lifetime, and moved the jacket to an upstairs wardrobe," suggested Deborah, amused at Maurice's amateur sleuthing. "Perhaps he got bored with pal stripy, and passed it on to a charity shop. Or perhaps he sent it out to the cleaner's."

"Yes, I thought he might want to get it cleaned."

"Maurice, are you telling me that you believe Calvin murdered my father, and is currently occupied with the task of destroying DNA evidence?"

"Absolutely not," protested Maurice, too hurriedly and too vehemently. "I'm so sorry I've made you remember. It was stupid of me. I wasn't thinking. Naturally Calvin wouldn't have harmed your father. After all, they were friends."

"Then what does it matter where Calvin's jacket is?"

"It doesn't; it doesn't matter in the least. I was just wondering why Calvin lied. But I probably made a mistake, as you said. There's no law decreeing that somebody who resembles Calvin can't have the same taste in jackets as him. I only glanced out of a window for a split-second, and didn't get a proper look. If Calvin maintains he was in London, that's most likely where he was."

"Except that you're still convinced he's lying," Deborah pointed out, more amused by Maurice's circular backtracking.

"Calvin prefers to lie. It's his nature to be devious, even when there's nothing for him to be devious about."

Maurice was correct. Deborah could think of no other reason why Calvin had kept quiet about knowing Gregory, and also why Maurice should have been left unaware of the existence of Babette until after her death. Calvin liked to be enigmatic, liked to divide up his life and keep the pieces in separate compartments. It was Calvin's method of staying in control.

"I better go, before that nuisance of a Chelsea turns up again," said Maurice, glad to abandon the tactlessness of his earlier choice of subject.

"Not many men would avoid a girl with her looks."

"Calvin certainly didn't. It's different for me because—because I'm—well, because you're—" Maurice hesitated, and Deborah felt embarrassed, fearing that he might be on the verge of proclaiming eternal devotion to her.

"Chelsea wants to be a fashion model," said Deborah, to move the conversation into safer territory. "It must be nice to have such a clear-cut aim. I just drift from job to job."

"You can't do any more drifting," Maurice declared, trying to sound jokily forceful. "Calvin would discover that you're the one who does the actual work, and I'm only a figure-head."

"A figure-head wouldn't be organizing an arts festival."

"I won't be able to organize anything, do anything, without you." Maurice paused again, and Deborah hastened to end a silence that he might hope was full of significance.

"Would you mind if I give your mobile number to the local media? It could mean you'll be pestered by journalists, but publicity's essential, and Calvin won't want his number handed out."

The thought of attention weaved its usual magic around Maurice, and he immediately straightened his shoulders. "Don't worry; I can cope with media pressure."

"They might even want you to go on television."

"Then I'll go on television," announced Maurice. "In fact, I'll handle all the media promotion from now on."

"It would help immensely," said Deborah, even though Maurice, as spokesman, was more likely to torpedo Seaborne's chance of acquiring some culture than guide the campaign onto triumph. However, if Calvin wanted to bask in the glory of founding an arts festival, he was indebted to his nephew, and should a few minutes in the media spotlight be contrived, Maurice fully deserved his share of them.

5

"Deborah, write me a speech for the town hall meeting," Calvin had ordered over the telephone. "Could you get something drafted out fairly soon, and come round to my place so that I can go through it with you? I'll need time to learn the words off by heart. There's nothing less authoritative than having to refer to notes as if you can't quite master the subject. Even worse to bury your head in a sheet of paper and forget to glance up at the audience. I intend to be fluent, purposeful, and totally compelling."

"You've left out dynamic and captivating," said Deborah.

"Those qualities are ever-present in my charismatic personality. But only bother with the speech if you're ready to start work again."

It was a mere show of sensitivity. Calvin expected a gripping oration to be completed within hours, and would probably have informed Deborah that work was the best therapy had she shirked the task. However, Deborah wanted to fill hours that had never before passed so slowly, and it was simple to exaggerate the possible benefits, both financial and educational, for the town should its inhabitants be overcome with a hitherto unsuspected yearning for the arts. She could not really believe that Maurice had dreamed up a project destined to grow into an annual event, but Calvin Canning did not usually involve himself with failure. Of course, the prestige of being known as a champion of high culture was a reward in itself, and the reason that Calvin had chosen to found a museum. The people who were impressed by money had ceased to interest him; he wanted to belong in the sort of company who took wealth so for granted that it was not an entry fee to their world, and the more insurmountable the obstacles between him and his goal, the more avid Calvin would be to conquer. He did not value easy victories.

****

The shoreline was the destination of every walk that Deborah took, but she had never before called at one of the monumental houses adorning the promenade. The area dated back to the mid-19th century, and abounded in turrets and battlements as though the householders expected to repel invaders from across the sea. Calvin had added to his defences with an iron-studded front door and an intercom system.

"Yes?" Calvin's voice demanded irritably, as he prepared to rout a salesman rather than a Viking.

"It's Deborah Wainwright. I've brought the first draft of your speech. Shall I declaim it over the intercom, or shove my notes through the letterbox?"

Calvin's reply was to open the door of a house ridiculously large for a single person: a declaration of status instead of a home. The hall was panelled in oak: carved oak that would not have looked out of place in an Elizabethan manor, but the pleasing simplicity of the effect was spoilt by the addition of a very modern radiator. Calvin had no intention of allowing décor to interfere with comfort.

"This speech of yours better be good," said Calvin. "My whole future as patron of the arts depends on it."

"The singer, not the song." But that had been one of Gregory's sayings, and Deborah hurried on. "If our fine townsfolk aren't persuaded to seize the opportunity to become discerning connoisseurs of culture, a lacklustre delivery of my stirring words might be to blame."

133

"Then come in, and I'll practise my rendition of your inspiring prose." Calvin led the way down the hall, past the door of an under-stairs cupboard, presumably the very cupboard through which his nephew had searched in vain for the truant blue jacket. Both Maurice and Rhoda had decided that Calvin was a murderer, but he was far too intelligent to make an appointment, with malevolent motive, in the grounds of a building so closely connected with him. Despite Maurice's suspicions, there would be a sound explanation to account for the elusive blue jacket, and Deborah could not resist the impulse to do a little digging.

"I think the right clothes will be as important as what you say in the town hall," Deborah remarked, in her most guileless tone. "Too formal, and you'll seem stuffily overdressed; too casual, and you'll give the impression you couldn't be bothered making an effort. You need to appear approachable, but not sloppy. I know what would be ideal: that blue jacket of yours, the one with the paler blue stripes."

Calvin stopped walking so abruptly that Deborah nearly collided with him. It was the first time she had ever seen him disconcerted.

"What's wrong, Calvin? Don't tell me you gave the jacket to the deserving poor this very day. Is there a problem?"

"No, not in the least."

"Then why have you come over all distracted?"

"I just remembered something," replied Calvin. "Deborah, I've got a jacket of Greg's here. Should I send it around to your mother's house? Or would that upset her too much?"

"I'm not sure. I think she'd like to have the jacket, but I'll have to check. How did part of my father's precious wardrobe go astray?"

"It didn't; he lent it to me." Calvin opened the door of a sitting room that could have featured in a shop window display. The furniture looked unused, and the ornaments were for show rather than representing a collector's cherished hoard, but the view between the floor-length curtains more than made up for the lifeless interior. Gulls circled against a purple sky, and the wide expanse of ocean was a swirling mixture of dark water and creamy foam. If Deborah could have chosen any view in the world to be seen from a house she owned, it would be that one. After growing up close to a sea that changed character with every hour, town and countryside vistas could seem very bland and stagnant.

"I'd be happy to live in a shack, if I could gaze out of my window at the sea."

"It's why I bought this place." But Calvin would always put the property above any view. The ocean had merely been an extra to him.

"Well, what's the story?" asked Deborah.

"What story?"

"How my father came to lend you a jacket, and the current unavailability of your blue one. I gather there's a connection. Did you swap for some reason?"

"Excellent deduction," said Calvin, but he spoke with reluctance. "I went to London for an afternoon meeting, and planned to buy myself a stylish new suit before I was due on parade, so I wore the blue jacket for warmth rather than elegance. However, I got a text message, while I was on the train, to tell me that the meeting had been brought forward. It meant I wouldn't have time to do anything but go straight there from the station, so I reigned myself to making an entrance bearing a strong resemblance to a provincial cousin."

"Are you talking about last Saturday?"

Calvin nodded. "The jacket your father wore was perfect, like all his clothes. I thought he'd scorn my blue stripes, but Greg said they made him feel young."

"That's when he told you about the girl who left her husband for him."

"Well, yes," admitted Calvin.

Gregory had fooled himself as much as Rhoda did. Phoebe would not have left Lucas because of Gregory; she had walked out of her marriage because she was bored. All the blue-striped jackets in the world, no matter how youthful an appearance they offered, would not be enough to secure Phoebe.

"He must have gone to the museum to return your coat," said Deborah, with sudden hope.

"No. I told him to keep the jacket, as it had such a rejuvenating effect."

Deborah's escape route was closed. Gregory probably had gone to the museum to see her, after all. It was a blow, but perhaps one that might be deflected a little. "My father wore your jacket on Sunday."

"Did he? Does it matter?"

It mattered because it gave a reason for Gregory's death that did not involve Deborah, even if he had planned to see her. The blue jacket and chance were to blame, should Gregory have been mistaken for Calvin. The actual location was unimportant; Gregory could have died anywhere in the town.

"No one lay in wait for me at the museum," protested Calvin, sensing what had passed through Deborah's mind. "That's impossible. Who on earth would want me out of the way?"

Maurice, thought Deborah. "I suppose I'm taking it for granted that successful businessmen must have ruthless enemies. I've seen too many films."

"Do you really believe I'm permanently identified with blue stripes?" demanded Calvin, feigning horror in an attempt to draw back from the topic of what had happened to Gregory on Sunday. "I'm shattered to learn that you imagine people only have to see a blue stripe, and immediately think of me. I was convinced that my image said modish, coupled with a certain pleasing charm. How can I face the world again after this mortifying revelation? You've so wrecked my confidence that now would undoubtedly be a good time to put in for a pay rise."

"Read the speech before you make any rash promises you might later regret." Deborah wanted to persuade herself that Maurice was guilty, even though she could not seriously picture him ever being decisive enough to attack his uncle, no matter what the cause. The very idea of Maurice as murderer was absurd, and yet it would not go away. She recalled that he had looked astonished, rather than thankful, when Calvin reappeared at the museum on Monday, and there was a possibility that Maurice's astonishment could actually have been bewilderment. If he had killed someone he believed to be Calvin, and yet his uncle was in front of him very much alive, it would seem as confusing as a nonsensical dream. Maurice needed time to think of a means to cover his tracks, and told Deborah about a fictitious search for the blue jacket to establish his ignorance of what the victim had been wearing. At the same time, he also attempted to throw suspicion onto Calvin, with the claim of a positive sighting. The plan was too devious and intricate for Maurice to have invented, but managing to eliminate the wrong person because of a striped jacket was precisely the sort of mistake blundering Maurice would make. However, it was the one and only part of the whole mess that could be described as typically him.

"This speech is exactly what I want," declared Calvin, after a quick scrutiny of the text. "No need to alter a word."

"With the exception of—?" prompted Deborah.

"Well, you could mention how the idea of a festival came to me like a flash of lightning."

"It didn't; Maurice was the one struck by lightning."

"A technicality," claimed Calvin. "I was listening to a CD—no, I wasn't; I went to a concert in London, and remembered how deprived of good music I'd been as a child. I wished I had the power to bring the beauty of the classics to all those as deprived as once I was, and then came my moment of pure inspiration. By starting a festival destined to become a celebrated annual feast of culture, I can ensure that no local child is ever again denied the opportunities I missed. What do you think?"

"That it's a bit unfair on Maurice, but otherwise commendably public-spirited of you. Anyone who objects to the scheme will sound like the sort of villain who'd slug Little Orphan Annie in the mouth."

"Then get writing," ordered Calvin. "And don't worry about Maurice. He owes me."

A debt Maurice was expected to repay for the rest of his life. Deborah could understand why he had not been overwhelmed with grief when suggesting that Calvin might be the courtyard casualty. Resentment instead of gratitude was perhaps an inevitable result of Maurice's isolated childhood, although liquidating his uncle would still be something of an overreaction. But even if Maurice had killed by mistake, Deborah remained the reason why Gregory was at the museum in the first place.

****

"Perfect!" Calvin announced after he had read through the second draft of the town hall speech. "This really establishes my visionary credentials."

"Then I can go on my way, knowing that I've earned my wages," said Deborah.

"I'd offer you a drink, but I can sense Greg's disapproval all around me. If I attempt to ply his little girl with strong liquor, no doubt with lecherous intent, a thunderbolt will hit me."

Deborah smiled, but she was unable to recognize Gregory as protective father, despite being well acquainted with the chameleon-like tendencies of a poseur. "I have to visit my mother anyhow. I'll find out if she wants the jacket."

"I wish I—" Calvin hesitated, and then said briskly, "But never mind what I wish. Thanks for doing such a good job on the speech."

"What do you wish?" asked Deborah, curious to know what had made the supremely confident Calvin unexpectedly dither in front of her.

"That I was better at handling this situation," admitted Calvin, as he opened the front door. "I hope I'm not hurting you when I talk about Greg."

"Of course you're not. In fact, I'd like you to tell me more: how you came to meet him, for example."

"I'm glad I haven't upset you," said Calvin, ignoring the second half of Deborah's reply. The door closed before she could ask any questions, but that was no surprise when dealing with Calvin the reticent.

After the stifling mugginess of central heating, the salt air was wonderfully fresh and free, almost strong enough to whirl away anxieties along with its cargo of plastic bags and sheets of newspaper. Deborah crossed the promenade to be even closer to the ocean, but she had only walked a few steps before being confronted by a sullen Chelsea.

"What were you doing in Calvin's house?"

"Writing a speech for him," replied Deborah. "What are you doing on the prom? Stalking Calvin?"

"Don't be silly. I just happen to be out for a bit of a stroll." But Chelsea's teeteringly high heels and tight skirt told a different story. She was presumably there in the hope of staging a chance encounter with Calvin, during which the glamour of her appearance would re-ensnare him. Maurice had refused to co-operate, but Chelsea could not be defeated that easily. She was annoyed and windswept, yet determined. She was also suspicious. "Do you often visit Calvin at home?"

"Chelsea, you know perfectly well that I can't compete with you in either face or figure. Phoebe Vale's your rival, assuming

139

you have one, and the novelty of a relationship wears off very quickly with Phoebe." Deborah found it odd to feel sorry for somebody who had such striking looks, but Chelsea was out of her league with Calvin Canning. She had been a temporary distraction, and Calvin would be astonished if he ever learnt that he was expected to finance her dreams. Deborah longed to advise Chelsea to persevere with Maurice, a soft touch for every tin-rattling charity collector in the town, but it seemed an insult to suggest that any man could be resistant to the attractiveness on offer.

"I bet Phoebe Vale is aware what side her bread's buttered on," declared Chelsea. "She'll never let Calvin go."

"You don't know Phoebe. She's had money all her life, so she doesn't think about it."

"She will," Chelsea said bitterly. "Rich people always end up with even more."

"That's true, but I think Phoebe's going to drift away from Calvin quite soon." Jason had no money worth mentioning, but Phoebe was unlikely to notice.

"I've got to get out of this town; I've got to." There was sudden desperation in Chelsea's voice, and she looked up and down the promenade as though the bars of a cage surrounded her.

"You'll get to London one day."

"One day! It's always one day. I'm so fed up waiting. I've been waiting for years and years."

It had probably been how Gregory felt as he chased the stardom that forever evaded him. Chelsea's ambition was no less compelling, and she too would be unable to compromise, since life without success, without fame, seemed pointless, just as it had done to Gregory. Because of his thwarted hopes, Deborah feared that Chelsea might have to face similar frustration, but not to try at all would be a worse failure. "You'll escape this town," said Deborah. "You'll find what you're looking for. Don't let anyone or anything stand in your way."

Chelsea's face crumpled, as if she were about to cry, but then she turned and tottered away on her high heels, more waddling duck than gliding supermodel. For a moment, Deborah wanted to cry as well, for all the disappointments that Gregory had refused to acknowledge and for all the rebuffs he had ignored. It was not stupidity but courage to fight on: a courage that she should have recognized long before. His casual treatment of Rhoda still mattered, mattered very much, but Gregory would not have had a chance to achieve anything without leaving home, and that chance was the driving force of his existence. He had been as desperate as Chelsea to take flight, and if Deborah could understand Chelsea's craving, she ought to have understood Gregory's, just as Rhoda had done.

Rhoda. Rhoda was on Deborah's conscience. Another visit had to be made, whether or not Rhoda wanted to see her daughter. It was a pretence of family support, Gregory's type of pretence, although he had never needed to wonder what Rhoda's reaction to him would be. Deborah's footsteps became slower and slower, but putting off the visit only postponed it, and the longer she left seeing her mother, the more difficult the excuses would be for not having made an earlier appearance. Gregory could have breezed back into Rhoda's life after an absence of months, but Deborah was and remained an outsider.

As Rhoda opened her front door, Gregory's voice filtered out into the street. Every so often, when particularly frustrated with his career, he had made a demo disc to send to music producers and DJs, all of whom embezzled the enclosed return postage and never bothered to reply. Perhaps the discs were simply thrown away unheard, or perhaps Gregory's lack of originality did not rate a response, but at least the ventures had left his wife with a personal treasure trove.

"I've just had the most brilliant idea," announced Rhoda. "I'm going to have Gregory's songs played at his service, instead of some dreary solemn stuff that's got no connection with him. It'll be a celebration, a party, and you know how Greg adored a party."

The thought of having to listen to Gregory's voice throughout his own funeral horrified Deborah, but it was Rhoda's decision to make, not hers, and might have been Gregory's choice as well, were it possible to canvass his opinion. He would have liked the idea of a captive audience unable to walk out on him.

"Jason brought over the loveliest speech about Greg for the service," continued Rhoda. "There were a few details left out, but I helped Jason add them to what he'd already written. He's such a nice boy. I'll never understand why you didn't consider him good enough for you."

It had been the other way around; Deborah did not consider herself good enough for Jason. He deserved better than to be inflicted with somebody who fled in alarm from close relationships and the duplicity that she regarded as an inevitable part of them; but it was impossible to explain to Rhoda that Gregory had wrecked his daughter's trust in men, and so Deborah smiled instead. "You were the one who told me that I had to hold out for absolute perfection."

"Well, I can't blame you for listening to me." The confrontational tone that had crept into Rhoda's voice began to evaporate, and she too forced a smile. "Come in, and help me choose which songs to have."

"Why not all of them?" asked Deborah, knowing that her suggestion would please Rhoda.

"You're right. It's Gregory's farewell concert, and so it should be him from start to finish. Can you put the demo discs on a single CD? Then I could give a copy of it to everybody when they leave."

"No problem." As Deborah went into the front room, Gregory began to praise the wonders of Hollywood, a place he had never managed to see for himself, although there was no need for Gregory to travel to the reality while old musicals filled his imagination. It was a world he had once shared with Deborah, as they tap-danced and twirled around the kitchen impersonating Astaire and Rogers, Kelly and Charisse, Rall and Miller. Gregory maintained that he had been born several generations too late for the type of career he coveted, but even in the right time and the right place, imitation would not be enough. Astaire already existed; a copy was unnecessary.

"I used to be so envious of you," said Rhoda, the song presumably having taken her as far into the past as Deborah. "I could never dance."

"I wasn't exactly Cyd Charisse."

"Greg thought you were even better. I wish I had your kind of childhood memories."

Deborah immediately felt in the wrong, because it was a privilege to have had happiness to lose, and Rhoda could not be nostalgic about any aspect of her youth. Even a husband's wandering ways could not compare with the neglect of a child abandoned to social services foster care, and Gregory had had to embody every person missing from Rhoda's life: a responsibility anyone might shirk. "I can understand you being envious of me."

"If you're so very understanding, why did you break Greg's heart?" Rhoda had demanded before she could stop herself, but then continued less heatedly, "I know I'm talking rubbish. You'll have to ignore most of what I say. I can't think straight right now."

"It's OK." But Deborah suspected that Rhoda's true feelings were the ones on show. The perfect marriage to the perfect man could not include a daughter who saw her father as a deceitful sponger.

"The police brought round Gregory's stuff from the Grand," said Rhoda, as if attempting polite conversation. "I thought it would upset me, but I'm really glad to have things of his."

"There's a jacket still to come back. He lent it to someone."

"Greg was always generous," claimed Rhoda at once. "Who did he lend the jacket to?"

"Calvin Canning," Deborah said reluctantly, knowing what her mother's reaction would be.

"How dare he get his hands on one of Greg's jackets!" Rhoda sat bolt upright with indignation. "Thieving murderer!"

"Calvin couldn't have been at the museum on Saturday morning. He was in London."

"Don't make excuses for him," ordered Rhoda. She needed to turn her anger against someone, and Calvin Canning would do as well as anybody else. "If he hadn't started that stupid museum, Gregory would still be alive."

The point was unarguable, and Deborah tried to divert her mother from it. "Did the police say why he was staying at the Grand?"

"No one tells me a thing," Rhoda said bitterly.

"That probably means there's nothing to report." Deborah hoped that her mother would remain ignorant of Gregory and Phoebe's relationship. Although Rhoda had managed to fool herself for years about his devotion to her, infidelity with a daughter's friend might be more difficult to gloss over than the usual dalliances with more anonymous females.

"You know something you don't want to tell me," said Rhoda. "I suppose there was a silly woman in pursuit of Gregory, and that's why he had to hide out at the Grand. She was planning to come here for a big confrontation scene, of course, but Greg knew he could rely on me to get rid of her."

"Didn't you ever worry that he might fall for one of them?" ventured Deborah.

"Why should I? Other women made the mistake of trying to trap him. It became a joke between us. Gregory said that I was the sole person who could ever control him, and I did that by giving him complete freedom, never asking questions or nagging." Rhoda laughed at the contradiction, but Deborah guessed that Gregory might not have been joking. If a wife had hemmed him in, carped, criticized and shouted, he could have walked off without blaming himself, but Rhoda's compliance with his wishes came from vulnerability, and meant that Gregory knew he could destroy her by leaving home for good. Rhoda had acquired the only hold over him that any woman could: a stifling hold that he was unable to escape.

"Why did he bother getting married, if freedom was his heart's desire?" asked Deborah.

"You don't know a single thing about love. Why, Greg loved me with such fervour, he even suggested we got a divorce." Rhoda sounded so proud that it took Deborah several seconds to register what had actually been said.

"He wanted a divorce?"

"Of course he didn't want one. He was worried about me being lonely, especially now you've moved out. He thought I'd feel freer if we were divorced, and that I might meet somebody more domesticated. I told him there were no other men in existence, as far as I was concerned."

"When did he suggest this divorce?" But Deborah knew the answer even before Rhoda replied.

"When he phoned on Sunday morning. Greg hated the idea of me being on my own." Rhoda smiled in triumph at the proof of her husband's concern. "I was so touched."

"Yes, I can imagine." If Rhoda really had convinced herself of the altruism of Gregory's motive in seeking a divorce, she was safe. Whatever came out could not hurt her, because she would remain in the pink-tinged fairytale world of unending true love.

"I only had one rival for Greg's attention: his daughter," declared Rhoda. "He adored you from the first moment, and entirely forgot to ask me how I felt, because he was too busy ringing up everybody to announce your arrival and taking hundreds of photos of you. He even insisted on choosing your name."

"Not the most imaginative of choices when he didn't think any further than his own mother's name."

"Greg only agreed to Deborah later on, when your grandmother started flouncing around in a huff because we hadn't called the baby after her. The name he actually chose for you was Babette."

"Babette!" repeated Deborah in astonishment. "How on earth did he come up with that name?"

"He knew the owner of some clubs in the north: Babette Anderson. Not that Greg was trying to curry favour, of course. He never needed to."

"Who did this Babette marry?" asked Deborah.

"Mr Anderson: Rod Anderson. He was the actual nightclub owner, and Babette took over the management after his death. Before that, she'd been a beauty queen, and then a singer. Gregory said she was nice to work for, very down to earth and never went back on her word. I suppose she's long since retired by now."

"What was her daughter like?"

"I don't recall Greg ever mentioning any children. What makes you think she had to have a daughter? It isn't compulsory."

Not compulsory, but probable in that case. It seemed too much of a coincidence that a couple of unrelated Babettes should wander into the lives of both Gregory and Calvin, especially as the two men had met in a northern nightclub. Calvin's wife was almost certainly the one-time beauty queen's daughter, and the younger Babette might also have attracted Gregory. He would be more likely to approve of a name if a pretty girl were affixed to it.

"Perhaps I should write to Babette Anderson, and tell her what's happened," said Rhoda. "All of Gregory's friends should be at his farewell concert. How can I find out where she's living now?"

"I'll ask Jason to track her down," said Deborah.

****

"I've been trying to get hold of you for hours." Jason had snatched up his telephone on its second ring, and sounded so eager that Deborah hoped the information she had managed to gather would not seem too meagre. "Tell me everything, especially the part that proves Calvin Canning is an absolute charlatan, fully deserving of the headlines I'll get him."

"Sorry, but I can't oblige," said Deborah. "It's a lot milder than that, and rather sad. He married a girl called Babette Anderson, but she died. Her mother, another Babette, owns or used to own nightclubs in the north somewhere, inherited from a husband named Rod."

"So that's how Calvin got his start. He married money."

"I'm not sure that there's wealth beyond the dreams of avarice in northern clubs, and he was only a son-in-law. The elder Babette might have had other children." Picturing Babette as a devoted mother brought Rhoda to mind, and made Deborah wish that she could force life on a year without experiencing the interim; but even then Rhoda would still be a reproach to her daughter, no matter how far into the future they were. "Thanks for doing that eulogy, by the way. My mother's very pleased."

"She's asked me to read it at the service."

"You don't have to. The gen on Calvin isn't that startling."

"I think perhaps your mother hasn't got anyone else to ask," Jason suggested.

"I suppose not, but you still don't have to do it. After all, you never met my father."

"I wish I had. It's quite intriguing. Was he your mother's picture of excellence or your feckless wastrel? Which one is the true version?"

It was a good question. Who had really known Gregory? Everybody in his life saw a different person, but Rhoda had to lead the field for inaccuracy. Even Calvin, with his unexpected talk of trustworthiness, had not pretended that single-minded devotion to wedlock was the mainstay of Gregory's existence. "I think you've already made up your mind about my father," said Deborah.

"Perhaps I have," Jason admitted, "but that doesn't mean I can't reassess an opinion. Where did your father meet Calvin?"

"In one of Babette Anderson's clubs: well, I assume that was the location. Calvin told me that they met in a northern nightclub."

"I'll be quite disappointed if Calvin's big secret is just that he married for money, and is too proud to acknowledge the fact. But acquiring an heiress would explain a lot. Once you've got your hands on some dosh, anybody can get at more. The start is the tricky bit."

"That sounds suspiciously like the voice of bitter experience."

"Indeed it is," Jason declared ruefully. "Each time I think I'm ahead, along comes another bill to swallow everything up. There's never any extra."

"I know what you mean. It's difficult to progress further than merely muddling through, without a helping hand from fate."

"And fate's hand gave Calvin a shove in the direction of a lucrative marriage, it seems."

Deborah understood why Calvin would not want to publicize such a convenient alliance, but he could nevertheless have been sincerely fond of his Babette, even while appreciative of opportunities accompanying her, and the details were nobody but Calvin's business. Deborah had not previously thought about the consequences of speaking to Jason, but if Calvin had wed money, he would feel humiliated by no longer being able to parade as a self-made man. He could well have chosen Babette for herself, but the bonus of money would be the only part of his story registered by the readers of the local newspaper. It sullied a relationship that might have been genuinely close.

Calvin had described Gregory as trustworthy, presumably because of secrets that were kept, and if a personal life became public knowledge, it would be the fault of Gregory's daughter. "I don't think Calvin would have got much money through marrying his Babette," said Deborah, in an attempt to reclaim ground so heedlessly relinquished. "It was years ago, and her mother would control the purse-strings."

"Why are you backtracking?" asked Jason. "It's a little late to do that, right after you've told me who he married. Has Calvin dumped you for another, so you want revenge, yet still yearn for his love?"

"No, I'm simply feeling guilt-ridden for having supplied a muck-raking hack with information about my employer. I should have had more loyalty."

"What about loyalty to the muck-raking hack? Have I been utterly superseded by the fascinating Calvin?"

"Oh, utterly. And I imagine I've been superseded in your loyalties by the alluring Phoebe."

"I never name my sources," declared Jason.

"Does Phoebe work undercover on your behalf, studying Calvin's accounts by day and dating him by night, in order to relay nuggets of info to you?" Deborah could imagine Phoebe relishing the intrigue that would add spice to her relationship with Jason. However, he was unlikely to be given the equally interesting intelligence that Phoebe had known Gregory rather better than was generally assumed. "Of course you won't confirm or deny what I've just said, so I'll tactfully change the subject. Have you heard of any well-paid jobs in need of an applicant?"

"I'll ask around for you." Jason paused, and then said, "I'm sorry, Deb. I shouldn't expect you to dig out stuff for me right now. It isn't fair."

"And you'll struggle with those scruples up to the very moment your copy gets into print," predicted Deborah.

"My sensitiveness, although uncharacteristic, is nonetheless real," protested Jason, but he too was amused. "OK, so I'd sell my grandmother into slavery to get an exclusive of her experiences, but that doesn't mean I admire the way I am."

"You're ambitious; live with it."

"No problem. Deb, as you know the worst about me, can I ask a question that I shouldn't bother you with?"

"You're going to ask anyway. Why shilly-shally?"

"What do you think happened to your father?" Jason tried to sound tentative, but he wanted the answer.

"I haven't a clue." The details had started to seem unimportant to Deborah. The fact of Gregory's death, Rhoda's reaction, and the ordeal of the funeral service ahead were more than enough to fill her mind.

"Did your father have any enemies?"

"Only if a few indignant husbands were in pursuit of him. He wasn't the type anyone hated." Indeed, the only person who had thoroughly disliked Gregory was his own daughter, but Deborah hurried away from the thought. "He didn't make enemies, or particularly close friends. He just knew people.

I think he felt trapped by relationships, and preferred to drift through life unhampered."

"When I asked your mother that same question, she gave me a very different answer."

"You're right; you would sell your grandmother into slavery. How could you have asked that?"

"But Rhoda didn't appear to mind any of my questions. Actually, I think she wanted to talk, needed to talk, unless I'm fooling myself to soothe an uneasy conscience, of course."

"You haven't got a conscience to ease. Did you believe the tale of jealous adversaries determined to thwart the brilliant career of England's foremost talent?"

"It did sound a tad on the far-fetched side."

"There were no bitter jealousies and no bitter rivals." Gregory had been self-centred and careless, forgetful of anybody out of sight, with Rhoda the only person to see his character as intensely complex, and she had also been the only person in his life with passion enough for love to fragment into hatred. And Rhoda had said something about going past the museum on Sunday morning, when on a quest for champagne to celebrate the return of her prince among men. Deborah's mind raced off in wild speculation. Could Rhoda have gone to the Grand, and seen Gregory with Phoebe? Did Rhoda back away unobserved, and later engineer a supposedly chance meeting with Gregory? Had she insisted that they went to the museum together to prompt some sort of reconciliation between father and daughter? Then what? A furious Rhoda, slaughtering her beloved? It was an impossible scenario. She would blame Phoebe, not Gregory, and regard the liaison as insignificant. Rhoda could never leave her dream world because, without it, she would be the one to perish.

"You've gone very quiet," Jason commented.

"I can't think of anybody who'd hate my father. It's too deep an emotion. He lived pretty much on the surface, and there weren't any feelings profound enough to lead to tragedy."

"But a tragedy happened, and there has to be a reason why it did."

"Invent your own explanation. Accident, wrong place at the wrong time, mistaken identity—that reminds me. Did I tell you my father was wearing a jacket of Calvin's on Sunday?"

"What!" A crash of wood against floor came from the other end of the telephone line. Jason's chair must have been teetering precariously on its hind legs, and surprise had restored equilibrium with abruptness. "You never said a word about jackets."

"He and Calvin met by chance at Liverpool Street station on Saturday morning. They swapped jackets because Calvin was unexpectedly summoned to a business meeting, and didn't want to turn up in blue stripes."

"Blue stripes!" The excitement in Jason's voice promptly evaporated. "The one consensus about your father is how well dressed he always was. Blue stripes would be beyond the pale."

"Apparently not. He said they made him feel young; at any rate, that's what Calvin told me."

"Your father looked rather like Calvin, didn't he?"

"No."

"Well, both dark-haired and tall: from a distance they'd resemble each other, especially in the celebrated blue stripes." Jason was attempting to talk himself into a story he wanted to be true, presumably because it could mean that Calvin had a secret in his past beyond the dullness of having married for money. "Do the police know about the jacket swap?"

"Only if Calvin's said something, and he doesn't volunteer information. You might be the possessor of an exclusive bit of gen. Do you really think Calvin could have been the actual target?" But that brought Deborah back to Maurice, the world's least likely assassin.

"I don't think; I research and report," Jason declared loftily. "Facts and more facts, to quote my editor: no speculation. Did your father arrange to go to the museum to return the jacket?"

"He probably knew Calvin was still in London," said Deborah, reluctant to acknowledge that Gregory might have been trying to see her. "Anyway, Calvin told him to keep the jacket."

"Data courtesy of Canning?"

"Yes." However, Deborah could not even pretend to believe that Calvin had told her a lie. There was no way out. For some unfathomable reason, Gregory had decided that it was time to talk to his daughter again, after years of silence.

"Do you have any idea why your father should choose to go to the Grand, instead of straight home as he normally did?"

"There's no need to be tactful."

"OK," agreed Jason, but he sounded awkward. "I wish I knew the identity of the girl he was seen with."

"Investigating is your department," Deborah pointed out.

"Nobody answering her description is staying at the Grand, so I guess she must be a local. Who did your father know?"

"Half the town. He grew up in Seaborne, remember."

"I meant young and female."

"You're on your own," said Deborah, wondering how long it would take Jason to unearth Phoebe's secret. "I can't help. Besides, she had nothing to do with whatever happened at the museum."

"I'm not assuming a thing until I find out who she is."

"Merely the last in a long line of attractive women who flitted through my father's life, leaving not a trace behind them."

"Did he mention her to Calvin?"

"No," lied Deborah.

153

"I don't suppose Calvin would tell you who she is, even if he did know."

"And Calvin is considerably less likely to discuss the matter with a journalist."

"You're right. The appealing warmth of my personality just didn't convey itself to him. Get Maurice to ask his uncle about the girl."

"Maurice doesn't ask his uncle anything. Maurice obeys orders. The only possible way into Calvin's good books is to report the town hall speech, with some fulsome praise of his altruistic benevolence. But even if you throw in all the elaborate compliments you can invent, I doubt if Calvin will ever make you his confidant."

"Then I won't lose a friend on the day his past fills the papers, hopefully in national as well as local headlines."

It seemed to Deborah that Jason's wishes were built entirely without foundations. Calvin was secretive by nature, when even his nephew had been ignorant of the existence of an aunt until it was too late for the fact to be of any use. A pointless concealment, and therefore typical of Calvin.

****

"I've heard that you went to visit Calvin," said Maurice, as Deborah opened her front door.

"Then Chelsea must have caught up with you again. I was talking to her on the promenade for quite a while. She seems a nice girl, and very ambitious. That's to her credit, after growing up in this town."

"The ambition is probably to lift money off Calvin," declared Maurice. "Why did you go to see him?"

"To deliver a speech he wanted written."

"A speech for the arts festival meeting, I suppose." Maurice walked down the hall and into the kitchen as though he had returned to his own home. He also appeared to think that Deborah had betrayed him. "How often have you visited Calvin?"

"You're as bad as Jason, rapping out questions." Deborah went into the front room because, in there, she could pretend to look through files and only half-listen to whatever Maurice said. The tactic was uncomfortably close to Gregory's method of shirking a situation, but while Maurice remained Deborah's boss, she could not afford to alienate him. "Talking of hot-shot journalists, have the local radio and television reporters contacted you?"

"Not yet." Maurice abandoned the kitchen, and trailed after Deborah into the front room. "What about Calvin?"

"What about him?" Deborah began to sift through a pile of letters, conscious that Gregory's next ploy would have been to change the subject, and keep it changed. "I've made an appointment for you with Mrs Palmer. It's in your diary."

"Who's Mrs Palmer?" Maurice asked sulkily, perhaps detecting the strategy that Deborah had adopted.

"Surely you know the fearsome Mrs Palmer, headmistress extraordinaire? She terrified me for years, but if you want the town organized, she's the one to do it. Get her on the team before the meeting, and your arts festival is as good as established."

"Then tell Calvin to talk to her. It's his festival now: nothing to do with me."

"You'll be expected to carry out any behind-the-scenes work."

"How can you get involved with him when you know what he's like?" demanded Maurice.

"Of course I know what he's like." Deborah tried not to overdo the absent-minded tone as she hurried towards the escape route that had presented itself. "I've known Jason for absolute years."

"Jason?" repeated Maurice, taken aback.

"Who else but Jason?" Deborah glanced up from her letters with a fine show of surprise.

"You finished with Jason Clenham," protested Maurice. "You said you'd finished with him."

"It doesn't seem to matter how many times Jason and I split up, we always get back together again. He's clearly my fate."

"Is this why you're looking for a new job? Are you planning to go to London with him?"

Maurice's tone was flat, suggesting that life had deflated like a post-party balloon, and he made Deborah feel uncomfortable for having lied, even though it would hardly improve the situation to inform him that time spent in his company was time wasted. People had been an encumbrance to Gregory as well, and Deborah feared she was becoming more like her father with every day that passed. Gregory had managed to remain committed to only one person throughout his life; that person was himself, and his daughter appeared to be heading down a similar path. "Jason aimed at London right from the start; you know that."

"But what about your mother? You can't leave her at a time like this."

"She'll probably move with us: a brand new beginning." It sounded so rational that Deborah almost wished the story could be true: almost, but not quite. She was convinced that she would make a mess of any marriage, and also knew that Rhoda could never be moved from the house that held all that was left to her of Gregory.

"You shouldn't entrust your life to Clenham," objected Maurice. "If he really cared about you, he wouldn't have risked losing you, even temporarily, by letting you get away."

"There wasn't any risk of him losing me." The words were an imitation of the sort of thing Rhoda would have said of

Gregory. Their relationship could not be ended, even by his death, because he was the lifeline that had come to the rescue after Rhoda's bleak childhood, and to let go would mean sinking back into a loveless world. Maurice's own austere experience of boarding school had presumably left him equally desperate for affection, and he too needed someone on whom to base his whole existence. It was just unfortunate that he should fix on Gregory's daughter. "Jason and I seem to belong together, no matter what happens. We don't have to explain or pretend to each other, so it's a rest cure, being with him."

"This might not be the right time to make long-term decisions," ventured Maurice.

"Or it could be the best time, when trivia gets pushed out of the way."

Maurice obviously wanted to tell her something, and Deborah guessed that he had picked up rumours concerning Phoebe's transfer of attention from Calvin to Jason. But Maurice could not bring himself to shatter Deborah's hopes, and he moved onto a new topic with clumsy haste. "Lucas Rudd spoke to me again, and I had to say that I saw Calvin at the museum on Sunday. It was a direct question, and I'm useless at lying. I go red in the face and start to stammer, even if I try to gloss over the most minor of details. Calvin was livid with me, but I had no choice."

"Calvin won't be bothered now. You didn't see him on Sunday; you saw my father. He was wearing Calvin's jacket."

Maurice stared at Deborah in astonishment. "That's impossible."

"Not according to Calvin. He told me there was a jacket swap at Liverpool Street station on Saturday."

"I saw Calvin," declared Maurice.

"You saw blue stripes, and assumed Calvin was inside them."

"No." But Maurice was more puzzled than positive, and spoke to convince himself. "It had to be Calvin; it couldn't have been anybody else. He must be lying about the jacket. Calvin wouldn't recognize the truth if it jumped up and hit him in the face."

"He wouldn't be able to lie, because the police know what my father was wearing," Deborah pointed out.

"But it doesn't make sense if I didn't see Calvin," said Maurice. "I don't understand any of this."

"Jason has a theory—but he permanently yearns for melodrama."

"He thinks your father was mistaken for Calvin," stated Maurice, suddenly angry. "That would be so like Calvin. Everyone except him has to suffer the consequences of what he decides to do, and I bet you anything he deliberately gave your father the jacket on purpose, fully aware what would happen."

"You don't believe that any more than I do. A person who accumulates a bit of dosh doesn't automatically have to be a villain."

"You don't know Calvin," Maurice had said before he quickly reined himself in. "I'm sorry. I shouldn't have mentioned any of this to you."

But all subjects led back to the museum courtyard, and Deborah felt as if they would for the rest of her life. There was not enough time in the world to relegate Gregory's death to a past so distant, it no longer dictated her thoughts and memories. Rhoda would remain shackled to the man who could never divorce her, and Deborah began to fear that she too might be unable to say goodbye to Gregory. His ghost haunted her mind, rather than limiting itself to a precise geographic spot, and he would refuse to be left behind wherever she journeyed.

"Oh no, it's that awful female," Maurice said in exasperation, retreating from the window. "I told her to go home. I told her to take the rest of the week off. She just won't listen."

Deborah followed Maurice's gaze, and saw Chelsea crossing the road, her destination the house that Maurice had regarded as his sanctuary. "Chelsea's not awful, and she clearly likes you. Give her a chance."

"Not if you'll let me out of the back door."

"No problem, but you're one of the very few men in town who'd flee in horror from the prospect of an amorous Chelsea Pritchard."

"When you're in love with somebody, it makes you immune to other people." Maurice was not telling a lie, but his face acquired a pinkish tinge, and he looked self-conscious. "Even if there weren't someone else, I wouldn't like Chelsea. She doesn't ring true, and she's in cahoots with Calvin. She's as ruthless as him too."

"I think Chelsea and Calvin have parted company, and rather acrimoniously on her side. She simply wants more than this town's got, and you can't call ambition a fault." Deborah suspected that Maurice was hoping that she would ask who had so captivated his heart, but a strident series of thuds on the front door sent him scurrying towards the kitchen. "I'll keep Chelsea talking to give you a head start."

"Thanks." Maurice lingered for a moment, but Chelsea began to knock again. Deborah went to the door, and there was no time for him to elaborate on the reason for his immunity to the charms on offer. The explanation had merely been postponed, however, because Maurice believed that Jason was betraying a Deborah who might be vulnerable enough to turn to another for comfort. The fact that Maurice had not found his own consolation in Chelsea, he conveniently ignored.

Seeming too apathetic and frail to have been the cause of so strenuous an employment of the door-knocker, Chelsea asked, "Is Maurice here?"

"He was," said Deborah, "but I don't know where he is right now. Surely you don't need more posters? There must be one on display in every shop window the town possesses. You're evidently very persuasive."

Chelsea smiled, liking the description, but then the habitual resentfulness returned, and she hunched her shoulders against the wind. "I got fed up, waiting for Calvin on the prom, but when I went to his house, he pretended to be out."

"Unless he really had gone out."

"I'd have seen him."

"Not if he left via his back door," said Deborah, only too conscious of Maurice's speedy exit. "Why bother with Calvin anyway? You can get to London by yourself. Find a job with accommodation attached, and save up for your modelling course."

"But that'd take forever," wailed Chelsea.

"Of course it wouldn't. We can do an internet search, if you want." Deborah was unable to picture Chelsea as the ideal domestic help or child-minder, but the work would not be a career choice, just a means to an end.

"At least I'd get away from this town," conceded Chelsea, glancing down the road that, to her eyes, was inferior to any London street. "And I couldn't be more bored than I am at the museum. Do you think I'd get enough money for my modelling course though?"

"You'd rake in some extra cash if you did a few hours in a second job," suggested Deborah.

"I'd do anything to get to London, anything."

Chelsea spoke with a fervour touched with desperation, and Deborah hoped that the modelling course would be an entrée to the fame and fortune confidently anticipated by Chelsea. There were so many attractive people, so many talented people, but without exceptionally good luck, they remained as unappreciated as Gregory had been. *Gregory! Gregory!*

Gregory! Gregory was once more in the front of Deborah's mind, and as though to prove the pointlessness of fighting her fate, Lucas Rudd got out of a car on the opposite side of the street, and called Deborah's name before she had a chance to close the front door behind Chelsea.

"I'd like to check a few details with you, if that's OK."

Lucas did not expect a refusal, whether or not it was OK, and Deborah held the door open for him. "Of course, you remember Chelsea."

"Yes." But Lucas spoke automatically and with indifference.

"I'm off home," announced Chelsea, trying to push past Lucas.

"Actually, I'd like a word with you too." The shrill voice must have helped Lucas to place Chelsea, and since their previous encounter, Calvin's activities had become of considerably more interest to Lucas. "You said you left the museum early on Sunday to meet Calvin Canning."

"You won't tell Maurice, will you?" Chelsea demanded, turning to Deborah. "He might not pay me for the whole morning if he finds out that I bunked off early, and you know I need the money. Besides, I was only in the way after ten o'clock because I was dead by then."

Lucas appeared to take Chelsea's unusual claim in his stride, yet Deborah felt compelled to explain. "The disaster exercise casualties picked cards telling them what they had to act out."

"I had nothing to do once I died, so I sneaked away. You won't tell anybody, will you, Deborah?"

"If Calvin didn't object, Maurice isn't going to." The hall was uncomfortably small with three people crowded in it, and Deborah ushered Lucas to the front room, and then wished that she had chosen the kitchen instead, although Lucas gave the impression of being oblivious to the clutter. He leaned against the mantelpiece and watched Chelsea, who stood in the doorway, ignoring Deborah's offer of a chair.

161

"Had you arranged to meet Calvin Canning at ten o'clock?" Lucas managed to make a straightforward question more of an accusation, but Chelsea remained unfazed. A hectoring tone of voice had been a normal part of her childhood environment; it was consideration that would have disconcerted Chelsea.

"I've already told you," she replied truculently.

"Refresh my memory," said Lucas.

"I didn't arrange any particular time with Calvin. He just said Sunday, after he was back from London."

"But you expected to see Canning before midday."

"No."

"Don't try to cover for him."

"I'm not," protested Chelsea.

"But you must have thought he'd be back some time during the morning. Why else would you go to his house at ten o'clock?"

"It was later than ten, because I had to go home and get changed first. I couldn't wear anything special to the museum that day: not when I was meant to lounge around dusty corridors as a casualty."

"Then what time was it, when you got to Canning's house?"

Chelsea shrugged. "Elevenish, I suppose. But Calvin wasn't there. He didn't show up until after twelve."

"How did he seem?"

"Seem?" repeated Chelsea.

"Was he agitated, happy, sad, worried—"

Chelsea shrugged again. "He was just Calvin."

"And what is 'just Calvin' precisely?"

"Just Calvin," Chelsea said with belligerent stubbornness.

Lucas believed he was being deliberately thwarted, but Deborah guessed that he could be as obstinate as Chelsea once he had made up his mind, and he had definitely made up his mind that Calvin Canning was not going to escape whatever punishment he deserved for dallying with Lucas's estranged wife. "How long have you had a relationship with Canning?" he demanded.

Chelsea frowned, as if trying to recall far distant years. "He asked me out to dinner the Wednesday before."

"The Wednesday before what?" snapped Lucas.

"The disaster exercise."

"And did you go to his house after the dinner?"

"Surely Wednesday evening is irrelevant," Deborah pointed out, as Lucas's tone became louder and more intimidating. "Chelsea can't help you."

"No, I can't," agreed Chelsea. "And I've got to go home now."

"Then go." But Lucas was clearly reluctant to let such a source of information get away from him. He wanted the dirt on Calvin as much as Calvin had wanted it about him, and both were inclined to be bullies.

"Still trying to stitch up Calvin?" asked Deborah, when the front door had slammed behind the released Chelsea.

Lucas smiled unwillingly, and his guarded expression relaxed, but perhaps Phoebe's automaton had moved onto a jocular programme, because he said with ponderous good humour, "I could run you in for making a comment like that about me."

"Only if it's untrue, and you were beginning to hound poor Chelsea."

"Canning maintains he didn't get back until Sunday afternoon, yet Chelsea Pritchard says she met him at twelve o'clock."

"After twelve, she said, *ergo* after noon. Calvin's story is confirmed by Chelsea. A triumph of detection. Well done."

"Canning should be ashamed of himself. That girl's more than half his age." Lucas lacked irrefutable evidence to nail his suspect, but he was quite prepared to console himself in the meantime with a moral tirade against the lecher. "Men like Canning imagine they can do anything, just because they got their hands on a bit of money."

"It's the way of the world, and always will be," said Deborah, thinking of Phoebe and Gregory: a liaison in which wealth had played no part. "You don't have to worry about Phoebe though. Money's never impressed her."

"She went out with Canning last night," said Lucas, with a reprise of his surliness.

"Phoebe would go out with Ivan the Terrible if the alternative is to stay at home." There was no point in telling Lucas that Phoebe could be consorting with Calvin simply to acquire information that might otherwise elude an ambitious young reporter. The jealousy would merely be transferred from Calvin to Jason, and while Lucas was brooding on journalists and their wily seduction techniques, Phoebe's attention would have flitted elsewhere. "Besides, Calvin's not that bad."

"He was at the museum on Sunday morning, for all he claims not to have been in Seaborne," said Lucas. "His nephew saw him."

"Actually, he didn't. Maurice saw my father."

"Nonsense. How could he possibly confuse his own uncle with a complete stranger?"

"Because my father was wearing a jacket of Calvin's: a rather distinctive blue-striped jacket. That's right, isn't it?"

Lucas stared at Deborah as though tempted to arrest her for collusion with Calvin. "What makes you think the jacket belonged to Canning?"

"It did belong to him. Ask Maurice, who saw the jacket and assumed he'd seen his uncle too. It was a mistake anyone could have made. Calvin's been devoted to those blue stripes for months."

"Then how is your father supposed to have come into possession of it?" demanded Lucas.

"Calvin met him in London, and they swapped jackets there."

"I gather the information was supplied by Canning himself."

"That doesn't make it untrue. Calvin will explain the whole thing."

"I'm sure he will, and very plausibly. Unfortunately, it's difficult to catch up with the golden-tongued Mr Canning."

"When you do, you'll find that he still has my father's jacket."

"How very convenient."

Deborah guessed that Lucas, like Maurice, was weighing up the chances of Gregory having deliberately been sent to the museum in a jacket exclusively identified with Calvin Canning. The idea presupposed the existence of a plot to eliminate Calvin, that he had been aware of it, and that he was quite prepared to save his own skin at the expense of somebody else's life. It was Maurice's picture of his cold-blooded uncle, a portrait that Lucas would eagerly recognize, but Deborah shook her head. "If Phoebe weren't muddled up in this, you'd know that Calvin's not the criminal mastermind you're imagining."

"I leave flights of fancy to other people," declared Lucas.

But whatever Phoebe's husband did or did not imagine, solid evidence ranked above grudges, and Calvin was more than a match for Lucas. "Prior to being sidetracked by Chelsea, you said you wanted to check some details."

"I hoped you'd be able to tell me how to get hold of the elusive Mr Canning. I've left phone messages, been to his house, and even sent word via Phoebe. Nothing works."

Lucas should have realized that Phoebe was unlikely to accept the role of obliging messenger from the husband she regarded as ex, just as he ought to have known that Calvin would not bother to return telephone calls unless a business deal were involved. A more fruitful method for Lucas to hunt down his fleet-footed suspect might be to loiter outside Phoebe's place, prepared to clamp a heavy hand on Calvin's shoulder the moment he appeared, but Deborah had a suspicion that Lucas might already spend part of his time keeping Phoebe under surveillance, and he did not need encouragement to add to his paranoia. "Calvin isn't avoiding you. He's a busy man, and often out of town at meetings."

"Who with?"

"Haven't a clue. I didn't even know he was a friend of my father's. If you want details of Calvin's life and times, I'm not the person who can help you."

"What does Phoebe think of him?" asked Lucas, trying to make the question sound casual.

"I don't know that either." Deborah was uncertain whether Phoebe ever really thought about anyone but herself. Even Gregory's death, hours after Phoebe's rendezvous with him at the Grand Hotel, had apparently left her unscathed. If Lucas were picturing Phoebe as a naïve victim of the corrupt Calvin Canning, he was wrong; he was very wrong, and perhaps Inspector Atherton ought to be asking whether or not Detective Sergeant Rudd had an alibi for Sunday morning. Should Lucas have followed Phoebe to the Grand on Saturday evening and seen her with Gregory, a revenge programme might have been triggered inside Phoebe's automaton that led onto far-reaching consequences.

6

Deborah could not settle to do any work, and yet idleness was unbearable. She seemed to be waiting, but had no idea what could end the vigil. Jason's arrival at the front door was a respite, although, when he left, Deborah knew that she would still be waiting and still uncertain why.

Jason opened a large brown envelope, shook its contents over the kitchen table, and then sat back, his expression triumphant. "Guess who I've unearthed."

Deborah found herself looking at computer copies of newspaper pictures and articles. The top print-out showed a pretty girl, long fair hair in rigid curls, ample charms fully displayed by the skimpy bathing costume she wore. "This must be Babette, the beauty queen."

"Of course it's Babette: Babette Atkin, in those days. She won quite a few beauty contests 40-odd years ago."

"I'm not surprised. She was very good-looking." The pictures were all of a perfect girl, with perfect figure, perfect face, and perfect hair. Nature had been generous to Babette, and she smiled for the camera, obviously pleased with the attention she was getting.

"She sang a bit too, but that career never really got off the ground. It helped her meet Rodney Anderson though, a good catch for an ex-shop assistant."

"There's no need to overdo the cynical journalist. There is such a thing as love, I'm reliably informed, and if Babette's daughter took after her, it's no wonder that the philandering Calvin was reined in for once."

"Babette didn't have a daughter," said Jason.

"Then who was Calvin's wife? A niece?"

"There's only one Babette Anderson in this story, and Calvin married her." Jason had the appearance of someone presenting a trump card, and presenting it very smugly. "She was more than 20 years older than Calvin, and yet he married her. It's wonderful the power of love: the love of money."

"A girl gets congratulated if she marries a rich man, even when he's a lot older than her," Deborah pointed out.

"There's no need to overdo the realistic PR; although, coincidentally, Rodney Anderson was 23 years older than Babette, so I congratulate her. Anyway, after his death, the beauty queen became a wealthy widow, and then along sauntered Calvin the stripling who, in one crafty move, took over Babette and the nightclubs she now owned."

"I can't imagine Calvin marrying somebody he despised, no matter how much money she had. You don't know him."

"Nor do you."

"Well, if his treatment of Maurice is anything to go by, Calvin prides himself on speaking his mind, and Babette would have flung him out at the first hint of criticism. No beauty queen is going to put up with superciliousness and contempt. Besides, my father said she was down to earth, and that doesn't sound the type who'd be fooled by a fortune-hunter."

"Why are you so determined to rubbish my incredible find?" demanded Jason. "And what's this amazing power Calvin has over women? Phoebe's another one under the impression that he's a man of sterling integrity. But I suppose she has to believe that, or the fine name of Vale and Son could be dragged through the mire by having accepted a dodgy client."

"If there's been any sort of financial shenanigan, Phoebe

will spot it. She knows what she's talking about when it comes to accountancy."

"That doesn't make Calvin's romantic method of latching onto money any less interesting, especially as Babette conveniently shuffled off her mortal coil only a year or so after acquiring husband number two."

"You have got it in for Calvin," observed Deborah. "I reckon you hope that he was the cause of the shuffling."

"I merely report what happens, and what happened was Babette's car skidding off a road and into a tree for no apparent reason. Calvin, still in his twenties, became a widower; but everybody has to shoulder life's sorrows, and Calvin bore his with exceptional fortitude. He sold the nightclubs, then took off for London with dosh enough to launch his business career; not doing any actual work, of course, but moving money in and out of various companies so profitably that Phoebe says either he had a brilliant financial adviser or Calvin was a natural whiz-kid."

"At least you know the money's legit."

"But I'm not as sure about Babette's death."

"Yes, you are. You simply want Calvin to be the complete baddie who'd stop at nothing to further his dastardly schemes." It was also the version of Calvin that filled Lucas's mind, and Deborah wondered if he too had managed to track down Babette, thereby increasing his suspicions.

"Don't you think it's odd that Calvin should be surrounded by unexplained deaths?" Jason probably knew he was clutching at straws, but that had never before stopped him from chasing the slightest possibility of a scoop.

"Babette's accident is easy to explain. She could have swerved to avoid an animal, or even another car whose driver didn't wait around to get caught."

"Exactly," said Jason. "However, Calvin was able to produce

a fortuitous friend who gave him an alibi for the time of the crash, so obviously he's beyond reproach."

"Then no unexplained deaths surround him, unless you're going to cite Maurice's parents. They died in a car crash too."

"When?" demanded Jason. "Did Calvin inherit anything?"

"Only Maurice. I suppose you'll be claiming next that Calvin got the idea how to wipe out Babette from his brother's fate. Jason, you'll have to accept it; there are no unexplained deaths."

"There's your father's."

Jason made himself sound reluctant to mention Gregory, but Deborah could sense that her opinion was required about something: something that Jason anticipated might not be to Gregory's credit. "Was my father the friend who gave Calvin his alibi?"

Jason nodded slowly.

"And now you're going to ask if my father would supply a fake alibi, then threaten to go to the police years later, thus giving Calvin an excellent motive for murder."

"It's nothing more than a theory," Jason said defensively.

"My father cheerfully told lies to everyone he knew, so if he had given a phoney alibi, no crisis of conscience would ever urge him to make truth his shield. Your only alternative is to suggest he might have been a blackmailer. I'm sorry, Jason, but he just wasn't that Machiavellian. He needed people to like him; it's why he told so many lies. He couldn't cope with anybody who saw through his façade." Yet Gregory had gone to the museum to visit the daughter who no longer believed his lies. Deborah shrank from the thought, and hurried on, "Anyway, Calvin told me that my father was trustworthy."

"Why did he say that?" demanded Jason, pouncing on what he clearly deemed to be some type of clue.

"You'll have to ask Calvin if he was gratefully recalling what he considers to be the supreme gesture of friendship: a false alibi."

"I still find it curious that your father should never utter a word about this purported friendship between him and Calvin."

Jason found the silence curious because it was curious. There seemed no reason for Gregory, who had readily talked of Babette, to keep quiet on the subject of her new husband, a man from Gregory's home town. He had also failed to speak about Babette's death, and therefore the marriage, the death and the alibi could have been linked in Gregory's mind with strict secrecy. Jason might be closer to a story than even he realized.

"Don't look at me for an explanation," said Deborah. "I can't throw light on it."

"Deb, do you think there's a chance your father might have supplied a fake alibi?" No doubt an attempt was made during Jason's childhood to instil good manners, but any respect for others' feelings had long since been overridden by journalistic tenacity. "I don't mean to imply that he was in on a plot to kill Babette—"

"I should hope you're not implying that conspiracy to murder lurks in the Wainwright genetic make-up."

"But would your father have lied to the police, if he believed he was simply helping a friend out?"

"Yes." Deborah knew perfectly well that a friend's gratitude would have been more important to Gregory than what he regarded as minor bureaucracy. "Not in the least out of character."

Jason was taken aback to get support for his theory, having expected Deborah to be more protective of her father's reputation, and he asked tentatively, "Then I'm not being ludicrously melodramatic, in your opinion?"

"In my opinion, you are, but I can't deny that my father needed approval the way the rest of us need air, though it doesn't automatically follow that the alibi was phoney. He might genuinely have been with Calvin when Babette died, and you can't prove otherwise after so many years."

"I could underline the odd coincidence that the alibi should meet an equally abrupt end as the wife."

"You wouldn't get your copy past the newspaper's lawyer. It's hinting Calvin's a murderer, and that's wishful thinking on your part, not research."

"Well, it's true he married a rich widow who was more than 20 years older than him. I can get that into print, and I don't have to say Calvin was pursuing her dosh because everyone will take it for granted. I can also add details of the mysterious car crash—or should I say crashes in the plural?—and then reveal that your father was Calvin's alibi. Nothing but fact after fact, and I won't be held accountable for whatever conclusions are drawn by our astute townsfolk. I could even send Calvin a copy of my notes, and ask if he'd very kindly check the details for accuracy. His response should be interesting."

Deborah felt sorry for Calvin, knowing how much he would hate the inference that he was more gigolo than self-made man. If Calvin lost the status he believed he had in Seaborne, his pride was going to be hurt, and he valued admiration as much as Gregory had done. Adopted ancestors and lavish donations to charity would not help, nor would his pursuit of local dignitaries. He had always been something of a hanger-on, tolerated for his willingness to open a cheque book, but now Calvin would realize he was looked down on, and it seemed cruel that such small-town vanity should be punctured merely to satisfy Jason's ambition. "You need more evidence, a lot more evidence. Besides, if Calvin's really the serial killer you've convinced yourself he is, then it might not be a good idea to upset him. Dispatching another victim would hardly be a challenge to someone so persistent."

"Calvin Canning is a crook," Jason stated. "Why can't you see it?"

"He's phoney, I'll grant you that, but most people pretend they're better than they actually are, and Calvin's no exception. You should join forces with Lucas Rudd. He's an adherent to the deranged Calvin theory as well, though primarily because Lucas is under the impression that his already doomed marriage can be saved if he trashes Calvin's good name."

"At least Rudd's making an effort, which is more than can be said for Atherton at the moment."

"Lucas told me that the Inspector's got problems at home: a son who dropped out of college or something."

"Not any old college, but an Oxford one, no less." Jason usually had the low-down on the latest gossip, often the only way to keep his news-collecting skills honed in a town where whole months could go by with little but idle talk to fill empty hours, and passing on information was not just Jason's job but his mania. "Roderick Atherton decided, in the middle of his third year, that he'd prefer the simple life to being a high flyer, and so abandoned his studies for a succession of part-time pointless jobs; although why he imagines that struggling to pay his bills should class as a stress-free existence, no one can fathom. After years of boasting about his clever son's brilliant prospects, poor Inspector Atherton has sunk into the depths of depression and cannot be consoled. Roderick's the only child, to make matters worse; no second chance for Atherton to brag."

"A lesson to us all: never live vicariously," Deborah said, thinking of Rhoda. "Any other gossip doing the rounds?"

"Well, I've heard that we're engaged to be married, and soon to leave town for the bright lights of the big city."

"Did you perhaps encounter Maurice on your travels?" inquired Deborah, smiling.

"I hope that the removal of inconvenient people isn't a Canning family trait. Still, I should be safe enough from Maurice. He's a born loser." Jason spoke with patronizing pity, confident of his own ability to succeed.

"Maurice tries to be like Calvin, and just isn't. If he got away from his uncle, he'd find life easier."

"Maurice Canning will never find life easy," predicted Jason.

****

Rhoda had been making lists: lists of flowers, of food, of people, and even a list of lists still to be made. There were also notes written to herself to remind Rhoda of details so unimportant, they could safely be ignored; but the flurry of activity was nothing more than an attempt to pass vacant time, and Deborah wondered how her mother would cope when Gregory's final party was over, although Rhoda's capacity for living in a fantasy world seemed infinite.

Deborah had had to force herself to compile the CD of Gregory's songs, and then make a second effort to deliver the finished product, certain that her mother would spurn the offering as unworthy of the singer, but Rhoda was surprisingly appreciative.

"It looks quite professional: like something a music company might produce." However, Rhoda could get no further than the picture of Gregory she had selected for the front of the CD. Photographs of him would never upset her, because his lengthy absences had given her a first-rate preparation for surviving on dreams alone. "Why didn't we do this ages ago? Greg could have sold hundreds of copies after his act. He always had such an electrifying effect on an audience."

"I didn't get time to listen to all the tracks in full, so you'll have to check them," said Deborah, but lack of time had not been her problem. Unwillingness to hear Gregory's voice again was the real reason she could not bring herself to play the CD. "If everything's fine, I'll go ahead and burn some copies."

"How many can be made?"

"As many as you want."

"What about a thousand?"

"A thousand!" repeated Deborah, staggered.

"To start with. I might need more. It depends on the number of people who come to the service. And I've decided that Gregory must have his own website, so his fans can download the CD. It's going to be really popular, especially with all the publicity surrounding him right now."

Rhoda's determination to turn a negative into a positive had long been familiar to Deborah, but even she was startled at her mother's ability to regard any part of what had happened as an opportunity; yet something that might keep Rhoda occupied in the weeks to come was worth encouraging. "I'll show you how to set up a website, and then you'll be able to organize it yourself."

"Why didn't you suggest this before?" demanded Rhoda, with a lightning switch to resentment. "It would have helped Greg's career immensely."

"He was on his agent's website," said Deborah, but Rhoda's glare showed how feeble an excuse she considered that to be. A quick change of subject was essential. "Jason's been telling me about Babette Anderson, but I'm afraid it's a sad story. She died a while back in a car accident."

"Greg never mentioned it to me." However, Babette's fate was of no interest to Rhoda; only Gregory's connection with it mattered. "I suppose he thought the news too upsetting to pass on. Greg was always so sensitive."

"He gave Babette's husband an alibi for the time she was killed."

"Why would anyone need an alibi for a car accident?" It was plain that no memory at all had been revived in Rhoda's mind. For some reason, Gregory must have stopped talking about Babette before she married Calvin. "How soon can I start the website?"

"As soon as you like. It's odd you weren't told of Babette's accident."

"Why odd? I never met her," said Rhoda, dismissing the matter without further thought. "Would you ask Jason if he'd write a memoir of Gregory for the website?"

"You'll be able to ask him yourself. I imagine he'll be around fairly soon to find out what you know of Babette."

"Why should Jason be interested in her?" But Rhoda spoke absently, her attention focused on more important concerns. "I'll go through all the pictures of Gregory, and pick out the very best for his website. Not that there is a bad photo of him. The camera adored Greg."

"Jason discovered that Babette married Calvin," Deborah began, but Rhoda was still taking, still not listening.

"It's such a pity that Gregory didn't keep a diary. I could have put it on his website, and I know it'd be fascinating to read. He led such an exciting life."

"Jason would certainly have wanted to read a diary. He's working on a piece about Calvin for next week's paper."

"Why ever is Jason wasting time on that murderer? He'd write a far more interesting article if he chose Gregory as his subject," declared Rhoda, offended that her husband had yet again been rejected. "Greg's the one who ought to be in the paper. It's his story."

"Calvin's a part of that story; he married Babette."

"Nonsense. She married Rod Anderson; Greg told me."

"Calvin was her second husband: the husband who needed the alibi. That's why Jason will want to talk to you. He hopes to jog your memory."

"It can't be jogged if no memory exists in the first place. Gregory never mentioned a second husband or a car accident. Anyway, Babette wouldn't have married Calvin Canning. She was old enough to be his mother."

"If Jason says Calvin married Babette, then Calvin married Babette."

"For her money, of course," Rhoda declared sourly, "and then he killed her. I bet he did something to the car."

"But that would have been spotted at the time. Babette skidded into a tree, so the police are bound to have checked the brakes etc."

"Then Canning paid somebody to force her off the road, and deliberately picked your father to be his alibi because it's well known that Gregory never told a lie."

Well known to Rhoda perhaps, but not to anyone else who had been acquainted with Gregory Wainwright. Honesty was unlikely to be the first word that sprang into the minds of most people when describing him. Calvin had said trustworthy, but that could mean something different, and probably did. Yet the secret kept by Gregory might simply be the origin of Calvin's wealth because Jason was quite correct when he said that everybody would assume a young man must have married an older woman solely for her money, whatever Calvin felt for Babette. Rhoda's unreliable husband had turned out, if only for once, to have been dependable, but his death would expose Calvin's past to local tittle-tattle, and it was Gregory's daughter who had given the Babette connection to Jason.

****

When Deborah arrived home, lugging carrier bags filled with packets of blank CDs, there was a telephone message waiting. "I'm a bit miffed with you, but congrats," said Phoebe's voice. "Catch you later. Bye."

On the assumption that Phoebe must have dialled a wrong number, Deborah deleted the message and did not bother to return the call. She had a thousand copies of Gregory's CD to manufacture, and no time to waste. It was monotonous, repetitive work, but the sole type she seemed able to tackle, and the opportunity to please Rhoda brought concentration enough for the task. When the telephone rang, Deborah only answered it because she thought that her mother might be calling with further instructions.

"Hi, Deb," said Phoebe. "I'm rather peeved to be cut out, but I'll survive. Congratulations."

"What for?"

"For goodness sake! You and Jason, of course. When's the wedding?"

"Where did you pick up that gossip?" asked Deborah, amused at the speed with which the rumour had spread across town.

"Jason told me."

"Jason?" repeated Deborah in surprise.

"Was it meant to be a secret? Too late, I'm afraid. I've passed the news onto dozens of people."

Either Jason was getting a spot of revenge for having been so unexpectedly confronted with Deborah's story or he was using it as an excuse. But why on earth would Jason choose to shun the glamorous Phoebe? He was not sending a hint to Deborah that she remained the one he loved, because Jason never hinted; he spoke openly and confidently when prepared to speak at all. If camouflage were necessary, it could mean that he was currently involved with a woman who valued discretion, presumably a married woman, and in case he wanted back-up, Deborah said, "My mother hasn't heard the news yet."

"You should tell her right away. She'd have something different to think about. Are you worried that she'll associate Jason with this awful time? I suppose it is a risk, but she's known him a while, hasn't she? Or don't they get on? But I'm sure they will in future." Phoebe could have been switching between credit and debit columns as she clarified somebody's financial standing, and it was a pity that life never arranged things so tidily. "Your mother's bound to like Jason when she gets to know him better. Everyone likes Jason."

"Calvin doesn't."

"Oh, Calvin!" Phoebe dismissed him with a bored sigh, and then continued, "You ought to have told me that Jason was unavailable. It's not fair on susceptible females to let them think they're in with a chance, and then snatch away the prize without warning."

Why should a mere purported fiancée daunt Phoebe, when she had been able to ignore the fact that Gregory was married? Deborah found it difficult to keep a certain barbedness out of her voice. "You never let an inconvenient female stand in your way before."

"Alas, I can't overthrow this particular female. Jason made it very plain that I was out of luck."

Gregory had made it very plain that any woman was in luck with him. The teenage Phoebe would have been flattered by the attentions of a handsome man, had possibly considered the situation akin to a romantic film, and the outcome was inevitable. She owed no loyalty to Rhoda, and Gregory had not regarded marriage as a reason to stop him from being as unfettered as a bachelor. Whatever the precise definition of the relations between Phoebe and Gregory—affair, friendship, need, infatuation—it had lasted for nearly ten years, right to the end of Gregory's life. The rendezvous at the Grand proved that. "Why did my father want to see me on Sunday?" Deborah asked abruptly.

"I don't know."

Deborah had not expected Phoebe to admit to the assignation at the hotel, but there was no reluctance to reply, and so Deborah tried again. "He didn't mention planning to go to the museum?"

"Not a word. I only knew you worked there when Lucas told me."

Deborah realized that she would hardly be even a fleeting topic of conversation when Phoebe and Gregory met, but it was still a frustration not to understand why he had chosen to seek out his daughter. "Did he ask you to marry him?"

"Did who ask me to marry him?"

"My father. He was under the impression that you ditched Lucas because of him."

"Wherever would he get hold of such an extraordinary idea?" demanded Phoebe. "I ditched Lucas solely to get away from Lucas. No one else was involved, and definitely not Gregory."

"But you arranged to meet him at the Grand."

"No, I bumped into him outside the hotel, completely by chance."

But Deborah remained unconvinced by the glibness. Phoebe had been very fluent in her excuses at school. "You're saying you weren't the girl he was with that night?"

"What made you think I'd be out with Gregory?" But all at once Phoebe's tone was guarded in a most un-Phoebe-like manner.

"My father was seen at the hotel with a fair-haired woman."

"Why should you assume she was me?" Phoebe attempted a light laugh to show how absurd such suspicions were.

"Then who was the girl?"

"I only saw her from a distance. Later on. She was in the lobby with Greg."

The girl had not been quite so distant, in Deborah's opinion, and bore a striking resemblance to Phoebe: a mirror image, in fact: Phoebe's reversed yet identical twin. "There's a huge, old-fashioned looking-glass in the hotel lobby, I seem to remember."

"That's right," agreed Phoebe, ignoring the sarcasm. "It's an absolute monstrosity, with a gilt frame made up of overweight cupids scattering rose petals more like dinner plates. For some peculiar reason, I used to think it quite beautiful as a child."

"You can't put a name to the girl you saw, of course."

"No. Why ever did you imagine she had to be me? Did Greg really say I'd ditched Lucas because of him?"

"According to Calvin."

"Calvin claims I walked out on Lucas because of Greg?" Phoebe was shrilly astonished: astonishment that was possibly a little overacted. "Calvin must be hallucinating."

"He told me that my father talked of a girl who was divorcing a husband because of him."

"Not guilty," declared Phoebe, but then added with noticeably more prudence, "How did my name happen to come into their conversation?"

"It didn't."

"Then what are we discussing? I'm not the sole fair-haired woman in the country who's ditched a husband of late. Why would you, or anyone, imagine that Gregory was involved?"

Phoebe's words were a barely disguised challenge, but there seemed no point in unearthing the past when the only person betrayed was Rhoda, and she would always be secure in her world of make-believe. "None of this matters now that it's all over," said Deborah.

"What's all over?" asked Phoebe, reprising her carefree light laugh.

"If you don't know anything, how can I?"

"Is that meant to be a mystic decree? Well, I'm certainly mystified. You apparently want me to admit something, yet I haven't a clue what that something is."

"Then we don't need to talk about it."

"What exactly are you saying?" demanded Phoebe.

"That we're going around in circles, and there's somebody at my front door."

"OK. I'll phone you later."

"Yes." But Deborah was fairly sure that Phoebe did not intend to phone later, or ever. They had drifted away from friendship after school, and would again because there was now nothing to say to each other.

****

Calvin, armed with another bouquet of pink roses, stood on the threshold. He thrust the flowers at Deborah, and said, "I refuse to congratulate you."

"What for?"

"My opinion precisely. Of course you'll come to your senses in a day or so. Greg's daughter couldn't be fool enough to marry an evil-minded hack."

"You might be speaking of the man I adore," Deborah pointed out.

"He targeted you at a weak moment, when you felt alone and vulnerable, but already you're beginning to regret the irrational decision, aren't you? However, before you hurl the obnoxious scrivener back into the primeval sludge he crawled out of, I want you to do me a favour."

"I can guess what it is," said Deborah, following Calvin down the hall and into the kitchen, where pink roses from his first bouquet were adorning the window sill. Yet again the vase shortage had become acute. "I haven't got any influence with Jason, I'm afraid. Ambition is his chief characteristic."

"What's ambition got to do with him nosing into matters that don't concern anyone but me? There's no story in the notes he sent, only innuendo: very unpleasant innuendo."

"That's what I told Jason, but he wouldn't listen. You should talk to his editor."

"And have them all think I'm running scared?" Calvin looked scornful.

"It's the secrecy that's intriguing Jason. He believes you've got something to hide."

"What secrecy? Do I have to tell everybody I pass in the street about Babette? Is it a legal requirement?"

"It practically is, in Seaborne. No emotion is too profound for words here." Deborah put her latest supply of roses into the sink, and then sat down at the table to face Calvin. She felt guilty not to have warned him about Jason's research, although such an action would have brought equal guilt for siding against a friend.

"You're the PR expert," said Calvin. "How do I silence the vulture?"

"I presume you mean my fiancé."

"I mean the scavenger you can't seriously consider marrying. How do I sink his ship?"

"You go public. Found a charity in your wife's memory, and announce your plan without delay. Chase the media, and they run for cover, especially if you insist on talking in detail. By the time the next edition of the local paper gets printed, the Babette story will be old news."

"I knew Greg's daughter had to be resourceful," declared Calvin. "That's why I gave you a job on the strength of your surname. How soon can you get a press release out?"

"As soon as you tell me what charity you're founding."

"Oh, just invent something. I'll agree with whatever you decide." Calvin was suddenly relaxed, pleased to have his life under control again.

"Was your wife interested in any particular cause?"

"Babette threw money at all the charity appeals going. She couldn't bear to hear a sob story, so feel free to distribute my largess where you like."

"Something local would be best: something that gets the town on your side," said Deborah, stunned to have a Lady Bountiful capacity to aid the parish's deserving poor. "If there's a link to the arts festival, it won't look so contrived. What about supporting a youth orchestra? Schools don't do much with music nowadays, so the Babette Canning Foundation could offer free music lessons to children who can't afford them, and supply violins, glockenspiels, clarinets etc on loan for as long as the kids stay with the orchestra."

"Fine. Write down the details and get them out as soon as possible."

"The media will want some information about your wife," Deborah said hesitantly.

"I know, but that's being forced on me anyway." Calvin spoke with resignation, but there was still anger behind his tone. "You really can't marry that muck-raker. I won't allow it."

"Are you even prepared to stand up in a church and forbid the bans?" asked Deborah, smiling.

"If I have to. It's what your father would have done. I bet you never had the nerve to introduce that scribbling weasel to Greg."

"He'd have jumped at the chance of access to a journalist who had to listen to him. The opportunity to get some free publicity would have been enough to ensue that Dr Crippen got a welcome as a son-in-law."

"Don't you believe it. There was no chance of any man being considered worthy of Greg's daughter. If he'd known you had a job at the Canning Museum, I'd have been subjected to a lengthy interrogation about my exact motive for employing you."

"But he must have known where I was working, and even that I'd be there on a Sunday. It's why he went to the museum."

"Then your mother must have told Greg after I met him in London. It was so unexpected, seeing Greg, that I didn't think to update him with regard to you. I wish I had. He might have gone straight to the museum on Saturday afternoon, as it was obviously important for him to see you. Perhaps he wanted to explain about—well, explain."

But Gregory would never have chosen to explain anything if he could avoid the situation entirely. He had bragged about marrying his young and impressive status symbol to Calvin, but she was unlikely to have been mentioned to a daughter, even if Gregory hoped that Deborah had powers persuasive enough to talk Rhoda into a conveniently uncomplicated divorce. Deborah ignored Calvin's remark, and said, "I must add details of the Babette Canning Foundation to your town hall speech."

"The Babette Canning Foundation," repeated Calvin. He spoke so slowly that Deborah waited for his objection.

"It could be the Canning Scholarship if you think that sounds better."

Calvin shook his head. "It has to be in Babette's name or the whole thing's pointless. Don't imagine for one second that I'm softening towards the pernicious reptile who's temporarily hoodwinked you, but I'm becoming quite reconciled to Babette's music school."

"There are a few rooms not in use at the museum that would do for lessons or practising, and the central hall could easily be cleared for orchestra rehearsals. Maurice will be pleased. He wanted the museum to develop into a centre for the arts."

"Maurice! Maurice mustn't be involved in this," declared Calvin. "No need to doom Babette's charity to oblivion before it's started. You can do whatever has to be done without even going near the museum—or the Babette Canning Arts Centre as I suppose I should rename it. In fact, you ought to have a completely free hand. I'll get rid of Maurice, and put you in charge of everything."

"You can't do that to him," protested Deborah. "It'd break his heart. Maurice is devoted to the museum, and nobody works harder."

"Or less productively. I'll tell him he's being promoted to—to—oh well, I'll invent an excuse to get him out of your way."

"But the Seaborne Arts Festival is Maurice's idea, and it was only his scheme to expand the museum into a concert venue that made me think of a youth orchestra."

"So his work is done. It's a PR job from now on." Calvin's tone was final. Maurice had just lost his dream.

"But I'm leaving the museum."

"Put that right out of your head. You chose Babette's charity, so it's your responsibility to make her orchestra a success. I know Greg's daughter won't let me down."

But Greg's daughter had created the present crisis in Calvin's life. Deborah was responsible for the Babette Canning Foundation in more ways than one. "You must have adored your wife to establish such a memorial to her," said Deborah, hoping to pick up some information that would demolish Jason's hypothesis of Calvin as killer, and make her feel less uncomfortable.

"Babette was—she was very—exceptionally—" Calvin looked awkward, and then smiled. "I'm English. I don't do feelings out loud. All that I'll say is, everybody liked Babette. That was her real name, incidentally. She once said that no pensioner could possibly be called Babette, so her parents had stymied her chances of reaching old age. She was right, as it turned out."

"I'm sorry." Deborah did not know how good an actor Calvin might be, but the regret in his voice seemed genuine, and her apology was for having spoken to Jason about Babette. However, Calvin assumed he had been given an automatic condolence, and disregarded the words.

"A long time ago now," he said, with a shrug of his shoulders, "although I wish it could have remained private. Still, at least the town's children get an orchestra out of this mess, and Babette enjoyed music, especially dance music."

"And the pink rose was her favourite flower," added Deborah.

"How did you know?" asked Calvin in surprise, then he smiled again as Deborah indicated the vase on her window sill, and the more recent bouquet close by. "Yes, Babette trained me to buy pink roses, so I never look further than them."

Pink roses were a favourite with Rhoda too, so perhaps Babette had been another incurable romantic, confident enough to believe that an age difference did not matter, and that Calvin's interest was in her, regardless of how much money she had. If pictured as a second Rhoda, Babette's view of the marriage could be explained, but not Calvin's. A Rhoda would bring out his impatient scorn, rather than produce offerings of pink roses, so there had to have been more to Babette than a sentimental belief that love conquered all.

"Get the press release circulating this afternoon, and I'll take you out to dinner," Calvin said, as though conferring an honour. "It'll give me a chance to make you realize the wretched misery your life will become if you don't ditch the repulsive snoop."

"Phoebe won't want me there as a tag-along third." But it was Deborah who objected to the company. She could not face any more of Phoebe's chatter than day.

"Ms Vale regrets she is unable to dine tonight, or tomorrow, and refuses to commit herself to any evening in the near or distant future." Calvin made a mockingly rueful face as he spoke, but could not disguise the annoyance of somebody unaccustomed to failure, and Deborah guessed that she owed the dinner invitation to his need to show Phoebe and the town how untroubled he was by the desertion. His pride had been hurt, and pride mattered to Calvin. "Do all Phoebe's relationships end so abruptly?"

"Sometimes: although one lasted for nearly ten years, on and off."

"She must have started young then."

"She did." The excitingly clandestine nature of an affair with a married man might have been why Phoebe had stayed interested for so long; however, Calvin brought no such drama with him, and Phoebe was not a woman to linger. Impossible for Deborah to explain to Calvin that at least his rejection meant he had one less thing to worry him, because Jason would not have made his excuses to Phoebe and left, had she discovered something irregular in Calvin's finances. The accounts were apparently kosher.

"I'll call for you at seven o'clock," said Calvin, pushing back his chair as he stood up.

"I gather the dinner is conditional on a press release doing the rounds by then."

"I've absolute confidence that we'll dine together this evening." Calvin walked down the hall, but stopped at the sight of so many CDs surrounding Deborah's computer in the front room. The multiple pictures of Gregory, waiting to adorn each case, made it obvious what Deborah's task had been. "You're compiling a CD of Greg's songs."

"My mother wants to give a copy to everyone at the funeral service. She's going to be very disappointed if only a handful of people turn up."

"There'll be more than that," promised Calvin. "I'll see to it."

****

A knock on the front door, well in advance of seven o'clock, made Deborah assume that Calvin had arrived early, so she swiped her hair with a comb, and then struggled into a coat while hurrying down the hall. To her dismay, the caller was Maurice: a distraught Maurice. "Calvin's sending me to work in the north somewhere."

"A new challenge," said Deborah, trusting that the use of one of his favourite managerial phrases would comfort him.

"But I don't want to leave Seaborne."

"Then stay."

"How can I?" demanded Maurice in anguish. "Calvin's arranged for me to start next week."

"What will you be doing?"

"I've no idea. I was too taken by surprise to listen."

"It must be promotion though. Congratulations."

"Promotion!" Maurice replied bitterly. He strode past Deborah, and began to pace up and down the hall. "It isn't promotion. Calvin's getting rid of me, so that he can claim credit for the arts festival. He's making sure nobody will ever know that the whole thing was totally my idea. It's not fair."

"But you don't have to go," said Deborah, closing the front door as Maurice clearly had no intention of departing to pace elsewhere.

"But Calvin said—!"

"He can't run you out of town if you don't want to leave."

"But he won't let me go back to the museum."

"Then find yourself another job."

So revolutionary an idea stopped Maurice in his tracks. "Another job?"

"Calvin doesn't own either town or county. There are other employers in Seaborne, and you've got a university degree as well as experience of running an organization. Your CV is really impressive."

Maurice looked startled to hear the news. "What sort of job could I get?"

"You'll be able to pick and choose," replied Deborah, although even more uncertain than Maurice about his capabilities. "I've applied for half a dozen jobs in the past few days, and I've never been a manager of anything."

"Calvin wants you to take over at the museum. I told him you were off to London soon, but he says you're dumping Jason."

"Calvin is too fond of making other people's decisions for them," declared Deborah, torn between amusement and exasperation at Calvin's imperious assumption that he was the supreme overseer of everyone else's life. "Getting free of him is the best thing you can do."

"But he paid for my education," objected Maurice. "I cost him thousands over the years."

"No more than his duty. You owe him nothing."

"Calvin expects me to leave Seaborne this weekend." However, Maurice wanted to be talked into defying his uncle. It would be a very late and long deferred adolescent rebellion, yet essential if Maurice were to stand on his own feet. He did not realize it, but a revolt might actually make Calvin more inclined to let Maurice stay at the museum; stubbornness could easily be mistaken for initiative. "I'm meant to be ready to begin work on Monday."

"We're talking about what you'll choose to do, not Calvin's *diktat*. Start a job search and see what turns up. It's what most people try."

"And I will too," announced Maurice, but sounding more bewildered than liberated.

"It's a matter of positive thought," said Deborah, knowing that the self-help books, read so avidly by Maurice, had already filled him full of mantras about thinking big and aiming high.

"I don't want to hurt Calvin though." Even on the very brink of mutiny, Maurice dithered as he sought a third way that would please everybody. "Calvin's the only family I've got."

"And you're the only family Calvin's got. He shouldn't push you from job to job without asking your opinion. If you don't fight this, he'll imagine you're quite happy to be posted around the country like a parcel."

"You always make things seem possible. Jason Clenham doesn't realize how lucky he is." Maurice hesitated before asking, "Is it true that you've finished with Clenham?"

"Ignore whatever Calvin says on the subject. He's annoyed because Jason plans to do a profile of him for next week's paper."

"So you and Jason are still—?"

"Still," agreed Deborah.

"That's good news," Maurice declared, his voice dejected. "We'll all be making a new start then."

There was a knock on the front door, and Deborah opened it, wondering how soon Maurice's temporary bout of courage would be annihilated by the sight of his uncle.

"Forget the rest of the flower world. Like one of Pavlov's dogs, I can't defy my conditioning," said Calvin, handing Deborah yet another bouquet of pink roses. "What are you doing here, Maurice?"

"I was just telling Deborah—" Maurice's words faded away as he looked at the flowers and then noticed for the first time that Deborah was wearing a coat, ready to go out.

"Goodbye, Maurice," said Calvin, indicating the open front door.

Maurice turned to Deborah in astonishment. "What about Jason?"

"He's history," said Calvin.

"Don't underestimate Jason," advised Deborah.

"Don't underestimate me," retorted Calvin.

****

Remnants of Seaborne's better days lingered on in the crimson plush chairs and velvet curtains of the Floral Restaurant. It was not as pretentious as the Sea View, but expensive enough for Calvin to parade in front of people he imagined, quite correctly, were gossiping about him. His attempt to save face would not succeed, however. Deborah Wainwright was known to be Calvin's employee, and one unlikely to have ousted the beautiful Phoebe Vale. Deborah was also an embarrassment. While they were being ushered by a waiter to an alcove table, Calvin greeted several diners who nodded to him but pretended not to see Deborah. Calvin, thick-skinned and pushy, remained unaware that it was apparently a social error, akin to begging for money in public, to make people uncomfortable by forcing them into the presence of somebody recently bereaved.

The moment they reached their table, Calvin took possession of the menu, ordered the most costly items on it without reference to Deborah's wishes, then he leaned back in his chair and surveyed her. "I know you want to give me a piece of your mind. Being Greg's daughter, you'll find yourself compelled to speak freely sooner or later, so let's argue now to get it over and done with. I gather you don't approve of the way I've dealt with the Maurice problem."

"No, I don't," said Deborah, but Calvin had managed to defuse much of her animosity by his openness. "The museum is Maurice's whole world. He'll be lost without it."

"Maurice was born lost. I should never have put him in charge of anything, but I thought even he couldn't botch up a museum."

"And he hasn't."

"Only because I saw your name on a list of job applicants. Anyway, I'm not condemning him to starve in utter destitution. I'll give Maurice a wage, and ensure that he's kept busy where he can't do any harm. And now you look as if you'd like to sock me on the jaw."

"You just sound so patronizing," said Deborah, but conscious that her own attitude towards Maurice would hardly pass muster.

"You can't claim that he's an astute and dynamic businessman."

"All the more reason not to shove him around. He understands the museum. Let him have more time there."

"Time! Maurice doesn't need time; he needs a character transplant." Calvin sounded amused, but Deborah was uncertain whether her lame defence or the thought of his nephew entertained him. "It doesn't say much for education. Maurice has had every opportunity: schools that charge exorbitant fees and then university. All I got was the local comp."

The local comp and a wife with money, reflected Deborah. "It's lucky I've already decided to hand in my notice, or I might now be told to seek pastures new after criticizing my employer's treatment of his nephew."

"You're not leaving the job any more than you're marrying that scandal-chaser," declared Calvin. "Neither point is negotiable."

It had perhaps been Calvin's dictatorial manner that doused Phoebe's interest in him so precipitately, but Deborah was untroubled by the attempt at dominance. He only had power over her if she chose to allow it, and the choice remained hers. "What I like most about Jason is that he never tries to control my life," she remarked pointedly.

"That's because Jason Clenham is basically interested in Jason Clenham, not you," said Calvin, unable to recognize himself as the opposite of the description Deborah had given. "There's no future with a hack who's got as far as he'll ever get. Nobody has a good word to say for him."

"My mother has. She likes Jason."

"Then she can marry him. He isn't good enough for you.

He's not even honest." There was such stern disapproval in Calvin's voice that Deborah smiled.

"I'm not sure that my own existence has been one of sterling candour throughout. How did Jason manage to fall below your higher standards? Tell me the worst. You've obviously been digging up the dirt on him."

"If I'd heard anything, you'd have heard it as well." Calvin spoke smoothly: too smoothly. He had clearly picked up some nugget of information that was not going to be repeated to Deborah. As Calvin seemed quite happy to slander Jason's talents and integrity, she guessed that rumour linked Jason to another woman, and Calvin assumed Deborah to be a deceived fiancée.

"I don't mind what the gossip is," Deborah said with a cheerfulness that Calvin probably interpreted as deluded obstinacy.

"I think the gossip about me is liable to be worse," declared Calvin, to move the subject away from the Jason he had been only too eager to disparage seconds before. "People are jealous of success."

"Then nobody can be jealous of Jason because, according to you, he's a total failure, wholly lacking in ability and virtue."

"I'm glad you're beginning to take note of his gormless nature," said Calvin, as if he and Deborah were sharing a joke. "You must want more from life than being lumbered with a wastrel for a husband."

"No wastrel need apply," agreed Deborah, but then the restaurant fleetingly swirled around her, and she clutched at the table as a dizzy sense of unreality made everything seem preposterously wrong. If Gregory had died, what on earth was she doing in an unfamiliar place, laughing with a stranger?

****

Gregory had announced that he was treating his daughter to a meal in a restaurant to make up for missing her tenth birthday. He should have said to make up for failing to remember her tenth birthday as not even a card or a telephone call had marked the actual day, but Gregory's version of events became conveniently vague when he was at fault. Best clothes were always worn during his transitory appearances, but for a restaurant meal with Greg Wayne, soon-to-be superstar, a new dress was essential.

"It's part of my present to you, Debbie," said Gregory, although Rhoda was the person who actually paid for the dress, of course. She would also pay the restaurant bill, but that too was taken for granted. Rhoda had recently been promoted to manager of the gift shop that Gregory mocked for the cheap gaudiness of the holiday souvenirs it stocked, but his scorn of bad taste did not stop him benefiting from Rhoda's wages.

The Sea View was dismissed as benighted, and the Floral as trashy, because the only place in town worthy to be honoured with Greg Wayne's presence was the Grand Hotel. Close to the sea front, the Grand lived up to its name with an excess of crystal chandeliers and gold-tasselled curtains, thick carpet and shining mahogany. In the lobby's full-length mirror, Deborah had seen a happy ten-year-old girl, dark hair loose, wearing her first long dress: a pink dress, as it had been chosen by Rhoda. For once, Deborah looked exactly as she thought Greg Wayne's daughter should. She had become a part of the world Gregory had promised her, a world of luxury, of excitement, of magic: a world that her father was never to know.

On the night before his death, had Gregory seen Phoebe reflected in that same mirror, the young and alluring companion who ought to complement Greg Wayne? She represented the only way he was able to force life to give him at least a part of the future that stayed so tantalisingly elusive. Phoebe might perhaps have been less betrayal than a desperate need to cling to his illusions.

7

Inspector Atherton arrived, with Detective Sergeant Rudd in tow, before Deborah had a chance to do anything about breakfast. She was surprised at so early a visit, but both Atherton and Lucas seemed to regard the hour as unexceptional. They looked at the pile of CDs stacked around her computer in the front room, but neither made a comment, although they must have recognized Gregory's picture. Deborah assumed that she was to be informed of medical details concerning her father's death: details that she did not want to hear. Gregory was dead; no further fact was necessary just then.

"Where were you yesterday evening?" Atherton made his words sound so like an accusation that Deborah was taken aback.

"I went out to dinner at the Floral." It seemed a horribly frivolous thing to have done in the time between her father's death and his funeral: frivolous enough to make Deborah wonder why she had gone out at all.

"Who were you with?" Atherton asked, as irritably as if Deborah had wasted his time by prevaricating.

"Calvin Canning. Why?"

Atherton ignored Deborah's question. "You were with him the whole evening?"

"From seven-ish onwards. Why do you want to know?"

"When did you leave the restaurant?"

"Ten-thirty."

"Precisely at ten-thirty?" Atherton looked sceptical.

"Has something happened to Calvin?" Deborah turned to Lucas as Atherton seemed so hostile.

"Canning's fine." It should have been good news, but Lucas did not seem particularly happy to relay his information. "Why are you certain it was exactly ten-thirty when you left the Floral?"

"Because Calvin looked at his watch and said the staff would throw us into the street if we didn't leave. What's this about?"

"Someone tried to beat up Jason Clenham last night," replied Lucas.

"Is Jason OK?" demanded Deborah.

"A bit battered and bruised, but more shaken than anything. It happened around ten-fifteen."

Deborah did not need to be a detective to realize that they thought Calvin might have attacked Jason: or, more accurately, arranged for the attack, because Calvin had an alibi just as he had when Babette died. It appeared to carry coincidence a little far to have first one Wainwright and then a second as his alibis, although coincidences did occur, but if Calvin had form, then Jason would not have escaped with mere bruising to judge by Babette's fate.

"Why did you stay so late at the Floral?" asked Atherton.

"Ten-thirty isn't that late. We were talking. Is Jason really OK?"

Atherton nodded impatiently. "I've heard he's doing a profile of Canning for next week's paper."

"Yes. Calvin's organizing an arts festival for the town, so all publicity is welcome."

"Not all," objected Atherton. "Does Canning know what's going to be printed about him?"

"Jason sent Calvin a copy of his notes to check for accuracy."

"And were they accurate?" As Atherton must already have spoken to Calvin, to be in the process of verifying an alibi, the accuracy or otherwise of Jason's notes had been established. Atherton was fishing for gossip.

"You'll have to ask Calvin about accuracy, but if there's any sort of scandal brewing, Jason wouldn't have mentioned Calvin to you before next week's paper goes on sale."

"What makes you think Clenham would name Canning in connection with the attack?" demanded Atherton, pouncing on what he apparently considered a damaging admission.

"I imagine you're checking up on Calvin because you asked Jason what stories he was working on. But he wouldn't tell you if he thought he had a scoop, so I think you can rule Calvin out." Although Calvin had been angry that Jason should control his life in any way. Had Calvin been equally angry that Babette was in control of him because of her money?

"The local rag isn't usually filled with sensational exposés that lead to revenge attacks," said Lucas. "Do you know of anyone, apart from Canning, who Clenham might have upset lately?"

You, thought Deborah. Lucas would certainly be disturbed had Phoebe ever mentioned being attracted to Jason. "I can't think of anybody who'd want to hurt Jason. Surely it's more likely to have been an attempted mugging?"

"No." Atherton was annoyed that Deborah should dare to instruct him on how to approach his job, and she felt sorry for the errant son who had so disappointed by freeing himself from ambition. "The man called Clenham's name, presumably to make sure he had the right person. A passer-by heard him."

"Why did you go out with Canning last night?" Lucas's voice denoted disapproval of the answer before he heard it.

"Calvin asked me to have dinner."

"But you're engaged to Jason Clenham." Not even Atherton had managed to sound as accusing as Lucas did. He should have been pleased at the chance to inform Phoebe that faithless Calvin was two-timing her, but Lucas identified with the cruelly deceived fiancé and could not be assuaged.

"I'm not engaged to Jason," said Deborah.

"Then why did he tell us you are?"

"Perhaps he's engaged to me, but I'm definitely not engaged to him."

It was the sort of flippant reply that Phoebe might have made, and Lucas continued to frown. "Did you break the engagement because of Canning?"

"There was never an engagement to break. It's a joke."

A joke that neither Atherton nor Lucas found funny. Their faces remained frozen, like the sort of Monday night audience that had daunted even Gregory. It was far too difficult for Deborah to explain the whole truth, especially as that would bring Maurice and his punctured hopes to police attention when Jason's assailant was being sought, and a bungled attack would be so Maurice, it practically announced his presence at the scene. A ridiculous notion: as ridiculous as suspecting him of killing Gregory in mistake for Calvin, but still the idea lingered in Deborah's mind, although Maurice's admiration might have moderated, now that she was suspected of discarding Jason in favour of Calvin's riches. Calvin: the man with the convenient alibi, something that might owe less to chance than to design. Babette's husband, Gregory's friend, Maurice's uncle, Jason's target, Deborah's employer, the museum owner; all roads led back to Calvin.

"Does Clenham know that you date Canning?" inquired Lucas, and only one of his Puritan ancestors, when confronted with a scarlet woman, could have matched his severity.

"It wasn't a date: just a meal," said Deborah, but the stern Lucas continued to frown.

****

"I'm OK," said Jason, in a voice that implied stoic refusal to acknowledge suffering. Over the telephone, it was clear that he wanted to pose as an intrepid young reporter still valiantly on the investigative trail despite the attempt to frighten him off, and his attitude was even more reassuring than his words. "I'm pretty fleet of foot when danger looms. The mere sight of a fist, and I'm sprinting in the opposite direction with the speed of an Olympic gold medallist."

"Are you really OK?" asked Deborah. "Lucas Rudd said you were beaten up."

"How that man does exaggerate. Why did he go to see you, anyway? Has something happened?"

"Yes, you were attacked, and the police wanted to check Calvin's alibi."

"*You're* Calvin's alibi?" The thought seemed to amuse Jason.

"And the police now regard me as a brazen Jezebel, out on the town with a wealthy man while my trusting fiancé gets beaten to a pulp. Why did you tell Lucas that we were engaged? And why did you mention Calvin?"

"To see what Canning's reaction would be," replied Jason, adding smugly, "I'm a dedicated journalist, even with a nose swollen to twice its normal size, and this is a good opportunity to observe Calvin under pressure."

"If you really did think that he masterminded the attack, the police wouldn't have got a syllable out of you. I can't believe you're being pursued by a vengeful gardener because you uncovered his geranium sabotage at the local flower show, so I'm forced to the conclusion that you know exactly who wants to punch you, and why."

"No comment," said Jason, but he continued to sound smug.

"It's not fair to keep quiet and let Calvin be a suspect," argued Deborah, even though she doubted that anything would persuade Jason to become scrupulously honest when a few lies might get him some better copy.

"I didn't deliberately put Calvin in the frame," protested Jason, too ingenuously. "Atherton asked what I'd been working on lately, and I told him. It was my duty as a law-abiding citizen to speak out dauntlessly. But don't worry; I didn't name you as a source. I do have my professional standards to uphold."

The chances of a bigger story than Calvin's past rocking the town were remote, therefore the attack on Jason must have been personal, which meant that there was a man who imagined he would feel much better after punching the abhorrent Mr Clenham on the nose. Calvin certainly fitted the description, but so did his nephew, although there was no reason for Jason to shield Maurice, and Deborah grew impatient. "Oh, for goodness sake, tell me what's going on. I'm fed up with secrets and guessing games. I'll trade information, if you like."

"What information?"

"I know the name of the woman my father met at the Grand."

"Who is she?" demanded Jason.

"Your info first. This is a trade, remember, and I've known Jason Clenham long enough not to trust a word he says."

Jason laughed, but did not bother to contradict Deborah. "OK. I suppose you have a right to know that you're being used as a smokescreen."

"Our famous engagement?"

"Well, you started it. I merely endorsed your story. It was a convenient tale though, because there happens to be a woman, and this woman has a husband."

"And that husband strongly objects to living in a triangle."

"I didn't realize he was so clued up," Jason said ruefully.

"You should have told Atherton the truth. It'll be called wasting police time when they discover that Calvin had nothing to do with rearranging your features, much as he'd doubtless like to punch you."

"But I've got to pretend I didn't recognize Stacey's husband, and that the thought of him never entered my head, or his worst suspicions will be confirmed," argued Jason. "When Stacey told me that he had a bit of a temper, she didn't exaggerate. But never mind my sordid yet dramatic private life."

"It solves a mystery though. I wondered why you were immune to Phoebe's fascination. Most men aren't."

"But she's another one with a narrow-minded husband who'd be prepared to knock me into the middle of next week. Even when Phoebe's divorce is finalized, Lucas Rudd will still regard himself as married to her."

"You'd be quite safe at the moment. Our detective sergeant's concentrating on Calvin, hoping to prove that he's a raving psychopath."

"As he very well could be. Perhaps it's the capricious Phoebe who ought to watch her step," said Jason. "Did you hear that she's dumped Calvin already?"

"Yes, but he appears fairly resigned to the fact. Do you know he's starting a charity in Babette's memory?"

"I read your press release, but wasn't fooled."

"Calvin's motives might be phoney, but it means free music lessons are on offer," Deborah pointed out, defensive of her own idea. "The opportunity could enrich the lives of local children: well, some of them, anyway."

"Calvin's simply trying to pose as a grief-stricken widower before next week's paper gets printed: a widower whose tears promptly dried the instant he clapped eyes on Phoebe," declared Jason, impervious to PR spin. "But why are we wasting time on Calvin and Phoebe? You haven't fulfilled your part of our deal yet. I want the name of the fair-haired girl at the Grand."

"You've just said it."

There was silence on the other end of the telephone line, and then Jason stated, "You don't mean Phoebe. You can't."

"Why not?"

Jason laughed again, apparently under the impression that Deborah was joking. "We had a deal. You can't back out of it."

"I'm not. Phoebe met my father at the Grand Hotel."

"Well, she never said a thing about him to me." Jason spoke as if the matter had been decided.

"She wouldn't tell you, but Phoebe had a relationship with my father that began when she was in her teens. I only realized what had gone on after I added two and two together."

"And made five."

"I'm right," said Deborah, with absolute certainty.

"How can you be so sure? Your father wouldn't have discussed something like that with a daughter, and it's obvious Phoebe didn't offer enlightenment, if you had to rely on rather shaky arithmetic as your source."

"I did try to talk to Phoebe, but she pretended that they met at the Grand by chance; then she got annoyed, and wouldn't say any more. And that's the first time I've ever known her to clam up."

"You're wrong," said Jason. "You must be. I can't picture Phoebe and your father as an item."

"You never met him, or saw them together. They were—" Deborah struggled to find a way of describing her memory of Gregory and Phoebe as they ate ice cream in the High Street, unaware of the crowds around them because each saw the whole world in the other. "You'll have to take my word for it. They were alike: a couple who didn't need to make any commitments. Neither of them should ever have been trapped by marriage. They could only be happy with freedom, complete freedom."

"But even so—"

"Talk to Phoebe. Ask her outright."

"I intend to, though I think you might be overestimating your father's magnetic attraction." But Jason sounded apologetic: an unusual circumstance, as nature had not endowed him with an excess of sensitivity. He had no idea how handsome and exotic Gregory would have seemed to the teenage Phoebe. She saw a sophisticated man, who told tales of mingling with film stars and models: a captivating man who might be famous himself one day. The local boys, with their limited experience and humdrum prospects, could not even begin to compete.

"Phoebe's very good at telling lies," warned Deborah. "She can fool anyone. The teachers at school didn't have an earthly. Don't forget that when you talk to her."

"I'm the expert when it comes to seeing through a conjuror's tricks." Jason was boasting, but Deborah knew that there could be some truth in what he said, despite a tendency to make up his mind before gathering all the evidence.

"Phoebe's an expert too." In fact, Phoebe was as accomplished a liar as Gregory himself had been.

****

"Perfect," said Rhoda, gloating over copies of Gregory's CD, as she stacked them on her hastily vacated book shelves. "They're absolutely perfect."

It was a weight off Deborah's shoulders to have her mother's approval. For somebody who had chosen to work in PR jobs, Deborah remained oddly ill-equipped when adapting the skills to real life, but Rhoda clearly valued her CDs above jewels, and smiled at the cover pictures as if she saw a different likeness of Gregory each time. Deborah picked up the books that Rhoda had tossed in the direction of the sofa, and tried to start a conversation that would keep the harmony in full flow. "How's the website coming along?"

"Fine. Why didn't you bring the rest of the CDs? Haven't you done them all yet?"

It was a query, not a criticism, but Deborah immediately felt in the wrong. "I couldn't carry a thousand CDs here in one go."

"I'll need far more soon, but a thousand should do for the time being. Jason phoned to check some details, and he promised to mention the CD in his copy, so I've got the publicity going already."

"What details did Jason want to check?" Deborah spoke warily, although she could not believe that even scandalmonger Jason would be tactless enough to seek Rhoda's views on the exact character of Gregory's relationship with Phoebe.

"Jason asked more about Greg's career, the early days in particular."

"Babette Atkin-Anderson-Canning came into the conversation, of course," said Deborah. If Rhoda ever learned of the affair, she would blame Phoebe for chasing after Gregory, but it was a relief not to be accused of having brought Phoebe to Gregory's attention in the first place.

"Jason couldn't write about Greg's career and not mention Babette, especially as Canning killed her too."

"I don't think that's actually been established."

"Jason's very sure."

"Jason's very sure, even when he doesn't have evidence to back up his hunches."

"That doesn't mean he's made a mistake," retorted Rhoda. "Don't you realize you're working for a serial killer?"

"I'm doing my best to find a new job, I told you."

"A new job!" Rhoda said in exasperation. "You never stop looking for a new job. If I'd told Gregory how restless you are, he'd have been worried sick. At least I was able to spare him that. He thought you were still working for Yates Advertising."

"Yates? I'd forgotten I was ever there; but nobody stays long in the same job these days."

"Gregory was so happy to think that you'd have a secure future with an advertising agency; people always want to push some product or other, he said. I couldn't tell him that you walked out only months later, and then quit the next job as well. He was really pleased that you'd have regular money coming in."

Perhaps because he had hoped to lift some of that money off his daughter just as regularly as it went into her bank account, Deborah thought wryly, before taking in the full implication of Rhoda's words. "He didn't know I was at the museum?"

"Of course he knew. That's why he went to see you there," declared Rhoda. "If you'd stayed with Yates, Gregory wouldn't be dead."

"But how could he know I was at the museum if you didn't tell him?"

"I expect Canning told him to lure Gregory to his death."

"No, Calvin said he hadn't mentioned I was working for him."

"That's exactly what he would claim, the murdering maniac." Rhoda looked down at Gregory's face on the cover of the CD she held, and suddenly she was smiling again, back in an imaginary world. Ignoring reality would save her, just as it had eased the way through a difficult childhood, and Gregory was more her possession dead than he had ever been when alive. "I'm going to send a copy of Greg's CD to local radio by the very next post."

"Good idea." Despite her denial, perhaps Phoebe had been Gregory's informant about his daughter's whereabouts; or perhaps Calvin was the person who had lied to Deborah. But however Gregory found out, he had decided to go to the museum on Sunday morning, and Deborah would have to deal with the fact that he had died while trying to see her.

"If it's such a good idea, why haven't you already sent a copy of Greg's CD to the radio station?" snapped Rhoda, with the unpredictable bluster of a January wind, gone as soon as it had roared. "Oh, of course, you think that a letter from me will get the CD more attention."

"That's right," agreed Deborah, grateful to be handed a ready-made excuse. "They might want to do an interview as well. It'd be good publicity, but don't let them force you."

"If it's good publicity, then they can interview me all they like. I'd do anything for Greg. I'd have done whatever he wanted, right from the instant I first saw him." Rhoda paused for a moment to gaze at her final CD, reluctant to stack it with the others and lose sight of Gregory's face. "It wasn't simply his looks, though I'd never seen a man so handsome, it was more that I recognized him."

"How could you recognize someone you didn't know?"

"I haven't a clue, but that's what happened. I was walking down the High Street after work, turned into Beach Road, and there he was, chatting to a girl. The second I saw him, it all fell into place. 'That's right,' I thought, 'that's my husband.' I recognized his face, his voice, his laugh, his clothes: everything about him. I didn't know his name, but I recognized my husband."

"You told me that you met him at a friend's house," commented Deborah, unconvinced by her mother's claim of psychic powers.

"I did meet him at the Randles'. Greg hadn't noticed me as I walked by, but it didn't matter because I knew I'd be marrying him. I went to see Hayley Randle a few days later, and I wasn't a bit surprised when Gregory opened the front door. I'd known all along that we were going to meet somewhere."

Rhoda's tone was so matter-of-fact, she could have been describing the inevitability of a new year following the old one, yet Deborah suspected that her mother had invented the memory. Rhoda obviously believed everything she said about the preordained husband, but destiny might have had less to do with it than Rhoda's dismal childhood and her desperate need to escape to a perfect world. However, the most generous of fates could not have supplied Gregory with a more supportive or acquiescent wife because Rhoda had provided the adulation he craved, as well as the money that evaporated quicker than morning dew. Her whole-hearted devotion had offered Gregory both freedom and security, and perhaps little would have changed had Phoebe not proved to be his Nemesis. A young woman to make Gregory feel young, a young woman with the added advantage of possessing more money than Rhoda ever would, Phoebe was to be his new start, his chance to re-live a life that had become a disappointment. But Gregory deluded himself as much as Rhoda at her most romantic. Phoebe would no more be captured than Gregory could have been. He too should have looked at the mirror in the lobby of the Grand Hotel, for the resemblance between him and his companion was palpable.

****

As Deborah approached her house through the darkening late afternoon, Calvin got out of his car. "You're only the second woman I've ever waited for in my life," he remarked.

"Is that a compliment or a reproach?" asked Deborah. "Actually, I suppose I should be sitting in front of my computer from nine to five, as I'm meant to be working from home."

"And that implies freedom from office hours. Work when you like, when you can. You're the one in charge now."

"Temporarily. Don't forget I'll be leaving soon."

"I'm not listening to you," Calvin declared, as he held the car door open. "Get in. We're going to my house. I want you to interview somebody for a job."

"OK," said Deborah, climbing into the passenger seat. "Why is the interview at your place though?"

"I wouldn't ask you to go back to the museum, even for a few minutes." Calvin closed the door and walked around his car to the driver's side. He was probably conscious of being observed by one or other of Deborah's neighbours, because he adopted a purposeful stride, his back ramrod straight. He expected to be recognized as the successful and wealthy Calvin Canning, but would more likely be dismissed as just another friend of the Wainwright girl. His fame in Seaborne was not as widespread as he imagined, despite the efforts to publicize himself.

"What job am I interviewing for?" asked Deborah, as Calvin buckled his seat belt.

"Cleaner. Incidentally, what do you think of relocating the museum? The old watermill is up for sale, and it'd be large enough for an arts centre. Plenty of room for everything under one roof: museum, concert hall, theatre, gallery, dance studio, café—"

"Catering for the body as well as the soul," commented Deborah.

"We could use that as a slogan," said Calvin, smiling. "Do you think it'd pay its way?"

"It might when the holidaymakers are here spending money, but winter is always a problem in Seaborne. I suppose a concert hall could be hired out for wedding parties, quiz nights and so on: a community gathering place, perhaps. And if your café provided good solid food, and undercut the stupid prices at the Sea View and the Floral, you could offer some sort of package deal: a family day out at the Babette Canning Centre that includes a meal before the parents hear their kids play in a concert."

"I thought these families were supposed to be too poor to shell out for music lessons. Why am I subsidizing them, if they can come up with the dosh to stuff their faces in public?"

"Because they think that going out on the town is an essential, but paying for music lessons would simply be throwing money away. They've got limited lives, and see no reason to try and aim at something better for their kids. That's the trouble: no long-term planning."

"Just like Phoebe," muttered Calvin, weaving his car into the traffic stream.

"Phoebe's long-term plan is to live life as she chooses. I expect that's your own plan as well, so I wouldn't do any more waiting for her, if I were you."

"I never did any waiting for Phoebe. I wasn't with her long enough for the need to arise." It was plain from Calvin's voice that he had already written Phoebe off with a coldness that Jason would have linked to malevolence. Phoebe had transgressed, and Calvin was not going to forget the offence.

"What will you do with the old museum building, if you buy the watermill?" asked Deborah, in a tactful attempt to change the subject.

"Sell it, turn it into flats, open a hotel: I don't know or care. I've lost my affection for the place. If you think the watermill plan has got a chance, I'll put you in charge of the whole thing, even the café. Don't hesitate; it might be your once in a lifetime opportunity to dictate menus."

"That'd be a decision you'd come to regret if you want decent food. I'll eat any processed rubbish quite happily," said Deborah, dismissing the watermill scheme as an example of a rich man mentally spending money he had no intention of parting with in reality. "One query: is this another of Maurice's brainwaves that you've shanghaied?"

"Maurice has had a reprieve, so there's no call to bother about him," Calvin replied, neatly side-stepping Deborah's question. "I've promoted him to local area manager, a suitably vague title, and he's now surrounded by a mountain of paperwork to check that's already been checked. If he mucks up, I'll hold you entirely responsible for persuading me to pretend he's still in charge of something."

Deborah would have liked to inform Calvin that his nephew did not deserve such disparagement, but knew she might not sound convincing. Maurice as administrator was difficult to praise. "He'll be pleased that you're not sending him into exile."

"I'm not quite so pleased, but as long as Maurice is kept busy, he shouldn't be able to do much harm."

"If you speak to him in that supercilious tone, it's a wonder he hasn't long since punched you in the face."

"Talking of punches in the face," said Calvin with sudden glee, "I had the police around earlier to discuss your flattened ex-fiancé. I gather he is finally ex, as you haven't mentioned an anguished vigil at his bedside, or claimed you had to rush away to soothe his fevered brow. Atherton's going to have a job finding the culprit who laid the twerp out cold, as I imagine there are a lot of people who'd cheerfully queue in line to knock Clenham's block off."

"Jason wouldn't be much of a reporter if he worried about popularity."

"He doesn't need to worry. Clenham will never know what popularity is. I was under the impression that journalists weren't supposed to reveal anything to the police, yet he seems to have babbled on unrestrainedly about me." But Calvin sounded rueful rather than troubled. Jason was apparently an annoyance, not a threat.

"It's only their sources that journalists won't name," said Deborah, conscious of how much information she herself had supplied. "Atherton asked what stories Jason was working on. I guess it's the automatic first question when a journalist gets attacked."

"Atherton," Calvin repeated thoughtfully. "Yes, Atherton. What do you know about his son, Roderick?"

"The one who went to Oxford, only to walk out in his final year, neglecting to acquire a degree in the process? I've heard that the Inspector still has to recover from the blow."

"A Roderick Atherton has applied for the cleaning job at the museum." Calvin spoke as if his words had a greater significance beyond the mere fact of a job application.

"I suppose it could be the reprobate son. He's gone in for a series of undemanding part-time jobs. I believe. Perhaps he had an overdose of parental pressure from an early age."

"Or perhaps he's a layabout who thought it was more sensible to quit college than hang around and fail his exams. It doesn't matter which, though. Give him the job."

"But he won't stick it for long, if he's such a drifter," objected Deborah.

"So what? Hire him."

"Then why bother with an interview? I could simply have sent him a letter with his start date, and had more time for the role of ministering angel to my stricken fiancé."

"The job offer has got to look genuine," said Calvin.

"I doubt if you'll endear yourself to Atherton by hiring his once-cherished genius as a cleaner," Deborah pointed out. "If anything, you'll annoy the Inspector by encouraging what he regards as feckless behaviour. He intended his son to be a high flyer, not a cleaner."

"Yes, but if Atherton becomes even more of a nuisance than he already is, I can remind him of his son's lowly status in my employ."

Calvin so obviously relished the thought of his power that Deborah laughed. "For somebody who's our local philanthropist, you're not very charitable at times. Inspector Atherton might be tempted to improve the crime-solving statistics by framing you for something."

"He'd be unlikely to succeed, if his parental skills are anything to go by." Calvin turned his car onto the promenade, a privilege afforded to residents only, a privilege that would assure Calvin he was special as he parked in front of one of the most expensive houses in the town. Inspector Atherton did not live on the promenade, therefore Inspector Atherton could be discounted. Calvin Canning belonged to a different world.

They got out of the car and the vastness of the sea was before them, its salt tang making Deborah feel as restless as the ever-moving water that defied the twilight sky with a silken sheen. The ocean had offered her, as a child, the possibility of adventure: an invitation to be carried to magical Nordic lands of dark forests and enchanted castles, where fairytales became real life, and the everyday routine of school in a provincial town would fade to a far-off memory. Freedom meant the chance to sail away from everyone and everything she knew. It still seemed a good definition of liberty.

"I had nothing to do with Jason Clenham getting his just deserts," Calvin said abruptly.

"I know."

"You know because Clenham recognized his puncher, or you know because of my exemplary character?"

"Oh, your exceptional virtue, of course." As Deborah reluctantly turned her back on the ocean, she caught sight of a figure in the distance: a figure that, even through the dusk, was unmistakeably Chelsea Pritchard with her short skirts, long legs and flowing hair. If Calvin saw her too, he gave no sign as he activated the car alarm and then unlocked the front door of his house. Chelsea would suspect the worst, and the idea made Deborah feel uncomfortably like a traitor, although her conscience was clear, and she wished that she could explain the reason for being ushered into Calvin's hall. Chelsea might be sceptical, but to shut the door and leave her outside in the raw wind seemed unnecessarily cruel. Despite her good looks, or perhaps because of them, Chelsea appeared destined to live the thwarted life of a Gregory, and the idea was depressing.

"Son of Atherton is meant to be here at five o'clock, but with his track record, I suspect he isn't the most punctual of mortals," said Calvin. "What do you think the drop-out will be like? Arrogant and patronizing is my guess."

"He'll be relaxed but self-centred, with a secret desire to compose great music or write great poetry. He feared being trapped in a monotonous civil service or local government career, if he got a degree, so he freed himself to concentrate on ambitions that need time rather than money," replied Deborah, picturing a young Gregory.

"You sound as if you know him already."

"I just know the type."

Deborah followed Calvin down the hall, past the cupboard that presumably still contained Gregory's jacket, and into a room that had a large desk by the window, and two armchairs on either side of a bookcase. "This is my study," Calvin announced with pride. "For some inexplicable reason, I always yearned to have a study. I'm hardly ever in here, but I like to know it exists."

Deborah wanted a room, whatever it was called, that offered her a glimpse of the sea, but Calvin closed the curtains without apparently noticing the most attractive feature of his study: the view. "Atherton's son will be impressed," said Deborah, guessing that Calvin wished to establish the intellectual credentials he imagined were automatically implied by the ownership of a study.

"I hope he's more intimidated. Get the good-for-nothing talking about his father," urged Calvin. "No detail is insignificant."

"Is the room bugged, or do I tape the interview?" asked Deborah, amused at Calvin's determination to glean an account of Inspector Atherton as domestic tyrant.

"I rely on you to remember the salient points, and to read between the lines." It was an instruction that Jason might have given, and Calvin's motives were not dissimilar, as both wished to profit from the difficulties in other people's lives. "Leave the door open a bit, and we can compare notes later. Find out if there's a mother around, and whether she sides with the useless son. Perhaps Atherton blames her for spoiling the little idiot rotten."

"In my experience, people don't usually unburden themselves of family secrets during a job interview."

"Just sound sympathetic, and the dunderhead will be more than eager to spill the beans, because he's bound to have had months of carping from his father, and perhaps the mother too. Let him think he's found a soul mate who longs to be free of the stress and pace of modern life. Or, if he got kicked out of Oxford after partying his way through the place, tell him you were sent down from Cambridge."

"A slur on my pristine academic record, but you're the boss. Although, have you thought that I might be the person who gets quizzed? The Inspector could be trying to plant his son in the museum to learn more about you. Cleaners have unparalleled access to offices when nobody else is around."

Deborah had been joking, but Calvin's reply was serious. "I did consider it, but Atherton isn't likely to dispatch a spy so easy to connect with him."

"Perhaps that's what he wants you to think to defuse any suspicions: a double bluff."

"Could be, but Atherton must have a very low opinion of my intelligence if he imagines I'd be fool enough to leave incriminating evidence just lying around. Even if the degree-deficient son went through every computer in the place, what would he find, except staff rotas, wages details, and so on?"

"True. I'll exonerate both Inspector and son of devious motives."

"Anyhow, as your recumbent ex-fiancé is prepared to reveal my whole life to the world, Atherton only has to read a copy

215

of the local paper to do a background check," Calvin said gloomily. "My sole hope is that the mayor will be discovered in compromising circumstances with the town clerk before next Thursday."

But even if pictures capturing the entire town council *in flagrante delicto* covered the first ten pages, there would still be the rest of the paper to fill. Calvin's guarded privacy was going to be breached, no matter what scandal rocked the district. "It's publicity for the arts centre," Deborah reminded him.

"I suppose so." But Calvin did not look less resentful or in any way defeated. "Come on, tell me, who slugged Clenham? A pay rise in return for the name."

"I don't know a name. Jason might have described a bride's mother's dress as purple when it was actually crimson, or called a supervisor a secretary. The paper has had to print apologies for such offensive blunders."

"Nonetheless, I have the feeling that you know more than you're prepared to tell me."

"I wasn't entrusted with a name, I promise you."

"But you don't deny having a little extra information about the scribbler's comeuppance." However, Calvin sounded lenient rather than annoyed and added, "You're like Greg: trustworthy."

In Deborah's opinion, it was hardly a compliment to be told that she resembled her father, even though she could imagine Gregory being more loyal to a friend than to Rhoda, since friendship was not usually something that required much effort. Had any self-denial been involved, he might have proved less reliable than Calvin thought. Gregory had believed that sacrifices were for other people to make.

"Son of Atherton arrives at last," said Calvin, as the front door bell chimed its way up a scale. "He's a mere 12 minutes late, so I guess we should think ourselves honoured."

"Perhaps he knows that it's more difficult to get a cleaner than a chief executive," suggested Deborah.

"No, he's just a conceited little brat. Keep him hanging around outside a bit. There's no need to pander to his vanity."

While Deborah stood behind the front door, and waited for a suitably humbling time to pass before she acknowledged the stranger's summons, Calvin retreated down the hall. The renowned Mr Canning, who dined with the local MP and feasted at charity banquets, could not appear to take an interest in the appointment of a cleaner. Lesser beings than the celebrated Calvin concerned themselves with such trivialities.

Roderick Atherton, shoddily dressed in denim and scruffy trainers, was neither handsome nor ugly. He was of average height and build, with light-brown hair, and did not particularly look like his father; yet there was something familiar about Roderick, although Deborah could not recall having met him before. He gave no sign of recognizing her, and she struggled to place him in a memory, but he belonged nowhere in her life. Then, suddenly, Deborah was wary, alarm bells ringing wildly in her head, as she remembered Rhoda's account of the preordained husband. Not a wastrel, Deborah thought in despair; not a second version of the irresponsible Gregory. She would fight destiny with all her strength if it intended her to re-live Rhoda's experience.

Roderick sat down in one of the study's armchairs without being invited to, and Deborah promptly condemned him for arrogant over-confidence, because Gregory would not have waited to be asked to sit either. She left the door slightly ajar, for Calvin's benefit, and prepared to hate Roderick Atherton.

"Why do you want a cleaning job?"

"For the money, of course. Why else would anybody become a cleaner?" Roderick said, handing Deborah a completed application form. "I've done cleaning work before."

217

"Among a lot of other jobs," commented Deborah, glancing at the form. She ignored the second armchair, and sat at Calvin's desk to feel more aloof. "You haven't mentioned any qualifications."

"Not a single one," Roderick agreed cheerfully.

"Then how did you get a place at Oxford, if you've never passed any exams?"

Roderick laughed, not in the least disconcerted. "I don't know why people bother with application forms in this town. You probably know everything about me already."

"I don't know why you choose to go in for dead-end jobs." Deborah tried to seem interested, conscious of Calvin eavesdropping on the other side of the door, but instinct told her to send Roderick on his way as soon as possible. Whatever fate had up its sleeve could stay exactly where it was. "Surely you can find something more interesting than shelf-stacking and cleaning?"

"I plan to drift for a while before I decide what I'm going to do." It was a slick reply, and one that Roderick must have thought more suitable than admitting to no ambition at all. "I don't want to get trapped by mortgages and bills in a life I hate."

"I assume you didn't have a mortgage as a student," said Deborah, and, to her surprise, she found herself comparing somebody unfavourably with Gregory, who had at least pursued a dream. "Why didn't you get a degree, before starting to drift? A few qualifications in the background don't hurt, even if you never use them."

"You sound like my father," said Roderick, pulling a wry face.

"He must have been very disappointed when you left college early."

"It's regarded as the family tragedy, to be spoken of in despairing tones, but as I'm the person who has to live my life, I think the decision was mine to take," Roderick declared nonchalantly, and Deborah had to acknowledge to herself that he had every right to be untroubled. It was his choice, and presumably the right one had been made when he appeared contented with the result. Deborah, so often called a drifter by Rhoda, had to battle not to sympathize with Roderick.

"How did your mother take it?"

"No better than my father," replied Roderick, but he smiled as he spoke. "They're both sunk in gloom, only able to rouse themselves occasionally when they try to nag me into considering my time-out as a sabbatical before the prodigal meekly returns to college."

The condescending tone seemed callous, although Roderick might have been attempting bravado to pretend that his parents' opinion meant little to him; whichever, fate could forget it. Deborah had no intention of condemning herself to any future relationship that would need all of Rhoda's skill at inventing a Hollywood fantasy to make life bearable. "What will you do eventually?"

"If I knew that, I'd probably be doing it already," Roderick pointed out.

"But you must have an inkling of the direction you'll take. Are you interested in art or music or—or anything?"

"Not particularly." Roderick saw no reason to make an effort to impress, merely to get a cleaning job. There was enough minimum wage, part-time work in the town to keep him going, and he knew it.

Deborah would have given up, had Calvin not been in the hall listening; but he was, and she pressed on. "Do you still live at home?"

"Good grief, no. I'd have been driven completely mad by now; though, according to most people, I already am, so perhaps there'd be no discernable change. But out of sight, out of mind."

The saying could hardly apply to parents bereft of a boast-worthy son, therefore Roderick was obviously referring to himself. "You must feel guilty to have disappointed your parents," said Deborah, thinking of her own failure to remain in Rhoda's pink-tinged world as Gregory's devoted daughter.

Roderick shrugged. "I'm an individual, not an extension of somebody else. Anyway, no one requires a guilt-ridden cleaner. It doesn't go with the job, unless you're in an old French film."

Roderick had taken control of the interview because he did not especially want the job, but Deborah tried one last question on behalf of Calvin. "Surely it'd be easier to make a new start. Why come back here to live?"

Roderick shrugged again. "It's home."

"Do you have any questions about the museum?"

"No."

There appeared to be nothing left to discuss, and so Deborah thanked Roderick for attending the interview, said that he would hear the result in a day or two, and then restored him to the promenade. She could not imagine ever being drawn to a man who brought Gregory to mind, but the wariness persisted, simply because of a reminiscence that Rhoda had probably made up.

"So that's Son of Atherton," remarked Calvin, emerging from behind a door at the end of the hall. "He wasn't at the front of the queue when commonsense and logic were being handed out."

"University isn't for everyone. Perhaps he shouldn't have been pressured to go, just because he had memory enough to pass a few exams."

"Don't tell me that creep has a fatal attraction you're unable to resist?" Calvin demanded.

"On the contrary. I took an instant dislike to him, and can't picture myself ever altering that opinion. I doubt if he'll last long enough in a cleaning job for it to be of any use to you."

"It'll always be of use that I once employed Inspector Atherton's son as a cleaner, and I cherish the hope that the dim-witted offspring will turn out to be totally incompetent or such a bad time-keeper, he has to be sacked: something I'd have over the Inspector for the rest of his career. Talking of careers, where's the list of the blockhead's previous jobs?"

Deborah went back into the study to retrieve the application form, and had the uneasy feeling that, one day, she might be telling somebody how she recognized her future husband the moment she saw him on Calvin Canning's doorstep. "I don't like Roderick Atherton at all," declared Deborah, as she handed the form to Calvin. "He's going to con some unsuspecting female, and spend the rest of his days living off her."

"That'll be his sole chance of a future. Contact the past employers, and find out what they have to say," ordered Calvin. "Of course, he won't have mentioned anybody who actually kicked him out, but see what you can unearth."

"OK. I could ask Jason for further details, if you like." It seemed only fair to offer Calvin some recompense for having shopped him to the press, and there was the additional motive of perhaps garnering such unpleasant facts about Roderick Atherton that Deborah would never find herself weakening towards him. "Jason's good at picking up gossip."

"As I know to my cost," remarked Calvin. "Yes, unleash the tyke. Let him delve through the dregs of someone else's life for a change. With any luck, the Inspector might end up being the person who administers a second punch to your ex-fiancé's nose, when an Atherton family disgrace is spread across the local paper."

"Don't count on it, but I'll phone Jason when I get home, and then chase up Roderick Atherton's references. It shouldn't take too long."

"We make a good team." Calvin went to put an arm around Deborah, changed his mind, sighed and then laughed. "I'd have tried to start an affair with you weeks ago, if you didn't happen to be Greg's daughter; but you are, and so it's marriage or nothing. Which do you think it'll be?"

"Nothing. I'm not the sort who'd ever be a rich man's wife." Although even the self-important Calvin would be preferable to an idler: anybody would be preferable to Roderick Atherton. "You couldn't trot me out as a status symbol at fancy dinners or charity galas."

"Why not? You're years younger than me, and attractive. What more can I ask for?"

"Love?" suggested Deborah.

"Merely the icing on the cake."

"There are times when I'd consider icing an essential."

"In that case, let me know the minute you're bowled over by my charisma. Is it a deal?"

"A deal," Deborah said lightly, trusting that if she were ever fool enough to yearn for the indolent Roderick, prudence would head her in the direction of a more sensible relationship, whether or not love chanced to exist.

"I'll take you out for a meal to celebrate our understanding," Calvin declared, before adding with less flippancy, "I think we could make a go of it. I don't have to pretend with you, and I know you'd never let me down."

But, with his track record, would Calvin be loyal to Deborah? Any wife was going to have to adjust to him, while he continued to live as he chose. Perhaps Babette had refused to adapt, refused to be a cipher, because an ex-beauty queen would have a higher opinion of her worth than a Rhoda ever could. Impossible to tell Calvin that there might always be a doubt in Deborah's mind about Babette's death, and equally impossible to say that Rhoda, the mother-in-law presumptive, believed he was a double murderer.

The door bell started to chime again, and Calvin said

impatiently, "See who it is, and if it's unimportant, get rid of him or her."

Deborah immediately thought of Chelsea, who would have seen Roderick arrive and depart, leaving Deborah once more alone with Calvin. Had Chelsea known about Calvin's semi-serious semi-proposal of marriage, her suspicions would have some foundation, and Deborah felt oddly like a usurper. Uncertain how to tackle the intercom system, she opened the front door and discovered that self-consciousness was not necessary, because instead of a resentful Chelsea on the threshold, an astonished Maurice gazed blankly at Deborah.

"For goodness' sake, Maurice, don't just stand there imitating a codfish," said Calvin. "What do you want?"

"I finished going through the accounts," Maurice replied, too taken aback to register his uncle's imperious tone.

"Then give them to Deborah, and leave."

Deborah took the paperwork and, to gloss over Calvin's abruptness, said, "Congratulations again on the promotion, Maurice."

"Thanks. Calvin simply must persuade you to run the museum."

"I already have," snapped Calvin. "Deborah doesn't need your recommendation."

"No, obviously not," Maurice agreed with discomfited haste.

"Well?" demanded Calvin. "Is there anything else?"

"No, not especially."

"Then goodbye."

Maurice backed onto the promenade, and Deborah closed the door. "I'm afraid Calvin Canning's vaunted charisma isn't exactly noticeable at present."

"I do try," said Calvin. "I really try to be nicer, but there's something infuriating about Maurice. I can't help feeling annoyed at the mere sight of him, and it's greatly to my credit that he gets good money along with a fancy job title. Anyway, he's happy enough bustling around, thinking he's important."

The depiction was so utterly and indisputably Maurice that Deborah shelved all thought of defence. "Before I forget: my father's jacket—"

"Yes, of course." Calvin opened the under stairs cupboard and picked up a carrier bag: a Harrods carrier bag. Even with the most transitory objects that passed fleetingly through his life, Calvin had to impress.

"My mother will be pleased to have the jacket. I imagined reminders would upset her, but it seems to be the other way around. And don't say that's because the marriage was unhappy. She adored him."

"Perhaps that's what Greg found difficult. It's a terrible burden, being responsible for another person's entire happiness." Calvin stared past Deborah for a moment, as if somebody else had joined them; then he saw her again, and smiled. "You must promise never to adore me."

"Not a problem." Had Babette adored Calvin? Deborah was more inclined to picture a beauty queen being the one who expected adoration, but the oppressive idolatry had presumably belonged to a relationship that Calvin could not just abandon with the swiftness of a Gregory bored by a clinging girlfriend. Either a much younger husband had made Babette insecure about the looks that were part of a beauty queen's identity, leaving her in need of constant reassurance, or she had simply loved Calvin so whole-heartedly that he, like Gregory, had felt trapped by uncompromising devotion when the novelty wore off. Whichever was the true portrait of Babette, Calvin's release had come conveniently soon.

****

Chelsea still stood on the promenade, although the evening was dark and the wind strengthening. She had moved closer to the house, but Calvin ignored her as he and Deborah got into his car. If Chelsea continued to trail after him, Calvin would probably order her dismissal from the museum, and the prospective supermodel might find herself in even more straitened circumstances. Chelsea did not adore Calvin, but she had become as tiresome as the previous burden he had successfully shed, one way or another.

"We'll go to the Coastal Restaurant," decided Calvin, the sweep of headlights dramatically illuminating the forsaken Chelsea when he turned the car. "I was there a few days ago, and the food was almost worth the price they charged for it. Any objections to the Coastal?"

"I never have any objection to being spared the boredom of cooking," replied Deborah. It was typical of Calvin to wish to inform the town that Phoebe Vale had been merely another female passing through his sophisticated world. And typical of life that Deborah, who did not want anything from Calvin, should be in his car that night, while Chelsea remained out in the cold.

"I'll get a surveyor to have a look at the watermill tomorrow, and then put in an offer for the place."

"You're really considering the watermill plan?" asked Deborah in surprise. "I thought you were just talking."

"I never just talk," declared Calvin, proud to present himself as a man of decisive action. "The museum has to move; there's no choice. I'll make necessity an opportunity, even if that does sound horribly like one of Maurice's utterances. The Canning Arts Centre is going to take off. I've made up my mind to put Seaborne on the map."

Maurice would have to be content with the knowledge that he had started the whole scheme, because it was the only glory left to him. Calvin intended to nab the rest. "Who will you blame if the town is stubbornly resistant to a spot of high culture?" inquired Deborah.

"Everybody but me, of course," replied Calvin. "Like Roderick Atherton, I don't go in for guilt."

"Not even when you ought to feel guilty?"

"Are we on the subject of Maurice again?"

No, Babette, thought Deborah. "Can anyone be completely blameless?"

"Blameless and insipid go together. Self-contempt isn't a virtue, nor is letting other people rule you. You're responsible for your own life, nobody else's. Can you guess who once said that to me?"

"My father?"

"And how right he was. You have to fight to be yourself."

"You're sounding more like Roderick Atherton with every word."

"He has the right idea: just gone about it in a stupid way." Calvin said superciliously. "No plan, no forethought, no energy. If there isn't a goal, you're at a standstill. He thinks something will turn up, but you have to make life happen or it passes you by. Even failure doesn't matter much, as long as you go on making an effort."

But Maurice always made an effort, and Calvin had no praise for him, therefore the advice applied to Calvin alone, and ignored his opportune marriage to a wealthy woman: a marriage that might perhaps have been part of the overall plan. To Calvin's credit, at least he seemed content with the money he had already acquired, and apparently did not intend to waste time chasing after a superfluity, simply to be richer and have an even larger house in a more fashionable town. "Why did you come back here to live?" asked Deborah.

"To quote Roderick Atherton, it's home. No, that isn't a good enough answer." Calvin was silent for a minute or two, and then said, "In London, I'm merely another person; here,

I'm Calvin Canning, local boy made good: big fish in little pond. Anything not to be invisible."

"Well, you're certainly visible in this town," said Deborah. Calvin's pretensions meant that he was more of a laughing-stock than the towering colossus of achievement he imagined, but he would prefer any sort of reputation to anonymity. There was something of Maurice's inadequate pushiness in Calvin, and both entirely failed to see themselves as others saw them. Maurice would never understand why Deborah avoided him, and Calvin had no idea why Phoebe should have chosen to wander off, despite the wealth that he assumed gave him distinction. It was an undoubted likeness, but one that uncle and nephew would not be able to recognize in each other.

Calvin parked his car in a side street, and after the quiet darkness of the night, the restaurant was garishly bright and noisy. Deborah would have preferred somewhere more peaceful, but Calvin flourished when he believed he had an appreciative audience. He waved to people who barely acknowledged his existence, and appeared unaware that he was being snubbed yet again. To survive the petty snobbery of the upper echelons of Seaborne's society, Calvin would need every bit of thick skin he could produce. He did not realize it, but gatecrashers remained gatecrashers, no matter how much money they threw around. Calvin had been deemed a boorish outsider, and nothing would alter the verdict against him. He was an interloper, and his axiom about making an effort did not apply.

****

Calvin escorted Deborah as far as her front door, said goodnight, and then remarked gloomily, "You're going to ruin my reputation as a philanderer. I can't stop behaving like a complete gentleman."

Deborah was glad to hear it. Her life seemed complicated enough, without having to offend Calvin. She went inside, dropped the carrier bag containing Gregory's jacket behind her front door, then picked up the telephone and dialled Jason's number, in the hope of confirming her low estimation of Roderick Atherton.

"How's the battered journalist?" asked Deborah.

"Suffering in almost silent stoicism," replied Jason. "You sound cheerful. The thought of my agony obviously comforts you no end."

"It perked Calvin up as well, and mention of him brings me to the point of my call. Can you find out the latest gossip concerning Inspector Atherton's lackadaisical son?"

"Of course I can," declared Jason, as if his investigative skills were doubted. "The question is, why should I?"

"Because I interviewed Roderick Atherton earlier for a cleaning job at the museum."

"If he was on good terms with his father, I'd say Atherton junior had been sent along to spy on Calvin Canning."

"That's what I reckoned as well," said Deborah. "Any chance it's true?"

"Probably not. The Inspector would sooner Calvin walked free than his son became a cleaner. And while we're on the subject of spies, what have you got to report? I've heard you're living the high life with Calvin these days."

"Who told you that?"

"Phoebe. I fear she might be trying to stymie my engagement to Deborah Wainwright."

"She thinks I'm two-timing you, and so does *le tout* Seaborne by now. My good character's gone forever, but I'll survive. What did Phoebe tell you about my father?"

"That she wasn't his companion at the Grand on Saturday night. In fact, she gave the description of the girl to Lucas Rudd."

"Phoebe's covering her own tracks," said Deborah. "She doesn't want to sully the reputation of Vale and Son by admitting she was at a hotel with a married man, especially as their affair dated back to her mid-teens. I suppose Phoebe maintained that she hardly knew my father."

"No, she didn't."

"Then what did she say?"

Jason paused, before asking, "Do you really want the details? It's all in the past, and can't alter anything. The story isn't even particularly newsworthy: well, not unless Phoebe changes her account of what she was doing at the Grand."

"You don't have to reveal any more. I know Phoebe and my father had a ten-year relationship that was special to them both. I think I knew right from the time it started, but I went out of my way to pretend nothing was happening because I couldn't deal with the situation."

"Phoebe told me it only lasted one summer," said Jason, but the usual certainty was gone from his voice. "She hadn't seen your father in ages when she ran across him by chance at the Grand on Saturday."

"You don't sound entirely convinced," commented Deborah, but Jason had been correct when he said that it was all in the past. She no longer cared what Gregory had or had not done, because Rhoda was safe in the fortress of her imagination. Even Phoebe did not matter; she was just somebody Deborah once knew at school. The time had come to move on. "I'd take whatever Phoebe tells you with a pinch of salt. Actually, I'm surprised she admitted as much as she did, but you're very impressive with your journalistic standing in Seaborne. You simply bowl us females over."

"But the effect wears off quite quickly. Stacey's had a big reconciliation scene with her husband. She said she didn't know how much he cared. If I go and punch Calvin Canning, will you appreciate how much I care?" Jason was joking, but

Deborah could hear an undertone of aggrieved umbrage.

"Unlike Stacey, I'm not attracted to men who regard me as a possession to be fought over. Anyway, Phoebe's got her sights on you, so that should keep you fully occupied in the near future."

"No, thanks. Not while the unenlightened Lucas Rudd remains her husband, especially as he too might be the type inclined to aim a fist at anybody he suspects of admiring his wife, ex or not. I've decided to concentrate on unattached women from now on. This is all your fault, of course. If you'd accepted my proposal, I wouldn't be in this dilemma; but poor unsuspecting me didn't realize that talking about marriage was a way to send a woman racing in the opposite direction as if the hounds of hell were about to leap out at her. I still fail to understand why the idea of life with me so horrified you. After all, as you know, I'm in great demand, even with a nose that currently bears a strong resemblance to the Albert Hall. What's Calvin Canning got that I haven't? Apart from money, success, influence, and a possible history as a murderer."

"Jason, do you honestly believe that Calvin killed his wife?"

"You know him better than I do, it seems. What's your assessment?"

Deborah thought, but thinking did not help. There was only instinct to provide an answer, and instinct said, "No, he didn't kill Babette; I'm almost sure he didn't."

"But not a hundred per cent sure."

"No, not a hundred per cent," conceded Deborah. "Would you settle for ninety-nine per cent?"

"Would you?"

"No, but my opinion of Calvin isn't important. What convinced you that I'm about to commit my life to the man? What's Phoebe been telling you?"

"Facts," replied Jason. "I deal in facts. If you're so footloose and fancy free, why are you constantly gadding around the district's most exclusive spots with Calvin?"

"How many reasons do you need? One: he asked me out, and I don't want to offend the man currently paying my wages. Two: a free feed is OK by me, whoever pays the bill. Three: Calvin's talking about a new development at the watermill, with me in charge of the project." But Deborah was the person still looking for the reason why she had not chosen to refuse Calvin's invitation, and no answer sprang readily to mind. "Besides, you yourself told me to get some information out of him."

"So you're just meekly obeying my orders? Oh well, as it's the only comfort left to me, I suppose I should believe you." But even when pretending dejection, Jason could not forget that, first and foremost, he was a news gatherer. "What info have you gleaned from the irresistible Calvin?"

"Practically nothing. He won't talk about Babette."

"She's obviously on his conscience: or would be, if he had one."

"I think it's more that he doesn't want to acknowledge anything that clashes with the image he tries to project. Canny businessmen are meant to be ruthless, not sentimental," said Deborah, thinking of the flowers in her kitchen. If Calvin hated his memories of Babette, he would hate pink roses too.

"Are you telling me that he comes over all syrupy at the mention of a much older wife who left him loaded?" Jason laughed as he spoke.

"And you're coming over all cynical journalist," retorted Deborah. "I think Calvin might—no, I think Calvin probably did marry Babette because of her money, but he must have liked her, even so. Calvin wouldn't be able to tolerate someone he despised."

"The money would help to coat a bitter pill with saccharine."

"I doubt if Calvin's a good enough actor to disguise his true feelings." Yet Deborah was not sure how far Calvin's treatment of his nephew could be considered an accurate guide. When Calvin himself was the dependant, his behaviour might have been less arrogant out of sheer expediency. "Anyway, you're assuming that Babette was a gullible fool, when she must have had a good business head to be able to run a string of nightclubs successfully."

"That doesn't mean she couldn't be conned," Jason pointed out. "How angry was Calvin at having to provide an alibi for the time when my nose got its visitation from Stacey's husband?"

"Calvin didn't seem in the least angry. In fact, he was highly entertained at the thought of you being prostrated by an unknown fist."

"The man has no soul," declared Jason. "I imagine it'll give Calvin a real laugh, if my face never again resumes normal proportions. Ditch the unfeeling swine immediately."

Jason had reached an impasse in his investigation, and he knew it. He would be reduced to reporting police statements, unable to get closer to the night of Babette's death than he already was. Any secret would remain hidden, because Calvin only had to stay silent. If he were a double murderer, as Rhoda believed and Jason hoped, he was unlikely to face a charge of having killed his wife, no matter what the police might discover about Gregory's death. But there was a point in Calvin's favour that Jason seemed prepared to overlook. "I don't think my father would have helped cover up Babette's murder. He was quite fond of her, apparently."

"Then Calvin conned him too," announced Jason. "He took advantage of your father's naivety."

"Naivety?" repeated Deborah, amused by such a description of Gregory.

"Well, your father must have been very trusting. After all, Calvin managed to persuade him to give a fake alibi."

"Assuming it was fake."
"Why else would Calvin have killed your father?"
"Assuming he did."
"Yes, yes, yes," Jason said impatiently.

****

Deborah wished she could simply give the Harrods bag to Rhoda without seeing Gregory's jacket, but it was essential to check the pockets first to make sure Calvin had not left anything behind that could be linked to him, the hated murderer of Rhoda's sainted Gregory. For an alienated daughter to disturb a relic seemed sacrilegious, as well as insensitive, but it would be far worse to let Rhoda discover an item that might disturb her, so Deborah took the bag into the front room, and lifted out the jacket: a black jacket, as perfectly tailored as everything else that Gregory had worn, even in his rankest days of poverty. Reluctantly, she went through the pockets, but the only remaining débris was a scrap of paper, folded and folded again, that had managed to work its way through some slack stitches into the lining. Gregory had often scribbled telephone numbers on bits of old envelope that he then shed like autumn leaves, and Calvin might have the same habit; but when Deborah opened the fragment, she recognized the scrawl, so unlike Calvin's neat printing.. To hold something that Gregory had recently held made Deborah's hands shake, and a rush of memories jostled through her mind. Gregory, arm around his small daughter's shoulders, as he and Debbie walked by the sea; Gregory and Debbie dancing out of the kitchen and down the hall to the *Stardust* melody; Debbie ready to prompt from a script, while Gregory went through the ten lines he had in a touring production of *Carousel*; Gregory and Debbie running breathlessly towards the railway station because he was late; Rhoda and Debbie waving goodbye to a train until it disappeared from sight.

"He didn't wave back," said Debbie in anguish.

"Of course he did," declared Rhoda. "The windows were so grimy, we couldn't see him, but he saw us. Of course he saw us."

But whether he had seen them or not, Gregory was gone, and Debbie ached with the loss.

Gregory had gone forever, yet Deborah's heart pounded in apprehension because the phone number was local: not Phoebe's home, so presumably her office. If unaware that Gregory had parted with his jacket earlier in the day, Phoebe was likely to claim that she gave him the office number at the Grand Hotel on Saturday night, when they had met so amazingly by chance. Deborah could then choose to call Phoebe a liar, or pretend to accept the story. Easier, much easier, to tear the phone number in two, and then drop the pieces into the wastepaper basket, as a symbolic end of the connection between Gregory and Phoebe. It was saying goodbye to Gregory's real life, in which his family had played such a small part, because Phoebe represented all the attractive women who offered him a world far removed from domesticity: the world Gregory had believed was his by right, the right of a star.

****

When Maurice arrived at the front door, Deborah realized that she had been expecting him to call, because he would want to warn her against getting involved with his uncle. Maurice probably cared more about her than anyone else ever would, and it was just bad luck that she found his ineptness as irritating as Calvin did.

"I know it's late—" Maurice began.

"It's only a few minutes after eight," said Deborah.

"Is it? I thought it was much later than that." Maurice paused, and then asked warily, "Is Calvin here?"

"No."

Maurice promptly walked down the hall and into the kitchen, as though Calvin's absence gave him permission to enter Deborah's house, and she could guess what he was going to say next. "Calvin definitely had an affair with Chelsea Pritchard."

"Yes, I know."

"Oh." Maurice paused again, uncertain whether to consider Deborah extremely broad-minded or extremely forgiving. He glanced at the vase of roses on the table, and sat down to give himself further time to think, before continuing. "Calvin told me to sack Chelsea, so that it wouldn't be the first thing you had to do when you take over at the museum. I've sent her a letter, and used poor time-keeping as the excuse."

Deborah felt sorry for Chelsea, now even more out in the cold, but was forced to acknowledge, "Chelsea has been a lousy time-keeper."

"I suppose she imagined that she didn't have to make an effort with her and Calvin being—well, it doesn't matter now. But that's Calvin. When people become inconvenient, he simply discards them."

"That's him all right." Deborah sat down opposite Maurice and tried to sound chatty, although his attempted kindness felt more intrusive than thoughtful. "You can't tell me anything about Calvin that would surprise me."

"Yet you didn't believe me when I said he was in the museum courtyard on Sunday morning."

"You saw my father; I told you."

Maurice shook his head, "It couldn't have been your father."

"Why not?"

"Because he wouldn't be talking to Chelsea Pritchard."

"He would if he asked her how to find my office," said Deborah.

"I suppose so," Maurice admitted reluctantly.

"And if Chelsea lied to the police for Calvin, he'd hardly risk offending her with the sack a few days later."

"But Calvin thinks he can do what he likes, and everybody just has to put up with it."

"No; he'd be a lot more cautious if Chelsea could get revenge by shopping him to the law. What did Lucas say when he heard you'd spotted Chelsea in the courtyard?"

"I didn't get around to mentioning her. Rudd asked if I'd seen Calvin, and when I said yes, he hurried straight off. Besides what's the point of trying to make Rudd listen to me, when both Calvin and Chelsea are prepared to lie? I can't prove anything. I only know that I saw them together."

But Maurice had merely seen a dark-haired man in Calvin's blue stripes talking to Chelsea. "My father had never visited the museum before, so he'd have to ask someone where to find me, especially in the middle of the disaster exercise confusion."

"It wasn't in the middle. The morning had practically ended."

"Then you didn't see Chelsea. She asked me not to grass on her, but that's irrelevant now she's had her marching orders. Chelsea sneaked off home at ten o'clock, so you couldn't have seen her later on."

"Yes, I did, and it was after eleven, because the casualties had been cleared from the courtyard. I worked out the timetable myself."

Maurice spoke with confident authority, and he was certainly right about the schedule of disaster events that had preoccupied him for weeks beforehand; but if Maurice could mistake Gregory for Calvin, he could also mistake Chelsea for another fair-haired girl. A fair-haired girl young enough to be Gregory's daughter; Gregory had been talking to a fair-haired girl young enough to be his daughter. If she worked at the museum, he had gone there to see her: the girl with him at the Grand Hotel the previous night. In that case, his daughter might not be the reason for his presence in the courtyard. But Deborah's sudden hope was almost immediately dashed by the recollection that the story came from Maurice, hardly the most reliable of informants. Freedom could not be obtained so easily.

"There are three girls with hair like Chelsea's working at the museum," ventured Deborah.

"I saw Chelsea," declared Maurice, "and she was talking to Calvin. You know I don't make mistakes."

But there was one thing that Deborah could be sure of: Maurice made mistakes with such regularity, it could have been a pastime.

****

"As the local area manager for Canning Enterprises, I'll see you almost every day," Maurice said reassuringly. "Any time you need help, I'm only a phone call away."

"Thanks." Deborah opened the front door, and disliked herself for being eager to rid the house of somebody who meant so well.

"You can talk to me about anything, not just work. After all, we've been good friends right from the start. And when Calvin—when he—well, I'm on your side, whatever happens. Don't forget that."

"Thanks," Deborah said again, but she barely registered Maurice's words. Her mind was on the telephone number she had found in Gregory's jacket, and the moment after she had closed the door behind Maurice, Deborah hurried to the wastepaper basket and retrieved the pieces.

If the number connected Deborah to Phoebe's office, there would be no need to speak; Vale and Son's message service was going to confirm that Deborah had been responsible for summoning Gregory to his death. If one of the museum staff answered, Deborah might be freed. But even before she heard a voice, she knew that the phone number would be linked to some woman or other. It was inevitable. Deborah started to dial.

"Hello?" A woman's voice, naturally: a young woman. Trust Gregory.

"This is Deborah Wainwright—"

"What do you want?" The sullen resentfulness was unmistakeable.

"Chelsea!" exclaimed Deborah.

"Who do you expect to hear when you ring me?"

Calvin must have been the one who jotted down Chelsea's phone number, Deborah told herself; but the hieroglyphs next to the telephone remained obstinately Gregory's. "I have to see you."

"Why?" demanded Chelsea.

Good question. "Because—because I've found some jobs, London jobs, for you." It felt horribly like setting a trap.

"You want to get me out of the way," declared Chelsea. "You want Calvin all to yourself. I saw you at his house."

"I went there to do a job interview. You must have seen the man arrive and leave." Deborah was thankful that Chelsea's suspicions were so off-target, but the guilt lingered because Chelsea seemed more of a victim than anyone else, even Rhoda. Inspector Atherton had described the fair-haired girl at the Grand as young enough to be Gregory's daughter, but Gregory's actual daughter was more than seven years older than Chelsea who still retained a childlike vulnerability despite, or perhaps because of, her experience with men. "Calvin isn't interested in me."

"No?" retorted Chelsea. "Then where did he take you in his car?"

"He gave me a lift home," said Deborah, ignoring the detail of the lift having been via a restaurant. "I couldn't replace Phoebe Vale, any more than I can compete with you."

"That's what you say."

"Don't believe me then. It doesn't matter. What about the London jobs? Have you changed your mind about saving up for the modelling course?"

"I'm going to be a model," declared Chelsea, as belligerently as though her dream had just been scorned. "No one's going to stop me, even if you have got to Calvin."

"I'm not in the least involved with Calvin," protested Deborah. "In fact, I'm engaged to somebody quite other: a reporter on the local paper called Jason Clenham."

"A reporter?" Chelsea's mood changed with the swiftness of a coastal sky. "Could he get my picture into the paper?"

"I'll introduce you to him, and you can ask," said Deborah, seizing the opportunity: a traitor's opportunity. "Actually, Jason's on his way to my house now. Why don't you come over and meet him?"

"I might as well drop by; I've got nothing better to do." Chelsea tried to sound coolly sophisticated, but could not disguise her exuberance, and Deborah felt worse.

For all Chelsea's willingness to use her body to get what she wanted, she was more naïve than grasping; but any scandal would be trivial, a commotion lasting a few hours, to be left behind with the town when Chelsea went to London. It was Deborah who appeared eternally stuck in the past, and she needed a friend: any friend, even one prepared to trumpet Gregory's failings across East Anglia. Normally, Jason snatched up a telephone on the first ring, but that night he allowed a little time to pass before answering, and Deborah began to fear that she might not be able to contact him. To hear his voice at last was a tremendous relief, although she knew that a problem shared hardly meant a problem solved when Jason yearned for a scoop.

"Can you get over to my place as soon as possible?"

"What's wrong, Deb?"

"I think I've found the girl who was at the Grand with my father, and I don't know what I'm supposed to do about it."

"Confide in the nearest journalist, of course," Jason said cheerfully. "Who is she?"

"Chelsea Pritchard." Deborah started to elaborate, but she had underestimated Jason's mastery of his craft.

"Calvin Canning's Sunday companion and alibi? She distributes her favours with striking liberality if she spent the previous night with your father. I didn't realize they'd even met."

"They probably didn't," conceded Deborah. The whole scenario suddenly fizzled out to nothingness, and she tried to laugh. "I'm afraid part of my assumption hinged on information from Maurice Canning, the least dependable of sources. Lucky I haven't accused Chelsea of shamelessly two-timing Calvin. He's the one she wants, and she wouldn't risk alienating him by being seen with another man. Sorry, but I've jumped to a non-existent conclusion with the speed of a steeplechaser. Calvin obviously wrote the phone number."

"What phone number?"

"Chelsea's. I found it in my father's jacket: the jacket Calvin was wearing that weekend. I thought I recognized the scrawl, but I have to backtrack. There's no story here."

"I gather Calvin doesn't scrawl."

"He must have been in a hurry when he wrote it," said Deborah. "I'm glad I didn't mention any of this to Chelsea. She's on her way here at the moment. I regret to say that I bribed her with a promise of meeting you."

"Clearly a girl of sound good taste, if the mere thought of Jason Clenham has her scurrying across town."

"Scurrying in the hope that you'll be able to get her picture in the paper. Chelsea aims to be a model."

"I wouldn't mind talking to her about Calvin," said Jason.

"Yes, there are definitely a couple of questions I'd like to ask Chelsea Pritchard."

"She's very young."

"A distinct contrast to Calvin's wife then."

"I meant go easy on Chelsea," explained Deborah, but realizing that she had no influence whatsoever over Jason when he was chasing a lead.

"You were absolutely positive that your father had written the phone number?"

"Yes," admitted Deborah, "but you're right: Calvin must be a secret scrawler."

"I never said that," Jason pointed out.

"You didn't have to. I know I was wrong. Could you get your editor interested in an article about a local girl going to London to do a modelling course?"

"The story will have to compete with the Rotary Club whist drive and a postman's retirement shindig, but the more informative Chelsea is on the subject of Calvin Canning, the more fluent I'll be when lauding her to the boss." Jason wanted to strike gold, to win first prize, to sit at the top banqueting table, to get at least one of the traditional three wishes. He also wanted Chelsea to be the supplier of those dreams: the source who held the keys to all the doors he needed to open. He knew Calvin would not have spoken of Babette or Gregory to Chelsea, but still Jason hoped.

"Calvin won't have confided in her," said Deborah. "It wasn't a meeting of minds."

"You never know what she might have overheard or seen. Anyway, an account of Calvin's performance in bed might be enlightening: a taste for sadism, for example. I don't suppose you could supply details?"

"You suppose correctly, and I've no intention of trying to seduce Calvin so that you can sell the story to one of the sleazier Sundays," declared Deborah. "I hate to tell you, but Mr Canning has been a perfect gentleman throughout our acquaintanceship."

"A closer companion might have encountered a different Calvin," said Jason, unwilling to lose the chance he craved. "I'll be around to quiz the more obliging Chelsea in ten minutes, so prepare yourself for the distressing sight of my cruelly maltreated visage."

Deborah put the telephone down, and hurried to her computer to seek and print advertisements of job vacancies, any job vacancies, in the London area, despite being fairly sure that the excitement of talking to the press would delete all thought of boringly sensible employment from Chelsea's mind. Some of Gregory's CDs were still in the room, and Deborah packed them into a box, unable to cope any more with photographs of her father's confident smile, even though she knew that hiding pictures would not banish him. She picked up his jacket to return it to the carrier bag, and felt as if she were folding away a part of herself at the same time, because there was little to be learnt about Gregory's final day. Chelsea would know nothing, Phoebe was not going to talk, and the police had probably found out as much as they were ever likely to discover. Calvin's annoyance, when Chelsea's place in his world was revealed, would pass, and Jason might eventually give up the hunt for tittle-tattle. Gregory had been absent from Deborah's life for so long, it seemed that his death should make no real difference to her, now that the first shock was over, as she had actually experienced and survived the loss of her father years previously. There was also the slight comfort of knowing that he, who had found middle age depressing, would have hated to be trapped in the frailty of old age. If Deborah could forget the Gregory of her childhood, she might be freed from regrets, but forgetting would not be manufactured by willpower. Only temporary distractions gave fleeting holidays from him, and the minor distraction of her first visitor's arrival helped.

"My hair's a mess," wailed Chelsea in genuine anguish. "The wind absolutely wrecked it."

"There's time to do repairs. Jason hasn't shown up yet. By the way, I've printed out a list of London jobs for you."

"Thanks," Chelsea said absently, scrabbling through the objects in her shoulder bag for a comb and mirror as she hurried into the front room. "I would be looking my worst tonight."

But Chelsea's worst was better than most women's best. She certainly fitted the description given to Calvin of the young and beautiful girl, except that the young and beautiful girl had just ditched a husband. Although the most rational conclusion was still that Chelsea's telephone number had been put into the pocket of Gregory's jacket by Calvin, the scribble remained as emphatically Gregory's as a signature. "I need to write with more flamboyance," said his voice from the distant past. "My autograph mustn't be neat and legible: far too dull for Greg Wayne. Stars scrawl, so I have to cultivate as many loops and zigzags as I can."

If she had found the piece of paper in the street, Deborah was sure that she would have immediately thought of Gregory, though commonsense insisted that a mere series of numbers could not so easily identify a specific writer, even when the choice limited itself to either Calvin or Gregory. Calvin or Gregory? It had to have been Calvin.

As Deborah walked into the front room, Chelsea scooped up her hair in both hands, glanced at Deborah for an opinion, and then let the long strands fall over her shoulders again. "No, I'll leave it loose," said Chelsea, her tone suggesting that a momentous decision had been made. "I don't want to look like a schoolteacher."

"You'll never look like a schoolteacher."

Chelsea laughed, accepting Deborah's words as a compliment.

"I didn't know you were engaged: engaged to a reporter."

"And I didn't know you were married," said Deborah, to force the denial that would eliminate Chelsea as the girl at the Grand, once and for all.

"I'm practically divorced," Chelsea stated, with an abrupt return of her sullenness.

Deborah was taken aback, convinced that she must have misheard. "Divorced?" she repeated warily.

"He's a slob and I was a fool," declared Chelsea. "I wanted to get away from home, but marriage was worse. All he does is hang around pubs, bragging how he's too clever for the sort of jobs in this town, yet I was supposed to go out and slave to keep him supplied with money for booze."

"You must have been very young when you married," ventured Deborah, as Chelsea paused for sympathy.

"I was 16 and stupid. I'll never be that stupid again: never. Even having to go back home was better than being stuck with a thick-headed drunk." Chelsea glowered into the mirror she held, and rearranged her hair with angry swipes of a comb. "Dave told me he was a builder with his own company. A builder! He couldn't even build a bread board. He can't hammer a nail without demolishing a wall in the process. But I'm beginning to think that all men are swindlers and liars, and when I'm famous, I won't be treated that way. I'll show them. I'll show every last one of them."

Chelsea apparently judged men by how useful they could be in her progress towards the future she desired, and she was well aware of the need to persuade somebody as wealthy as Calvin to finance her dreams. Therefore, one of the men Chelsea had determined to show was unlikely to have been Gregory, whose constant monetary crises would rule him out as the provider of either London accommodation or modelling courses, and Deborah relaxed. If romance had ever inveigled Chelsea, marriage certainly cured her of it. "Sounds as though you made the right choice: going for divorce and a new start."

"Everything will be my choice from now on," declared Chelsea. "I've had enough of being pushed around. I'll find someone richer than Calvin: richer, and handsomer as well. It's all going to happen for me soon; it's got to."

Throughout his life, Gregory had been convinced that things were about to happen for him. Each job and each audition was to be the big chance: the big chance that never materialized. His lack of success did not mean that Chelsea was equally doomed to anonymity, but somehow Deborah could not separate Chelsea's hopes from Gregory's obscurity. Chelsea was very attractive, but every aspiring model would have a similar face and figure in a world where spectacular appearance had to be regarded as the norm, and getting her picture into the local paper might not be the tremendous boost that Chelsea believed must automatically lead on to fame and fortune. Beauty queen Babette had had her photograph surrounded by columns of newsprint, and yet had lived and died in the provinces, far from the glamorous world of Chelsea's imagination. Realizing just how uncomfortable she would feel at having played any part in the probable disappointment, Deborah wished that she had not phoned Jason; but events, once started, failed to stop because somebody had changed her mind, especially as Jason was announcing his arrival.

"Is that him?" Chelsea asked eagerly.

"I'll have to open the front door before I can answer that question," said Deborah, although the echoing onslaught that Jason deemed the only way to gain entry to a house was very familiar.

"Should I stand or sit?" demanded Chelsea.

"Sit. It's more natural: more casual and confident," said Deborah, knowing that Jason would prefer Chelsea to be thoroughly unnerved so that he had a better chance of tricking his victim into harmful admissions. Feeling utterly wretched,

Deborah went to open the front door, and found herself confronted with a Jason in all his glory as battered reporter.

"Don't say a word about my face. Quasimodo had nothing on me."

However, Deborah had been prepared for a worse sight than minor bruising, and even Jason's nose was not the bulbous horror of his earlier description. "Your word-picture was more dramatic than the reality, I'm glad to note."

"There's no need to belittle the agony I'm in, or deny me the compassion that's rightfully mine," Jason protested. "I could do with a bit of consolation for a change. If you won't oblige, perhaps the interestingly wanton Chelsea will be prepared to soothe my torment."

Deborah hastily flapped a hand to wave Jason to silence. "I made a mistake," she whispered, joining him in the street. "Chelsea can't have been the girl at the Grand Hotel."

"Why not?"

"Because she never met my father."

"Did she tell you that?"

"I didn't ask, but it's obvious. I shouldn't have phoned you."

"But you did, and I'm here."

"And I'm fully aware of the fact. You'll do a really flattering article for Chelsea, won't you?"

"All my copy is uncompromising in its searing accuracy and forthright realism. I refer you to my amazing exposé of the lord mayor's secret passion for chocolate biscuits." Jason hesitated, but then added, "Deb, do you really want to know the truth about your father's death?"

"I'm not sure," admitted Deborah. "It can't hurt my mother though; she lives in a fantasy world as far as he's concerned. Have you discovered something?"

"No, but I'll stop working on the story, if you like. I could just report the police statements, and leave it at that. The decision is yours." Jason actually seemed to believe his words, and he sounded genuinely sincere.

"You wouldn't be able to resist investigating," said Deborah, amused at an offer that Jason could not possibly fulfil. "Anyway, truth is supposed to set people free, so perhaps it would help me get on with my life. Yes; go ahead. Do your worst, and let a sensational scoop carry you onto London and success."

"Now I know why I asked you to marry me, although not why you went into appalled shock at the prospect. If I promise never to mention the word marriage again, could we try to recapture old times?"

Deborah had wasted much of the early teenage years frowning into a mirror, gloomily wondering if any man would ever find her attractive, and now three had turned up at the same time. If forced to choose between Jason, Calvin and Maurice, there was no contest, because Jason would be the inevitable winner; however, a choice did not have to be made, and Deborah led the way into the house. "You're just wallowing in sentiment after being dumped by Stacey of the indignant husband. Come and meet Chelsea. She might be your type."

Chelsea had solved the problem of whether to sit or stand by the compromise of perching herself on the edge of the table, short skirt displaying the length of her legs to advantage, as she smiled her best smile.

"This is Jason," said Deborah. "He doesn't normally resemble a prize-fighter, but he had a slight accident with someone's fist. Jason, meet Chelsea Pritchard."

"Chelsea Pritchard?" echoed Jason, his surprised tone implying that he had had no idea who would be in the room. "You're the girl seen with Deborah's father at the Grand Hotel."

Chelsea's smile abruptly vanished. "What?"

"Phoebe Vale was telling me about you," Jason continued, his voice warm with interest. "She saw you in the hotel lobby."

"How could she recognize me?" demanded Chelsea. "I've never net Phoebe Vale."

Deborah wanted to protest at Jason's bluff, but there was panic in Chelsea's eyes: the panic of somebody flailing in quicksand. "Did you know my father?"

"Of course not," cried Chelsea. "I haven't a clue what you're on about."

"Phoebe couldn't mistake you. There can't be another girl in the whole of East Anglia with your looks," said Jason, admiration in every syllable. "You're stunning enough to be a fashion model."

"I'm going to be a model," declared Chelsea, keen to change the subject. "I'll be an actress on television as well."

"That's what Deborah's father told Phoebe. He met her outside the Grand, and they had quite a chat. He said he was going to marry you."

"Rubbish!"

"Not according to Phoebe. Gregory Wainwright maintained that you'd left a husband for him."

"She's lying." Chelsea tried to appear untroubled, but she was frightened, very frightened, and Deborah made herself intervene.

"It's OK, Chelsea. You can speak freely. My parents didn't have a conventional marriage. There's nothing to worry about."

"Why should I be worried?" asked Chelsea. She was still striving to feign nonchalance, but her hands were tightly clasped together, the knuckles white.

"Men must chase after you all the time," said Jason, surveying Chelsea's figure in undisguised approval. Once he had duped her into a false sense of security, he would confuse

Chelsea with a few blunt questions to startle the truth out of her. It seemed unpleasantly close to Lucas Rudd's bullying tactics, and yet again Deborah interceded.

"I bet my father promised he'd get you into show business. He probably could have, but not at the level you were imagining."

"Infatuated men must be a constant problem for a girl as gorgeous as you are, Chelsea," said Jason. "When you're famous, it'll get even worse. Are you prepared for admirers who'll shower you with jewels and expensive presents as they bribe their way into your life?"

Chelsea smiled again, believing she was safely back on her own territory. "No man's going to con me again."

"But men will scheme to further their own careers by using your fame," Jason declared sympathetically: too sympathetically. "I suppose Gregory thought that acquiring a young and beautiful partner would boost his image."

"I don't know what you're talking about," Chelsea stated.

Deborah did not want to feel sorry for Gregory, knowing he would have seduced the attractive, ambitious but gullible girl with tales of the success that existed only in his mind. However, Chelsea never loved him, nor had she hoped for a permanent relationship. Gregory was to be her ticket out of a town she disliked, and they had probably deserved each other, but he would have been the person who got hurt for once.

"My father made a lot of assumptions about you, because he didn't understand that you'd ditched your husband for being an idle drunk."

"I never met your father." But it was Chelsea's desperate last stand, frantic and fidgety.

"You won't have any trouble proving that," said Jason. "Detective Sergeant Rudd is talking to the staff at the Grand now. They'll be able to confirm you weren't the girl seen with

Gregory Wainwright, but I know that Inspector Atherton plans to take you there so the staff can be absolutely certain it wasn't you they saw. Apparently, one of the waiters made the same mistake as Phoebe, and named you."

Chelsea dithered, breathing shallowly like a hunted prey, but she was neither a quick nor resourceful thinker, and capitulated after a few seconds. "I didn't want to hurt Deborah," Chelsea claimed, to give a respectable reason for her previous lies.

"Oh, don't bother about me. My father regarded himself as the complete Casanova. You must have made quite an impact for him to talk of marriage."

"Greg just assumed he was the reason I walked out on that git of a husband," complained Chelsea. "I couldn't say anything, because I thought Greg was famous then. He told me he'd been on television, made films, starred in the West End and knew everyone in show business. I only realized he was a nobody when I did a search for his name on the computer at the museum, and couldn't even find a mention of him."

"You can't blame a man for trying to impress the girl of his dreams," said Jason, still friendly, still sympathetic. "Where did you meet Greg?"

"At a club in Fenster a few months ago. He told me he lived in London, and was just obliging a friend by doing a provincial tour. He'd teach me to sing and dance, he said, and we'd be on television. He promised me I'd be a star; he promised me." Chelsea's voice became more querulous at the memory, and the deception had indeed been a cruel one: as cruel as dashing Rhoda's fantasy world would be. "Greg said he'd never met anyone like me, and the moment he finished his tour, we'd be together in London. I actually believed he meant it, because he kept phoning and sending presents and getting me to visit him whenever he was working nearby. He couldn't bear to be parted from me, he said; I had genuine star quality, he said.

But Greg didn't say he had a daughter years older than me. I thought he was still in his thirties."

"That's why he had to keep me a deep, dark secret." To Deborah, Chelsea's description of the obsessed Gregory seemed no more real than Rhoda's fairytale husband, or Calvin's loyal and trustworthy friend. Chelsea must have meant a great deal to Gregory, because it had usually been the girl who pursued the fleeing Greg Wayne, as he sped after a newer and therefore more exciting love. Chelsea had perhaps represented his final opportunity to storm the big time with a well-favoured partner, whose appearance would augment his own handsomeness, and convince him that he really was still in his thirties. Chelsea might even have symbolized the lost Phoebe.

"I didn't know that Greg Wayne was only a stage name, as phoney as the rest of him," grumbled Chelsea.

"I don't think he ever knew he told lies," Deborah explained. "My father believed what he wanted to believe: that he was a star, and that he could make you one as well. He certainly didn't send presents to other girls, or hope to marry any of them. You were different."

"What's the point of being different if he couldn't make me famous?" Chelsea demanded bitterly. "He didn't even have any money."

"And of course, in the meantime, you'd met Calvin," added Jason.

"At least he's genuinely rich," Chelsea retorted.

"So why were you at the Grand on Saturday night?" asked Jason. "You'd finished with Greg Wayne."

"Yes, but he wouldn't listen. He kept phoning and phoning, and saying he'd get a divorce, take me to London, do anything I wanted, but I figured that was nothing more than his usual guff. I told him it was over, but he rang again on Saturday afternoon from the Grand, said he'd arranged a film test for me, and ordered us a dinner to celebrate, so I thought I'd give him one last chance."

A last chance that had slotted neatly into Chelsea's busy schedule, coinciding as it did with Calvin's trip to London. In a sudden regression to childhood, Deborah could not bear to think of her handsome and poised father being brought so very low by an infatuation with a girl whose self-centredness rivalled his own. Even Gregory's make-believe universe, as vivid as Rhoda's, had not been enough to protect him from Chelsea's refusal to play her part as adoring protégée. She should have felt honoured that Greg Wayne, star, had deigned to glance in her direction, and she should not have called him a nobody. His lies had, of necessity, become wilder in sheer self-defence, because if he had had to face reality, it would have killed Gregory with the same implacability as whatever happened to him in the museum courtyard.

"When I got to the Grand, I asked Greg how soon the film test would be, but he said the exact date hadn't been fixed. I told him he could keep his bogus screen test, and I walked straight out of the hotel." Chelsea seemed to expect approval of so decisive an action, and she smiled again.

"Did you do your walking out before or after dinner?" queried Jason.

"Before. I never saw Greg again."

"One of the waiters said he spotted you in the dining room with—"

"The waiter made a mistake." It was a pointless claim, delivered with a vigour that dared Jason to contradict Chelsea's assertion. In her opinion, if one lie might help, ten would be even better.

"Greg must have been very upset—"

"What does it matter?" asked Deborah, unwilling to hear further details of Gregory's humiliation. "Chelsea was right not to believe in a screen test. My father couldn't possibly have arranged one for her."

"Anyway, I'd decided to be a model by then," added Chelsea.

"What was Gregory wearing when you met him at the Grand?" Jason's question sounded apropos of nothing, but it made Chelsea suddenly wary.

"I don't remember."

"You hadn't realized that he and Calvin were friends, had you?"

"Were they?" Chelsea was no actress. Even if Gregory had had the power to bestow screen tests on aspiring stars, she was unlikely to have been snapped up as a potential Oscar winner.

"But you recognized Calvin's jacket," said Jason.

"Calvin's jacket?" repeated Chelsea, her voice shrill with overacted bewilderment. Jason had ventured near an area that she wanted to avoid. "What do you mean: Calvin's jacket?"

"When I spoke to the hotel staff, they said that Gregory wore a blue-striped jacket. Not the most conventional of evening wear at the Grand."

"Oh yes, I think Greg might have worn a blue jacket. I'd forgotten." Chelsea tried and failed to give the impression of airy indifference.

"He and Calvin swapped jackets earlier in the day."

"Did they?" Chelsea made a second effort to portray unconcern, but it was tinged with apprehension, and she fought to regain control of the exchange. "Can you really get my picture in the paper?"

"Gregory wasn't aware that you worked for Calvin," continued Jason, ignoring the sidetrack. "And, naturally, you didn't want Calvin to hear of your relationship with Greg. It must have been a very awkward situation for you."

"What was?" demanded Chelsea. "Greg knew I worked as a receptionist. I told him."

"But he hadn't met Calvin in a while, and there was no cause for Greg to associate his friend with a museum."

Deborah's heart pounded as the door of a cell that had imprisoned her for days began to swing open with a slowness that was nerve-racking, and although she could not face reacquiring the burden of having been the reason for Gregory's presence in the courtyard, the reason for his death, the question had to be asked. "Did my father go to the museum to see you?"

"Why should he?" protested Chelsea. "I'd finished with him and his lies. Greg knew that."

"But perhaps he couldn't accept it," said Jason. "Perhaps he hoped to change your mind."

"No," retorted Chelsea. "It was over."

"Then why did Greg go to the museum?"

Chelsea glanced around the room in a desperate search for inspiration, and her eyes fixed on Deborah. "He wanted to see his daughter. Yes, he told me he was going to see Deborah: to see where she worked. That's what he said."

Although sure that Chelsea was telling another lie, still a doubt must have lingered, because Deborah felt the weight of guilt about to descend once more, and she struggled to escape, sick with fear that she might never be able to free herself from the thought of having played some part, no matter how minor, in Gregory's death. "He couldn't have said that. You didn't know I was his daughter."

Chelsea looked trapped for a moment, but then rallied. "That's because I thought his surname was Wayne."

"But there's no Deborah Wayne at the museum."

Chelsea hesitated again, unaccustomed to such rapid mental exercise, and Jason filled the pause. "Greg must have commented on what a coincidence it was: you and his daughter working in the same place."

Chelsea seized Jason's words with the eagerness of the drowning man his straw. "Yes, Greg did mention something about a coincidence. I remember now. Yes, a coincidence."

"But he didn't know where I worked," said Deborah.

"Yes, he did," Chelsea maintained stubbornly. "He told me he was looking forward to seeing you on Sunday."

Deborah wanted to cry with relief, because Gregory would never have risked encountering her while in pursuit of a girl, nor would he have revealed the existence of so aged a daughter to the juvenile Chelsea. Rhoda's attempt to shield Gregory from knowledge of Deborah's restless employment record had backfired disastrously, as a little information concerning his daughter's whereabouts that Sunday would have been enough to make him shun the museum entirely. Although Rhoda could easily filter out uncomfortable facts, it was essential she never realized that she might have saved his life by not creating a fantasy daughter with an exemplary work background. Rhoda would eventually cope with his death, since he had always been a daydream husband, as much of an illusion as Gregory's fabrication of his young and beautiful new love, but some secrets were worth keeping.

"I didn't see Greg on Sunday." Chelsea was speaking so rapidly that she had become breathless in the rush to convince her listeners. "I sneaked away from the museum early. Ask that detective; he'll tell you. I wasn't there when Greg arrived to see Deborah. I'd left long before eleven: closer to ten. I told the detective. Deborah was there when I said it, weren't you, Deborah?"

"Chelsea, how do you know when Gregory arrived at the museum?" asked Jason.

"I don't," stated Chelsea.

255

"But you said—"

"You're putting words into my mouth."

"No, I'm not. You said you'd left before eleven o'clock, when Greg arrived." Jason's tone indicated that an exceptionally trifling inconsistency had been noted, but Chelsea reacted with fury.

"You're lying, like everyone else. I told you that I'd gone home by ten at the latest, and Greg wasn't there then, so I couldn't possibly know when he arrived."

"OK, OK," said Jason. "Did you leave via the courtyard?"

"I didn't go anywhere near the courtyard," declared Chelsea with a belligerence that suggested more a fending off of an accusation than a mere reply. "I waited for a quiet minute, and then crept out the back."

Deborah knew that Chelsea could not have left the museum on Sunday in the way described, but to hassle her any more seemed cruel. Chelsea was silly, not vicious: an immature girl who wanted to gatecrash a future that she believed would lead her on to the happily-ever-after promised by her imagination. But Jason was somebody else with ambition, and he had no qualms about entrapping Chelsea.

"According to my research, there are two doors at the back of the museum, and both were locked throughout Sunday, with activated security alarms. How did you manage to bypass them?"

"I just did."

"Which door was open?"

"I don't remember." Caution replaced Chelsea's anger. She had guessed that too many details were dangerous.

"You must remember."

"Well, I don't. And I thought you were meant to be interviewing me about my modelling course in London."

"That's exactly what I'm doing, but I can't help being

interested in an unsecured exit at a time when the museum was supposed to be sealed tighter than a drum."

There had been no unsecured exits on the morning of the disaster exercise; Deborah knew that as well as Jason did. Chelsea might have left early, but not through a back door; clearly it was imperative to remove herself from the vicinity of the courtyard, the vicinity of Gregory's death. Jason glanced at Deborah, although he would go on, whether or not she could cope, and his keenness made Deborah feel old and weary. Chelsea was not clever enough to fool either Jason or the police, and running away might make things worse for her when the truth did emerge, and the truth was eventually going to fight its way free. "Chelsea, it'll make a real difference if you speak now," said Deborah, "before the police find out for themselves."

"Find out what?" retorted Chelsea.

"There are all sorts of DNA tests they can do. They'll place you in the courtyard with my father. Besides, Maurice saw you there."

"He's lying." But Chelsea was trembling, unable to keep the fear from her voice.

"Were you frightened that Greg would tell Calvin about your affair?" Jason was already mentally writing his copy, with Chelsea featuring as the innocent prey of lascivious, older men. Gregory could no longer be hurt, but Calvin remained very much in Jason's sights. The rich man seduced the ingénue with promises he had no intention of keeping, therefore the rich man must be the pantomime villain. Gregory might have lied to Chelsea as well, but he was already bespoke as another victim. In Jason's copy, Calvin would carry the can.

"I'm not afraid of anybody or anything. Why should I be?" However, the defiance was belied by Chelsea's face in which trepidation mingled with crumbling aggression, as she frantically tried to defend her ground. "I didn't see Greg at the museum, and if he had been there before I sloped off, I would have spotted that awful jacket a mile away."

"How do you know he was wearing it on Sunday?" asked Jason.

"I didn't." Chelsea had only one shelter left, if stout denial failed her, and she promptly began to cry like a child, openly and loudly, letting the tears run down her face without attempting to disguise or check them. "You want to frame me, but I haven't done a thing."

"Of course you haven't," agreed Deborah, although her words were empty because she knew that she was looking at the girl who had probably been the reason for Gregory's death. But Chelsea was too young, and too foolish to be held entirely responsible for her own actions. It would be akin to expecting Gregory not to have enticed an attractive female with lies about his success and influence. As Chelsea herself had a rather distant relationship with truth, the deception should have mattered less than usual; the upshot had simply run wild. "It wasn't your fault, Chelsea. My father ought not to have gone on chasing you, after he'd been told it was over."

"Yes, he should have listened," said Jason. "If Calvin had seen him with Chelsea, it could have ruined everything."

"Everything's ruined anyway," sobbed Chelsea. "I bet you're only pretending you can get my picture in the paper, and Deborah's going to tell Calvin that I'm a murderer so she can have him and his money for herself. And she doesn't even want to do a modelling course. It isn't fair."

"I can definitely get your picture into the paper. All you have to do is tell me what happened to Greg." Jason was again speaking softly and sympathetically, but Deborah could sense how much he relished the moment. He had his exclusive, and had managed to secure it before the police concluded their investigation. Chelsea's future was of no more concern to him than it had been to Gregory. She represented a means to an end for both of them.

"I didn't see Greg on Sunday." Even Chelsea was not convinced by what she said, and the tears became more profuse.

"Don't say another word," ordered Deborah. "You need a solicitor."

"Oh, there's no call to begin running up a sky-high bill with some greedy shyster," Jason said hastily, before his scoop could be snatched from him. "No one's going to blame you, Chelsea. After all, if Deborah understands, everybody will. And you do understand that Chelsea's the actual victim in this, don't you, Deborah?"

"Yes, I do." But Deborah could only understand Chelsea because she had understood Gregory.

"I can get a photographer here in five minutes, if you'll tell me the whole story, Chelsea," urged Jason. "Don't cry any more. You wouldn't want to be photographed with swollen eyes."

Chelsea paused in mid-sob. "Can you really get my picture into the *Seaborne Weekly*?"

"*The Seaborne Weekly!*" Jason replied scornfully. "I can get you into a national daily, with this story."

"The nationals! I'll be famous!" Chelsea gasped with joy, before wailing in sudden anguish, "My make-up! It's wrecked. I've got to re-do my make-up."

"There's plenty of time. I just need a few details," said Jason, his best coaxing tone fully employed. "How did Greg die?"

"I'm going to phone Lucas Rudd," announced Deborah. "I'll ask him to get a lawyer."

"No!" Chelsea and Jason spoke as one.

"It's important, Chelsea," argued Deborah. "You have to get some legal advice before you tell anyone anything."

"I'm not saying another word until that photographer takes some pictures of me," declared Chelsea. "And I want copies of them too."

"You'll get a whole portfolio of pictures," Jason promised at once. "When you're famous, you'll be able to flood the modelling agencies with photographs, and it won't cost you a penny."

"Don't listen to him," said Deborah.

"I want a portfolio. I need a portfolio," retorted Chelsea. She seemed to imagine that she was now in control of events: the person who made the decisions, and would go on making them. She knew the information she had was valuable, but did not realize how dangerous it could be for her. "First of all, I've got to re-do my make-up. When will I be in the papers, Jason?"

"The nationals? Tomorrow."

"Tomorrow? I'll be famous tomorrow?" Chelsea could barely speak for excitement.

Deborah hated to see so much enthusiasm over something that would have such grim consequences, and she was compelled to try another warning. "Don't listen to Jason."

"Can he get my picture in the nationals tomorrow?"

"Probably," admitted Deborah. "But you must talk to a solicitor before you decide anything." It was as useless as endeavouring to persuade Gregory to abandon his dreams would have been. Chelsea too craved fame because, without it, existence meant nothing. To be ordinary was failure.

"Phone that photographer," commanded Chelsea, hunting inside her shoulder bag for cosmetics.

"OK." Jason went out into the hall, and Deborah hurried after him.

"You can't do this, Jason. It's wrong. You know what will happen."

Jason closed the door of the front room before he spoke, even though Chelsea seemed too absorbed with lipstick and foundation to pay attention to anybody else's life. "Deb, she deserves to get clobbered by the law. Don't let that helpless little girl act hoodwink you. Chelsea Pritchard is a cold and calculating harpy."

"She's young and silly."

"Well, if she can fool her victim's daughter, she'll most likely con the police too, and get off with a caution, so stop worrying."

"I just can't believe she's malevolent enough to hurt someone deliberately. You're thinking of your own hope that Chelsea will turn out to be a female version of Jack the Ripper."

"Don't make me develop a conscience, whatever you do. It won't combine well with my job." Jason took his mobile phone out of a pocket, but then paused to put his arms around Deborah and hug her. "I know this whole mess is awful for you, but I can't change."

"I don't expect you to," conceded Deborah.

"Thank goodness for that," said Jason, promptly releasing her. "This could be my big chance, and I do wish that your father had no part in it. But he does, and I'm sorry, although not sorry enough to turn down such an opportunity; and, yes, I'm fully aware that I'm a rat."

"But an honest rat. Besides, everybody needs some ambition. Without hope, there's no point in getting up each day."

"Then let me phone that photographer before you commence summoning solicitors." But Jason paused again, even as he searched his mobile for the number he wanted. "You are going to forgive me in the end, aren't you?"

"I don't blame you to start with. Vermin can only act on instinct."

"I'm glad you're able to plumb the depths of my shallow nature. However, should I chance to mention any future togetherness, I suppose you'd turn me down flat again," said Jason, ruefully amused. "Yet you're the only woman who accepts me exactly as I am, and I haven't the least wish to alter anything about you. Don't you realize how important that is? Don't you realize what it means?"

It meant that Jason was the one person in her life who knew the actual Deborah. It also meant he might not inevitably reject her, and that she could have made a mistake when she chose to get her own rejection in first, before he could hurt her. She had let Gregory down by growing too old and cynical to be the adoring little daughter he required, and her inconvenient view of him had frozen Deborah out of Rhoda's cosy world. If parents could not be trusted to go on loving unconditionally, there seemed no chance that an outsider could be steadfast. Only fear stopped Deborah and Jason from becoming a couple, because she knew that if she linked her future to his, and then he walked away, it would be the worst betrayal of all. Much simpler to get involved with Calvin, as she did not love him: a thought implying that she might be in love with Jason. Perhaps Deborah had inadvertently spoken the truth when telling Maurice that she and Jason belonged together: assuming destiny did not plan to lumber her with the unmotivated Roderick Atherton.

"I have to phone the police," said Deborah, to repel the alarming idea. "Chelsea doesn't understand how serious things could get."

"Wait until Chelsea's had her moment of glory." Jason's coaxing voice was back in full force, even though he probably guessed that Deborah would not stymie his chance of an exclusive. "You don't want to disappoint Chelsea, and she'll be really upset if the police arrive in the middle of the photo session and confiscate the camera."

"You're all heart," commented Deborah.

Jason laughed. "Just let me secure my scoop, and I won't mind what insults you dish up."

****

"If I'd known I was going to be photographed for the newspapers, I'd have worn something decent," Chelsea said happily.

"Indecent gets the editors much more excited," remarked Jason.

Chelsea had been photographed to her heart's content, sitting, standing, and draped over the furniture. She appeared able to relegate everything else to insignificant detail, including the reason why she enjoyed the attentions of a photographer. Chelsea yearned to be famous, and how she achieved that goal was apparently of no concern. Even Deborah, the usurper of Calvin, could be ignored, as Chelsea smiled and pouted and posed, liberally displaying her attractions.

"Chelsea, I'll need some copy to go with your pictures," said Jason, the instant the photographer had left. "How did Greg die?"

"You don't have to tell Jason anything," Deborah pointed out, uncertain if her motive was to protect Chelsea or avoid details of Gregory's last moments. However, Chelsea, for all her excitement, had managed to work up a story.

"Greg must have fallen over and hit his head," decided Chelsea. "At least, I guess that's what happened. I'd gone by then. I told him we were through, and then I walked away. That's all I know."

"Why didn't you tell the police?" queried Jason.

"Because they'd try to pin something on me, of course. That's what they do. Ask anybody."

"Why did no one spot you and Greg together?"

"I was behind the fountain in the courtyard. I'd hidden there so I could sneak out the gate, after the casualties got carted off."

"Then how did Greg see you there?"

"I saw him." Chelsea's voice was suddenly wary, and considerably less glib, but her gaze remained guilelessly wide-eyed, and fixed on Jason's face. "I called Greg over, told him to stop chasing me, and went home."

"If he hadn't seen you, why call to him? Why didn't you ignore Greg?"

Chelsea shrugged to give herself time for thought. "I just didn't," she replied eventually.

"You were afraid that he might wander around the museum, asking for you," suggested Jason. "After all, somebody could have recognized Calvin's jacket, realized that he and Greg must be friends, and mentioned him to Calvin later on."

"I didn't think of Calvin: not once," claimed Chelsea.

"But you were leaving the museum early to meet him."

"I told you I went straight home. I wasn't seeing Calvin until the afternoon."

"So when you saw Calvin in the courtyard, it must have been quite a surprise," said Jason.

"Calvin?" The wide-eyed look became the goggle-eyed look as Chelsea stared at Jason in amazement. "Calvin wasn't there."

"Don't bother protecting him, Chelsea. He's not worth it."

"Nice shot at framing Calvin," Deborah commented to Jason.

"You can't blame a journalist for trying."

"Actually, Calvin might have been around." The ingenuous eyes acquired a hint of slyness, as Chelsea seized the lifeline thrown her way. "I didn't see him, but he might have spotted me with Greg and been jealous. Then, after I left, Calvin could have got behind Greg and hit him with a loose railing—I mean, hit him with something."

"Chelsea, how do you know that Gregory was attacked from behind with a piece of railing?" asked Jason.

"It was on television," Chelsea replied after a second's hesitation.

"No, it wasn't."

"Then it was on radio or in the paper."

"No," stated Jason

"It must have been. How else could I know?" retorted Chelsea, triumphant to be so unexpectedly quick-witted. "Anyway, Calvin's plainly worried I'll connect him to the museum on Sunday morning; that's why he's avoided me ever since."

"He didn't exactly avoid you on Sunday afternoon."

"He couldn't. It would have been too obvious that he killed Greg in a jealous rage." The escape plan was becoming clearer as it gathered detail in Chelsea's mind, and offered her the bonus of an image as a *femme fatale* who drove men to excesses of passion. "Calvin's so terrified I'll work out what he did that he's keeping his distance from me until he thinks it's safe."

"Calvin couldn't have done anything in the courtyard on Sunday morning. He was in London." Deborah felt numb with cold, although she was not hearing facts about her father's death; she was listening to lies. Gregory had lost his life because of a girl so paltry, even he should have noticed. Calvin had certainly treated Chelsea shabbily, but not as shabbily as she was returning the insult. The Gregory who had taught Debbie to wish on stars and dream unattainable dreams should not have sunk so low as to love a girl who was prepared to save her own skin at the expense of someone else's. Gregory had often failed his daughter, but never so grievously.

"Calvin *says* he was in London." Chelsea's tone implied that she knew better, and the wariness had entirely gone. "But Calvin says a lot of things that aren't true."

"He didn't know that my father would be at the museum," Deborah pointed out. "Why should Calvin slink around a place he owns?"

"I haven't a clue." But Chelsea made a visible effort to find a reason, biting the side of her lower lip before the welcome arrival of an answer. "Greg must have told Calvin he'd be there, looking for me."

"Why didn't Calvin confront him then, instead of choosing such a public place?" asked Jason.

"How should I know?" demanded Chelsea, sounding like a sulky five-year-old. "You want to trick me. I'm not talking to you any more; I'm just not."

"OK," said Jason. "Deborah, it's time you made that phone call."

"No, wait," cried Chelsea.

"What for, if you're not going to say anything else?"

"How can I, when I've told you all I know? Calvin killed Greg. You've got to put that in the paper, Jason. You've got to make everyone realize it was Calvin. You will, won't you?" Chelsea directed a coy, sideways glance at Jason, confident of the impact she usually had on men. Her appearance was her identity, and she relied on it to solve any problem, as a child might rely on magic and lucky charms. A seduced Jason would make everything right for Chelsea, because a seduced Jason would do her bidding.

"Once you've made a statement to the police, I can start writing my copy." Jason was offering a deal, and Chelsea recognized it as such. She had to acknowledge her presence in the courtyard with Gregory, or there would be no pictures in the paper; and, in Chelsea's mind, a newspaper picture equalled celebrity.

"What should I tell the police?"

"What you've told me," replied Jason. "There's nothing to worry about. I'll take you to the police station myself."

"The police station!" said Chelsea in alarm.

"You don't want them to think you're scared of making a statement."

"Of course I'm not scared," snapped Chelsea. "Why should I be? But I'm not going to any police station."

It might be more a police decision where she went, after they heard the saga of the courtyard and the accusations against Calvin, but Jason allowed Chelsea to believe that the choices would continue to be hers. "No problem. I'll get somebody to come here. In the meantime, why not do a search on Deborah's computer for modelling agencies? You'll need the addresses when you send your photos out."

****

It was Jason who made the telephone call to Lucas Rudd. Deborah went into her kitchen and sat down at the table, not wanting to play any further part in Chelsea's fate. Rain began to spatter against the window, and even though Deborah was chilled, she felt she did not deserve to be more comfortable, but it was too late for anything other than self-indulgent guilt over the fact that she had not insisted Chelsea kept quiet until the arrival of a solicitor. The omission seemed to place Deborah squarely in Chelsea's tawdry world, but only time could blunt the sense of having chosen to be callous. Once there had been a purpose to waiting, as Deborah waited for her father's return, for birthdays, for Christmas, for the end of the school term, for a future bright with promise. Now she simply waited to feel nothing and experience nothing, but that had become her everyday life as an adult. There was no longer a dream, no longer any aim except to keep her head above water financially. Debbie, dancing through the house with Gregory, would have been ashamed of her grownup self.

There was a knock on the front door, and Deborah heard Jason speak to Inspector Atherton as footsteps tramped into the hall. A blast of cold air accompanied them and it swirled around the kitchen, making Deborah shiver, while a confident Chelsea greeted Lucas Rudd like an old friend.

"I'll go and sit with Deborah," said Jason, although he was much more likely to stay in the hallway eavesdropping, but Chelsea had come to regard him as an ally.

"I want Jason to stay with me."

"OK," said Lucas, and the door of the front room closed.

Deborah went on waiting in the kitchen, where ten minutes might have passed, or ten hours, and she had to rouse herself as if from sleep when the door reopened.

"But I don't want to go to the police station," Chelsea protested shrilly.

"We'll get you a solicitor," said Atherton.

"Why does everybody keep harping on about solicitors?" demanded Chelsea. "And why can't Jason come too?"

"Because I have to work on my copy," said Jason, and the thought of her approaching fame must have comforted Chelsea because she made no further objection, and the front door closed behind her and the police escort.

Jason walked into the kitchen and sat down next to Deborah. He looked at Calvin's roses for a few moments, before saying, "Chelsea's gone."

"I know. I heard. I should have got her a solicitor before she spoke to you, before she spoke to Atherton, but I just didn't."

"Don't worry about Chelsea Pritchard. You must realize that she's responsible for your father's death. How else could she know details that the police didn't reveal to the media?"

"What's going to happen to her?" asked Deborah.

Jason shrugged. "It depends. Her best bet is to make a full confession as soon as possible. She isn't fooling anybody."

"My father never chased women; he didn't have to. Chelsea was the only one he couldn't bear to lose. The only one, and she isn't worth giving the time of day to." Deborah pictured the feckless Gregory, and could have cried in exasperation. It had been so like him to fall in love with the sole woman he should have discarded for his own good: so like him to mistake tinsel for gold.

"Chelsea has managed to do something that should please you. She's made me decide to back off Calvin. I can see myself in Chelsea's willingness to destroy somebody for her own benefit, and don't like that particular version of myself."

"You haven't got that much on Calvin anyhow, and you won't find more than you've already discovered. Calvin didn't harm Babette."

"How can you possibly know that?"

Because Calvin still buys pink roses, thought Deborah. However, it was hardly a clinching argument that Jason would accept, and Deborah's other reason was no more convincing. "Calvin told Maurice that Babette had died."

Jason waited for further enlightenment, realized it would not be forthcoming, and demanded, "What does that prove?"

"Maurice never gets told a thing normally, yet Calvin was compelled to talk about Babette when he could have kept quiet. Maurice hadn't even known that Calvin was married."

"And?"

"If Calvin had Babette's death on his conscience, he would have avoided the subject entirely. Maurice was only a kid at school."

"You're assuming that Calvin has a conscience."

"Well, he's never been a journalist."

"OK, so his integrity is all that mine now aspires to be, but I'll out-Calvin Calvin yet. If I ever get to work on a national paper, it'll be because of my ability, not the ruin of someone's reputation."

Jason's sanctimonious tone made Deborah laugh, and she felt better than she had done for days. "It's a noble resolve, but

I have a suspicion that you might be inclined to modify such lofty principles the minute a good enough scandal beckons."

"A reporter must live," argued Jason, but he too laughed. "Anyway, now that it's clear Calvin didn't silence his one-time alibi, it probably means there's less chance of him being a wife-killer. All right, my virtue could be on the temporary side, but today I'm haughtily above the taint of sleaze. If I asked you to marry me right away, you couldn't resist such a high-minded upholder of decency and good taste."

"Yes, I might consider marrying you," said Deborah, "but not because of your newfound integrity."

"No, it'd be because today is today, and you feel isolated and vulnerable. That's why it wouldn't be fair to propose right now." Jason spoke rather too hastily for one who had previously avowed that only with Deborah could he know true happiness.

"Coward," said Deborah. "You obviously schedule your proposals to coincide with the moment you're certain the female will refuse."

"A slur on my unswerving devotion to you."

"And to Stacey?"

"So I swerved a bit; but fate's given me a lesson I won't forget, especially if my nose decides to resemble Jimmy Durante's for good. Still, to prove my restored faithfulness, I'll make a regular appointment with you to propose at yearly intervals from now on. However, at this precise minute, I need to churn out some copy rather urgently. Should I go or stay?"

"Stay," replied Deborah. Even a Jason absorbed in his work was preferable to being alone, because then Gregory would invade her thoughts, and she wanted to escape the past. The past had made her avoid Jason, avoid commitment, avoid any risk of desertion, but avoiding risk meant avoiding life itself. Perhaps the time had come to let Debbie free again, and trust that she would be sensible enough to steer clear of Roderick Atherton.

"As soon as I've finished, we'll go around to your mother's, and break the news to her."

"There won't be any dramatic reaction for you to report," warned Deborah. "She knew that my father was a wanderer, and accepted it. Chelsea's the person who'll get the blame for pursuing him."

"This is the new, improved Jason. I didn't even think of reporting your mother's reaction."

"A brand new Jason indeed," said Deborah, not entirely convinced.

"Though I will admit to being intrigued as to what Calvin's reaction to the news is likely to be, and what he'll say when he learns that he spent Sunday night with the woman who killed his trustworthy friend."

"Poor Calvin; he'll feel dreadful."

"Oh yes, such a gentle and sensitive soul, like all hard-boiled businessmen," Jason declared with unrepentant cynicism.

"I'm not sure that the new Jason is much of an improvement on the old."

"Give me time," protested Jason.

8

"Page 5," announced Jason, presenting Deborah with a newspaper. Because the story was an important milestone in his career, it did not occur to him that she might wish to shun the tabloids indefinitely. "Page 5 in a national daily. Chelsea and her legs on full display; she'll be thrilled."

Deborah was not quite as certain, although Chelsea, like a child, could probably relish the moment while ignoring the future. "Has she been charged?"

"Even Lucas Rudd wasn't taken in by her claim of an invisible Calvin eliminating his rival in a jealous rage. If our enterprising town councillors aren't arrested in the meantime for collective fraud, Chelsea should get her picture on the front page of next week's local rag; and, believe me, it'll be a great comfort to her. Hard luck that sheer stupidity is no defence."

"It's a defence we could all do with," said Deborah, knowing that fame might have comforted Gregory too, no matter what the circumstances. "Chelsea will never be able to work out the difference between celebrity and notoriety."

"She won't need to; she'd be perfectly content with either." Jason glanced down at the newspaper, as though longing to read selected passages of his prose to Deborah, but even he sensed that it was not the ideal occasion on which to parade his talents, and he folded the paper under one arm. "Let's go out for lunch. We ought to do something to proclaim our non-engaged status."

It was inconvenient that Jason's triumphant day should also be one of the more difficult that Deborah might have to face. She could finally picture the detail of Gregory's death in the museum courtyard, and the force of Chelsea's blow would continue to reverberate through Deborah's mind for years to come. "I don't feel like going anywhere."

"In that case, it's essential we go out, if only to get your life moving again."

"I suppose so," Deborah admitted.

"Of course, nothing less than the Floral Restaurant will be acceptable, now that you're accustomed to the highest of Seaborne's high society."

But it was less the town's high society that Deborah feared, than any society at all. The news about Chelsea would have circulated, and Gregory's daughter was going to be watched and pointed at; however, the gossip had to be confronted, and the longer Deborah put off starting to live again, the worse the ordeal would seem. Deborah had to brave the tittle-tattle of Seaborne until she could ignore it as easily as Rhoda did. Jason had been right; going out to lunch that day was essential.

****

Journalist Jason made it a rule never to be impressed by ostentation, and in his company, even the grandiose Floral Restaurant was relegated to merely another eating place. While he studied the menu in a vain search for some reasonably priced food, Deborah glanced idly around the restaurant, and was suddenly transfixed by the sight of a formally dressed Roderick Atherton escorting a couple to an alcove table. Parted from the shabby denim and trainers he had worn for his job interview, Roderick was a different person, and she could understand why she had been unable to place him. "He showed Calvin and me to our table here," she said in amusement.

"Who did?" asked Jason. He put the menu down, and turned his head to follow Deborah's gaze. "Do you mean Roderick Atherton?"

"Yes. For some reason, he neglected to mention the Floral on his application form for the cleaning job."

"Then I reckon we're looking at a waiter about to be given the heave-ho, or one who means to depart without bothering with the minor formality of working his notice."

"I thought I recognized Roderick Atherton from somewhere." Deborah wanted to laugh with pure relief. She was not fated to marry a ne'er-do-well, nor would she be tempted to tie her life to either Jason or Calvin as protection against being encumbered with a second version of Gregory. She was not doomed to repeat Rhoda's mistakes, any more than she was doomed to automatic rejection. For the first time in what seemed years, Deborah felt happy. Predestination was not going to push her around. She could find another job, sell the house, move away from the town; or she could stay where she was, and organize the watermill project for Calvin. The actual decision appeared inconsequential; it was the freedom to make her own choices that Deborah valued. A few of Seaborne's ghosts had at last been exorcised.

Jason put his menu down with a sigh. "I've come to the conclusion that we can either pay for lunch here, or finance a trip around the world."

"I intend to do both," said Deborah.